THE ADVE

The Adversary

A. M. KABAL

ALLISON & BUSBY
LONDON

First published London 1986 by
Allison & Busby Limited
6a Noel Street, London W1V 3RB

British Library Cataloguing in Publication Data

Kabal, A.M.
  The Adversary.
  Rn: H.S. Bhabra   I. Title
  823'.94[F]   PR6061.A/

ISBN 0-85031-651-0

Set in 11/12pt Sabon by
Ann Buchan (Typesetters) Limited,
Walton-on-Thames, Surrey
Printed and bound in Great Britain by
Billing & Sons Limited, Worcester

for Nicolas Kinloch

Author's Note

This book is a work of fiction set against the background of contemporary political reality. With the exception of certain public figures, whose actions are kept mainly within the bounds of the public record, and on whom no judgement is intended or implied, all the people and events described within the novel are imaginary. Any resemblance to actual events or persons, living or dead, is entirely accidental. Only the places are real.

There is no generally accepted, consistent, system of transliterating Arabic to English. I have therefore always preferred simplicity to consistency.

A. M. KABAL, *Toronto* 1985

Contents

"Be sober, be vigilant; because your adversary the devil, as a roaring lion, walketh about, seeking whom he may devour."

The First Epistle General of St Peter
Chapter Five, Verse Eight

Prologue:
STRIKING AT PRINCES

Panama City: 6th October 1981

Anwar Sadat, President of Egypt, stood to attention. He looked as though he was about to take a salute. But it wasn't a salute the four men running in from the Soviet-built Zil-151 truck had for him. The two fragmentation grenades they threw into the reviewing stand failed to explode, but they were firing already, Kalashnikov AK-47 automatic rifles. Sadat seemed to be the only person who had noticed them under the thunder of the six Mirage 5-E jets completing their fly-past. Sadat half-turned and stumbled.

Ismail coughed, politely. "The Cardinal is here to see you, sir." David Medina's green eyes never flickered from the video-screen. He hardly ever watched television, but this was a special occasion.

"Tell him to wait."

Two more grenades. Shrapnel. Sadat was down. So were Vice-President Hosni Mubarak and General Abu Ghazala, who had stood automatically with the President. Two of the assassins were at the edges of the stand, their guns high over their heads, like harpoons, raking the platform with fire. The third ran up. Shot Sadat's photographer, Muhammed Rashwan. Now the fourth had joined the fire. The second, the leader, Islambouli, was down, hit. The others ran. Then chaos, as everyone moved in, to the pile of bodies, rubble and shrapnel where Sadat lay, already dying.

Fifty seconds. That was all. Fifty seconds.

No doubt about it, Islambouli was good. Very good. Or, rather, he had been.

Ismail, who had returned, appeared to agree. "They did a good job, Mr Medina."

Medina turned, acknowledging his private secretary's presence for the first time. "Yes. They did."

"Is it safe, sir? They survived. Three have been taken. What if they talk?"

Medina smiled, his green eyes hooded, dangerous. "Oh, they'll talk all right, Ismail. Especially Islambouli. As will the fourth one, who our friend will have arrested in three days' time. They'll talk. They'll do nothing but talk, to the instant of their execution. But what they'll talk about is the wonder and glory of Islam and the truth of the Koran. Not something we have to worry about."

Ismail nodded, as always accepting his master's opinion. Then Medina remembered he had business.

"I'll see the Cardinal now, Ismail. In the meantime, have the balance of the funds transferred as agreed to their account in Geneva. Also the other fee, to our friend's account, in Chiasso."

Part one:
THE FISHERMAN'S WILL

Cairo: The present day

The first thing Chas Winterton did that morning was throw up. He could not quite remember how he came to be curled up on the floor hugging a vast Edwardian toilet-pan, but he knew it made him feel happier and safer than he had done for several hours. A company of small malicious dwarves seemed to be locked up in his head and were tunnelling their way out. His tongue felt as though it had been used as a landing-strip by kamikaze flies all night. And his stomach. . . . There was a pause as he leaned over the pan again; his stomach had just returned from orbit somewhere out beyond Mars.

Oh, God, he thought. *This must be Cairo.*

His head ached as he tried to remember why he was supposed to be here; a dull sort of ache, as though his brain were considering applying for another job; something safe, with good future prospects, like an atom bomb casing.

Cairo, Cairo . . . . David Medina.

Christ!

He stood up sharply and his blood, unused to the altitude, bubbled up to his brain. Everything went grey again and his legs buckled beneath him.

The hell with it, he thought, a few seconds later, propped up against the bathroom wall, his legs tucked up to his chin. The cool tiles reassured him, and the bath-mat reminded him where he was.

Hotel Windsor, in the Sharia El Alfi. He always stayed here when he was in Cairo. Old colonial hotel, running a bit to seed now but nice people and quite cheap, and no bloody tourists. Martin Foster was supposed to be meeting him here for breakfast. Our Man In Cairo. Martin Foster, who was responsible for the way he felt right now. How had he got together with such a maniac?

11

Just one for the road. One for the Edgware Road and one for the Fulham Road. One for the Old Brompton Road and Kensington Church Street and six for Shepherd bloody Market.

Ewen Jones, the British Council man in Alexandria, had introduced them. And now Martin Foster was meant to be coming to breakfast, before taking him to meet David Medina.

David Medina, with all his lovely money.

There was a sound of scurrying and shuffling outside his bedroom door and then a pistol-shot knocking. He winced. Then he pieced together enough of his normally fluent Arabic to tell the porter to make Martin Foster wait. He would be down once he had showered.

Ten minutes later, he felt something more like a human being. Even so, the world seemed to have shrunk. He kept bumping into things. Everything seemed much closer than it ought to be, and more fragile. He remembered he ought to look respectable today, respectable enough to meet a billionaire. He found his linen suit, laundered the previous night, hanging outside his door. Cotton shirt. Real shoes (how old were they?), not basketball trainers or desert boots. Even a tie for the first time in (four?) years. Would it do? It would have to. All he was asking for was money.

The thought made him grin, but the sudden movement felt as though his eyes were being pushed back into his head. He stopped grinning and went down to breakfast.

As soon as he got down to the first floor he remembered why he always stayed at the Windsor. Foster was waiting in the bar beyond the ancient open-frame electric lift. There was hardly anything like the public rooms of the Windsor left in Cairo. Oak floorboards and Persian rugs, rattan furniture and elderly faded French embroidered cushions and curtains. Tables made from ships' barrels and candelabra made from ships' wheels. Sliding mirrored doors into the dining-room beyond, a long bar and, since the fez had been legalized again, waiters in starched white robes and red fezzes. It was cool, and not too bright; it was like returning to a distant colonial past, without

12

any nonsense about having to pick up the white man's burden. This was where he came when he wanted to be a burden himself, when he wanted to be indulged.

Foster was sitting at the other corner of the room, reading one of the newspapers folded on canes each morning and left at the rack by the door for guests. He was a small dark man in his forties, about ten years older than Winterton, who looked not so much tanned as weathered, like the stones of an ancient monument, and he smiled rather too much for Chas Winterton's liking. He smiled again now.

"How're you feeling? My God, we strapped one on last night, didn't we? Nothing like a new face, I always say, to make you appreciate the delights of Cairo."

Foster was supposed to be some sort of liaison man between the British Council and the Embassy but, for the life of him, Winterton could not imagine him making any cultural contacts outside a bar or brothel. He raised a big brown bottle of the local beer now, saying, "You look as though you could do with one for the road." Chas moaned and rolled his eyes up in disbelief. Foster laughed. "I thought you chaps who live out in the desert are supposed to be used to the firewater."

"I am," Chas replied sourly. "It's Scotch that does this to me now, and beer makes me fart."

Foster laughed uproariously at this, and even Chas managed a weary smile. He asked the waiter if they could breakfast in the bar, and the grave, military and entirely mute servant bowed in agreement. They were the only people present, for summer is the quiet season for hotels in Egypt, everywhere except Alexandria. Chas ordered a jug of black European coffee instead of the sweet sticky Egyptian kind (after generations of Ottoman rule it was still not done to call it Turkish coffee), a slice of watermelon and scrambled eggs.

"I don't know why you bother with coffee in Egypt," Foster muttered. "The local stuff's all crap. I have mine flown out from England."

It was true, Chas thought, the local stuff was all terrible, but what was it about Egypt (or was it the Diplomatic Corps?) which made people like Foster, who probably shopped at

13

discount stores back at home, behave like whining memsahibs in the vanished days of Empire? He said nothing, and reached for a newspaper.

The main stories and editorial were what they had been for months. Ever since the Camp David treaty with Israel, Libya had been built up in the government-sponsored press as the great enemy of Egypt. (*Quite right too*, thought Chas; Gaddafi's intentions had clearly been dishonourable for years and, whatever apologists might say, his brain was plainly permanently out to lunch.) In recent years the Americans had held joint manoeuvres with the Egyptians along the Libyan border, and almost all the conscript soldiers you met, sad but sadly proud in their dusty field uniforms, were on leave from Libyan border patrols. One step out of line by Gaddafi, Chas had thought for a long time, and it would be war. The army wanted it; the country would enjoy it, for a while; and the politicians needed something to take people's minds off what they laughingly called the economy. The Egyptians would win it, too. They might not have oil wealth and the latest weapons, but they had a bigger population, a bigger army, a lot of pride and, Good God, they had beaten the Israelis back in '73 at the Canal and in the Sinai, though it had never been polite to mention that anywhere outside Egypt itself. So the papers (and the radio, and the television, which reached deep into Egyptian villages now) went on building up Gaddafi as an atheist son of Satan whose every move was to be mistrusted.

And then there were the bombs. There had been occasional incidents ever since Sadat was murdered, but in the past few months. . . .

The papers screamed random accusations. Some blamed the bombings on Jihad, the group which killed Sadat, financed by Iran. Others were sure it was Gaddafi's doing. Last year he had hired English hit-men, it was claimed, to murder a former Libyan Prime Minister living in Egypt. He had been foiled by the secret service then (*But how could you be sure?* thought Chas; the whole thing smelled of dirty tricks and deep disinformation; it smelled of CIA); he would stop at nothing now. And outside the press, where the common people could not hear it, in elegant cafés and private houses, some whispered of darker

14

secrets; of Palestinians bored with diplomacy seeking to destabilize Israel's one uneasy Arab ally; of the dangers of religious fundamentalism to a country like Egypt with its urban poverty and its wealthy but vulnerable Coptic Christian minority; and, most secretly of all, some doubted the viability of Hosni Mubarak's government, while others dreamed wetly of military coups.

"Terrible, these bombs," Foster offered wisely as breakfast arrived. "I blame it on the politicians. They're holding back the army. You'd see, if they let them off the leash for a week. No quarter, no questions, just like a war. They'd soon sort these bastards out."

"Just like Ulster, you mean?"

Foster paused to spit watermelon-seeds into his palm. Chas could sense him wondering what sort of wimpish liberal he had on his hands. "That's more complicated."

"It always is."

They finished breakfast in silence. There had been another bombing the previous day, in Port Said. Six dead, fourteen wounded, one a four-year-old child who had lost both her legs in the blast. Christ.

He had come to love this country. It had been his real home for ten years now. More, if you counted the time he had spent here when working on his doctorate. Doctor Charles Winterton, of Cambridge University. Funny, how grand that still sounded to Egyptians; how little like failure. Though he sometimes missed the in-bred certainties of Gwydir Street parties and King's College Chapel, this was where he belonged now. This was what he knew. How could people do this to each other?

He thought back to Cambridge, with its wholefoods and vegetarians, its nuclear disarmers and madrigal singers, and wondered why respect there, through the long years of his researches, should have mattered so much more than the daily respect Egyptians offered him. People who were usually too busy with making enough for food and shelter to care about the moral whims and piping which seemed to matter so much in the city of his youth. And now, now that he had discovered something to make Cambridge sit up and notice, something to

15

justify what it thought of as his wasted years, he wondered if he really wanted it. He wondered if he really cared.

But that was silly. He had earned his share of fame and adulation by ten years in the desert. He wanted it all right. He wanted it all, right now. And to get it he would have to start with a little of David Medina's money.

The same thought must have occurred to Foster for, looking at his watch (it was a Rolex, Chas noticed; how could he afford that on a civil servant's salary?), he said, "We'd better go. Have you got the papers?" Without waiting for a reply, he unrolled a wad of notes and settled the bill.

Chas rose saying, "I'll go get my stuff. I'll see you outside."

Foster nodded without looking up, and as he did so added, "Remember, this meeting is arranged on the basis that whatever happens you say nothing to anyone without prior agreement. No announcements. No press releases. No letters to colleagues. Nothing."

The sweat sprang from them as soon as they stepped outside. There was, as always, dust everywhere, dust and sand. It got so bad that even the balconies on modern towerblocks had to have gutters through which to sweep the sand out. It got everywhere, like rain in England, thought Chas. It was a fact of life. He almost suggested calling into the café opposite, where he had spent so many evenings, for a glass of the local blackcurrant-and-orange cordial, but duty and ambition called.

Out in the Sharia El Alfi, all the colours were bleached by the flat light. The glare off the windows made it almost impossible to look at anything directly. Chas, who took no chances, wore sunglasses, but Foster's machismo reduced him to screwed-up eyes and hopping discomfort. He flagged down a black-and-white cab with relief. Chas bent down to talk to the driver.

"Zamalek. Sharia Kamel Mohammed."

The driver grinned and held up four fingers. "*Araba.*"

Chas grinned back saying, *"Mish maghnoun,"* I'm not crazy, and held up two fingers.

As the driver leaned forward to bargain Foster scowled "Sod this," and wrenched the car door open, settling himself in with cries of *"Araba, araba,"* to the delight of the driver and

16

Winterton's dismay.

Chas got in himself and, as the driver put the battered old Peugeot through a hideous squealing U-turn, said sadly, "You really shouldn't have done that, you know. The official fare's barely one pound fifty."

"Screw that. I'm not arguing about a couple of quid in this weather. Life's too short."

That, thought Chas, *is the trouble with people like you. You're so busy rushing through life throwing your money around that you never take the time to lie back and enjoy it.*

The drive was no more insane than most cab rides through Cairo. At least this time they at no stage had to get out and push, which happened often enough, and their lives were threatened in the race through the crowded streets by the hostile cornering of only two trucks, three buses and one donkey-cart. They were due at Medina's company flat on Zamalek Island in the Nile, where the city's grandees lived, at ten. They might have walked it quicker, thought Chas; or at least they might have done if there were no streets to cross. Cairo drivers felt much the same about pedestrians as good Muslims did about bacon sandwiches, and the authorities had long given up hope at the main squares and intersections, building rickety pedestrian bridges from which the true madness of the traffic could be surveyed.

Foster interrupted his idle thoughts. "I've been having a quiet, a very quiet, word with a few people about your case . . . ."

It isn't a case, Chas felt like saying; *I'm nobody's idea of a criminal.*

"You know the kind of thing. No names, no pack-drill. . . ."

Of course, thought Chas, he's just old enough to have done National Service. No wonder he sounds like Wellington all the time.

"And what you have to understand is that if you're right about this letter. . . ."

"I am right."

There was no stopping Foster, however. "If you're right about this letter, the whole thing could prove very sensitive indeed. You know what this place is like right now, and the

Muslims are always touchy as hell about the Copts." He must have wondered about the security of a public taxi suddenly for, nodding at the driver, he asked confidentially, "No chance of this chap understanding us, is there?"

"Oh, I expect so," Chas replied stony-faced. "I should think he works for the KGB."

Foster assumed his hail-fellow-well-met colonial accent and, patting the driver heavily on the shoulder, called out cheerfully, "No chance of that, is there, you pork-eating woggo bastard?"

He sat back reassured when he saw that the driver's only response was to grin in the mirror, and continued.

"The thing is, there are all kinds of people who might not be too happy to discover the Copts sit on the right hand of God, and who's to say how the Copts will react themselves if they discover they're the best thing since five loaves and two fishes? So while the whole thing's being verified, keep it hush, all right? And that'll give us a chance to sort out how to arrange the announcement."

"But what about Medina?"

Foster looked anxiously at the driver before answering that. "Well, Ewen Jones explained you needed some money, and I know Medina quite well. . . . He'll play along about secrecy, you can be certain of that."

Chas was well aware of it, if only on the basis of scattered news-magazine articles read over the years, and the little which surfaced about Medina in the non-financial press. If nothing else came of it, this trip would be worth it for the chance of meeting one of the richest men in the world. It was like meeting Midas himself. He tried to recall what little he knew of the man.

He tried to remember the layout of the article in *Newsweek* he had read a couple of years before. Single column photograph, colour, of Medina arriving at the private view of an exhibition of works drawn from his collection. What had it been that time? Pre-Columbian carvings? Or post-Impressionist masters? Hadn't there been some scandal about that? Something about him donating his post-Impressionists to the National Gallery of Art in Washington DC just weeks before

18

his company was allocated premium drilling and exploration rights in the Gulf of Mexico by the US government.

Remember that photograph. Looked much younger than his seventy-odd years. Was there a woman with him? Younger? *Can't remember.* Is he married?

Carries an American passport, as did his parents, though his father was born in the Levant, his mother in Ireland. Takes after his father, quite short, very powerful, but has his mother's eyes. Green. (*How did I remember that?*) Father's first millions were made in furs and whale-oil. (*Whalebone too? How much Innuit sculpture do we owe to old man Medina?*) Traded mainly with Canada and Russia before the Revolution. Saw the potential for the motor car and diversified into oil and gas in the early years of the century.

Eldest son killed by White Russian troops on his first trip to Russia in 1918. Broke his father's heart. Old man died a year later during the flu epidemic. David still a schoolboy. Mother ran the company till he was ready to take over. Till her death in the Sixties Medina's only close confidante.

Medina maintained close trade links with Communist Russia, and Eastern bloc after '45. How did he manage that without State Department approval? How did he keep clear of the McCarthy witch-hunt? Bribery, presumably. And services to the CIA? What about services to the KGB?

Parent company of the group now registered in Liechten-stein. Impenetrable to outside observers. American companies incorporated in Delaware, state with minimum disclosure requirements. Total group (name of group? Of course. International Trade & Industry. ITI) believed to be the largest private conglomerate in the world. Discounting the holdings of the Saudi royal family and perhaps six other royal families around the world. Total assets? Undisclosed, but estimated in excess of seven billion US dollars. Believed to be significantly greater than those of the Royal Houses of Windsor, Hapsburg and Bourbon combined.

How achieved? Used trade to gain the confidence of governments so as to be awarded mineral exploration rights. Maintained largest, and most brilliant, team of geologists of any company in world. Used mineral assets as collateral for borrowings to finance further trade. Rumoured use of bribery, corruption, punitive takeover bids and effective monopolies.

Chas sat back exhausted, his eyes closed, pleased at having remembered so much. Then he smiled, as he recalled the most important facts of all. David Medina was that rarest of things, a rich man who collected for pleasure, not for profit or out of pride. He could afford to indulge himself, it was true. Except for Armand Hammer of Occidental Oil, there was probably no other individual collector alive who could afford to buy a Gutenberg Bible, a Shakespeare First Folio and seventeen mature Raphaels, but, like Hammer, he was a genuine amateur. He had published a scholarly monograph on the Genoese School and prepared the Italian, German, Russian, Spanish, French and Swedish translations himself. He had personally financed six private press publishers in Italy and England. He awarded pensions to painters, sculptors, writers, and supported theatre companies through the Medina Foundation. He maintained a personal staff of art historian/curators. He supported opera composers he loathed and ballet companies he loved. His collection of scientific instruments and treatises was perhaps the finest in the world. And he was in Cairo for the opening of an exhibition of the works of early Arab cartographers and cosmographers which was to include his collection of astrolabes. The whole exhibition was drawn from Medina's collection, and he had written part of the catalogue himself.

Chas could not help wondering what political favours the show was supposed to pay off or purchase.

He was shaken out of his reverie by Foster. They had crossed on to Zamalek and were approaching the ITI flat overlooking the Gabalaya Park.

"Typical millionaire's view," said Foster snidely.

Chas was on the point of agreeing when he realized that, although nothing on Zamalek could be unfashionable, the flat overlooked the poorer West Bank of the river. Perhaps Medina did not care as much for show as he had guessed. He ignored the speculation. It did not do to be too generous to millionaires.

Foster paid off the taxi and the doorman showed them up to the flat on the first floor. Both of them found themselves fiddling nervously with their ties and the buttons of their jackets. The secretary, after a decade in Egypt, came as less of a surprise to Chas than to Foster. He was a Palestinian in his middle-twenties. Chas guessed he was American-educated, and that Medina chose high-flying graduates to serve as his secretaries; Chas thought it a charmingly nineteenth-century custom. What came as a surprise to both of them was the carpets. They were on the walls. In each room, at least one antique hand-knotted Middle Eastern carpet hung on a wall. There was no other decoration, save for the parquet floor and the lacquered furniture, from the Turkish period by the look of it.

They were shown into a drawing-room which ran the whole length of the flat and they settled into chairs by the window over the park.

"Mr Medina will be with you shortly," the secretary informed them in a faint Boston accent, which on its own made Chas feel under-dressed, and indicated to the other side of the room where, safely out of earshot, the old man was dealing with another of his secretaries.

What struck Chas immediately was that, although a reading table stood at his elbow, Medina did not use a desk. The second was that the room contained not a single telephone. He wondered how people got hold of Medina, and then he realized that was precisely the point. No one got hold of Medina. He got in touch when they could serve him, but he was permanently unavailable. Chas found himself impressed despite his deep distrust. Foster was just about to lean over to whisper something when they were interrupted by the return of the first secretary bearing a tea tray; English tea in blue and white porcelain. There was juggling with milk and sugar and lemon for Foster, and before they were aware of it Medina was seated by the window, forbidding them to stand to greet him.

He accepted tea himself and Chas was surprised at how much larger he was than he seemed in his photographs. His hands in particular were vast, with long powerful fingers and broad manicured nails. He waved the secretaries away and as they retreated the first one asked, "Shall I send in Miss Carfax, sir?"

21

Medina looked at Chas as he replied, without any trace of an American accent, "That won't be necessary, Ismail, but ask her to wait outside. Please call us at eleven, and inform the Chinese secretaries I shall need them at eleven-fifteen." He turned to his guests apologetically. "I'm sorry to offer you so little time, but I am required to draft a letter to the Chinese government before the opening of business in Beijing today."

Chas did a quick sum with the time zones. It made sense. He found himself impressed again. It gave Foster the chance to butt in.

"That's quite all right, David. Thank you for seeing us at all. . . ."

He had looked the old man in the eye and it had silenced him. Chas guessed the use of Medina's first name had been the unforgivable sin. Medina simply looked at Foster, and Foster seemed to diminish visibly. He did not speak again until he was leaving.

Medina turned to Chas as though nothing had happened and unfolded his huge right hand. "Dr Winterton, how do you do? I'm so glad you could make it." By the time Chas could remove his hand it felt as though a truck had run over it.

"It was good of you to see me, sir. I know how busy you must be, and as you don't know my work. . . ."

"Oh, but I do, Dr Winterton."

He's lying, thought Chas. *He's had somebody look me up.*

Medina continued without faltering or blinking. "Cambridge, wasn't it? A Two-One in Oriental Languages and a First in Archaeology and Anthropology under Henry Kircauldie. Your doctorate was on pre-Islamic Arab alphabets in Jericho. That led to comparative work elsewhere. Am I right so far?"

"Perfectly." *Whatever else he may be,* Chas thought, *he is immensely plausible.*

"I've read your papers on variant transcriptions of Hebrew and non-cursive forms of Pharaonic, of course, but I've been out of touch with your work since then. Perhaps you could bring me up to date."

Chas was stunned. All right, he had probably mugged it up without ever having set eyes on the papers, but if so, he had recited his lesson perfectly (something none of Chas's family could do) and his staff's research work had been impeccable. Chas thought quickly before answering.

"I'd be happy to, sir, of course, but I'm intrigued. How do you know Henry Kircauldie?"

Chas thought he saw the old man almost smile, as though he recognized the question as an attempt to sound him out, to find out how much of his knowledge was authentic, and how much specially got up for this meeting.

"I'm afraid the answer, Dr Winterton," he replied, "as so often in my case, revolves around money. Twenty years ago, when I first got interested in early examples of writing, it was a matter of great sadness to me that I was frequently forced to pay more than I desired for certain pieces, or to let them go altogether, because of the opposition of another purchaser with as good an eye and even more patience than myself and my advisers. I discovered that my opponent was the Museum of Archaeology and Anthropology at Cambridge and, on its behalf, Professor Kircauldie. I arranged a meeting, and we have been friends ever since."

Chas was surprised, almost shocked. "I thought auction arrangements were illegal."

"They are, which is why we never made one. All that has happened is that when the price of a piece seems certain to rise above what Arch and Anth. . . " Chas was impressed again; Medina used the Cambridge abbreviation, "could afford, they have agreed not to bid at all, and I, in my turn, have undertaken, should I be successful, to let them have the piece on semi-permanent loan."

"I'm impressed."

"As you should be. But you were telling me about your career."

Chas smiled. He had been doing no such thing, but he let Medina have his way. After all, he needed the old man's money. "Well, sir, I've been based in Egypt for the last ten years. You obviously know my early work. Since then I've been cataloguing the various Coptic collections of manuscripts. I finished the cataloguing of the Coptic Museum and the Cairo churches first. That was relatively easy. . . . "

23

"Even so," Medina interrupted, "money must have been a problem. I can't imagine there were many foundations or research councils which thought the job was worth the expense."

He had hit on Chas's favourite subject. "You're quite right. All the research money for Egypt goes to the sexy projects. Egypt under the Pharaohs, and the Arab Conquests. Still, Cambridge was very patient, and the Société d'Archéologie Copte did what it could, but I haven't been helped by the Coptic Authorities insisting I show good faith by spending four years cataloguing their minor monasteries before I was allowed into any of the great ones."

Medina was clearly appalled. "Four years!"

"Yes, sir. Down at Aswan and on the Red Sea."

"Even so. . . ."

"Well, quite. You see, in two cases I wasn't allowed just to catalogue the manuscripts. I had to prepare descriptive catalogues of their entire collections and transcribe all their manuscripts. So far, I've transcribed all or part of fourteen uncollected Gospels, and that was only the start."

The mention of uncollected Gospels had interested the old man, as it had been intended to. "Anything new in the Gospels?"

Chas shook his head sadly. "Nothing that isn't duplicated elsewhere. I have an arrangement with Cairo and Princeton to publish my work, but it's so intensely specialized, and money's so tight, that nothing's ever come of it. Just look how few of even the Dead Sea Scrolls have been published. That's an academic scandal and my work comes a long way down the list from them in terms of newsworthiness."

Medina smiled and sympathized. "Which is what really matters these days, as both of us know. Where does that leave you now?"

"I'm broke. My last grant ran out three months ago. I've survived by living at the monasteries at Wadi el Natroun, where I've been working for the past few years. I've used the last money I had to get here for this meeting. If you refuse me, I'll have to ask the British Consulate to stump up my plane-fare home."

24

Medina scowled and inspected his fingernails, not looking at Winterton as he spoke. "It's my policy, Dr Winterton," he said softly, "never to countenance personal appeals. My funding of academic research is dealt with by the advisory boards of the Medina Foundation. To be honest, I only agreed to see you because Mr Foster suggested that there might be something else, something quite specific, which might interest me, perhaps even as a collector."

Chas took a deep breath. This was it: the selling opportunity, and he would only get one chance.

"That is correct. There is something. Something I've discovered very recently, and which I don't think I would have found if I hadn't got into the habit of preparing comprehensive descriptive catalogues down at Aswan. I owe that to the Coptic authorities, but it's what's slowed down my work so much that I've finally run out of money."

Medina was still interested. *Right*, thought Chas, *I've played the humble bit. Now it's time for the transparent cunning.*

He leaned forward in his chair, crossing his arms over his portfolio case. "Martin Foster knows what it is, as does Ewen Jones in Alexandria, but they know only the barest details and, frankly, sir, that's the way I want to keep it."

Foster sat up, startled. Winterton pressed on.

"You'll realize, sir, that if I'm right, this is the biggest manuscript discovery since at least the Renaissance. Its repercussions could be vast. Until it's been authenticated, the fewer people who know the details the better. I have those details with me here." He patted the portfolio case. "And I don't want Martin Foster present while we go through them."

"For God's sake. . . " Foster protested.

"Shut up, Martin."

It was meant to make him angry and it did. "Who the hell do you think you are?" he began, but the instant his voice rose the door flew open and she was into the room heading towards him. Medina stopped her with a single imperious gesture.

"It's all right, Carfax. Mr Foster was just leaving."

My God, thought Chas, *who is she?* He had never seen anyone like her in his life. Or had he? Had it been her, half-glimpsed and half-remembered in the *Newsweek* photograph?

If so, who was she? Medina's mistress? If that, how did you get to keep a woman like her, besides by being one of the richest men alive?

Anger and suspicion still burned in her eyes. They were as green as Medina's, Chas noticed. *Daughter?* he wondered for a brief wild instant. Then Medina reasserted calm and his authority.

"See Mr Foster out, will you, Carfax, and rejoin us when you've done so. And please don't worry, Mr Foster. If anything comes of this business, you will be suitably rewarded."

She shimmered away, and was immediately replaced by Ismail. Medina was curt. "Postpone the eleven-fifteen meeting, Ismail. Call us again at twelve-thirty. If Dr Winterton and I are not finished by then, instruct the Chinese secretaries to prepare a holding telex to Beijing along the lines we discussed this morning. And Ismail, cancel all my other meetings today."

"Including the Finance Minister, sir? He's due at five this afternoon."

"No, not him. It will do him no harm if he has to wait a little." Then Ismail was gone and Carfax re-emerged. He got a closer look at her this time and it was better than the first. She was tall, with a calm, objective beauty which relied on nothing and no one. A small oval face in waves of heavy chestnut hair, green eyes, a strong straight nose, and a full mouth that looked bruised with kisses. Her silk suit was cut loose in deference to Muslim sensibilities, but she moved with a long sinuous pace that told it concealed a lot worth moving. She took her seat silently and never took her eyes off Chas. He felt his headache return, and the flushes, and knew it was her and not the previous night's drinking. She made him feel young and easily embarrassed again. Medina rescued him from his unease.

"I appreciate what you say about confidentiality, Dr Winterton, but I require a witness to whatever you may have to say." Chas doubted that. He guessed that all Medina's offices were wired for sound. "So Carfax will remain with us."

Chas managed to stammer some reply.

"Good," Medina said finally, dismissing the Foster episode altogether. "Now, you have something you want to tell me."

Winterton gathered his thoughts and turned to the old man,

26

ignoring his headache. The time had come to sing for his supper.

"Yes, sir, but first I'd better explain what I'm going to need, if you find yourself interested by what I have to show you. Whatever happens, the document will need to be authenticated by at least two independent scholars of international stature. As it happens, Henry Kircauldie and Jennifer St Clair of Arch and Anth will both be at the International Society of Antiquaries conference which opens in Athens in a fortnight's time. I estimate that clearing my lines of authority here in Egypt and going to Athens to see them will cost about a thousand dollars. They will want to come to Egypt themselves, since the document itself is currently immovable. Allow another thousand or fifteen hundred dollars for their expenses, and mine. Finally, even if they are interested, now all my grants are suspended you may have to finance the necessary tests. That could cost the Medina Foundation anything up to a further quarter of a million dollars. In return for whatever your costs may prove to be, you get equal status with the discoverer."

Medina laughed for the first time that morning. "Dr Winterton, I can assure you that if you are right I shall want a great deal more than that, though that is a matter for myself and the Coptic authorities, and a quarter of a million dollars will be neither here nor there. Your evidence, if you please."

Winterton unzipped his portfolio case, and paused before producing the first photograph. "I should explain that, for security's sake, I developed these photographs myself. They have their imperfections." Medina waved him on, and he handed over the photographs. The old man puzzled over them for several minutes before speaking.

"I recognize the script, of course. Cursive Alexandrian Greek. But the language I do not know. Semitic, I should say."

"You would be right. It's Aramaic, as used in Galilee."

Suddenly Medina laughed again, like a dangerous boy. "The rest of it, Dr Winterton."

Chas handed over his typescript. "This is a draft of my intended article on the letter. It contains all the necessary details of environment and provenance, a transcript, a transliteration and a translation. It's as well documented as I can make it until the tests are completed. Right now it's all I have to say."

Six hours later the three of them were still seated at the window. The telex to Beijing had gone, and the Finance Minister still waited in the ante-chamber, and David Medina was smiling.

"It's very convincing, Dr Winterton. Very convincing indeed, and quite enough to warrant an initial expense of two thousand dollars or so, but I have only one question to ask you: By all that you hold holy, and on your mother's grave, are you certain? Are you sure?"

Chas smiled back in return. "I'm not sure that what anyone holds holy is appropriate in the circumstances, Mr Medina, and the last time I heard, my mother was very much alive, but I will tell you this: I believe that letter is what it appears to be. With a decade's experience in the field and nearly twenty years in the academic discipline, I trust my own judgement, and my judgement tells me it is what it says it is. I believe it to be St Peter's Will."

Cairo/Wadi El Natroun

His headache was gone when he woke next morning, but he
had an erection the size of a tent-pole. He had been dreaming
of Carfax. He tried to forget it and her by going through the
events of the previous evening.

Medina had broken off their talks for an hour to deal with
the Finance Minister, leaving Chas with Carfax. He had found
himself with almost nothing to say to her. That was strange in
itself, for years in desert monasteries had made him grateful
for, and good at, the smallest of small talk. She, however, was
almost entirely self-contained. When she spoke at all, it was to
ask if he wanted more tea, or to check his material requirements. It was she who had arranged to have a car put at his
disposal (a Range Rover, he noted with approval; she knew
what was practical in this country). He had been surprised to
discover that she was English, or so her name and accent
suggested. It was a warm voice, he recalled, which hinted at
shamelessness and great reserves of patience. It had taken him
aback, for he had always vaguely thought of professional
mistresses as being raucous Americans or Italians, or silent
Swedes or Swiss. Her greatest attraction was her independence, though. She had rejected his friendly approaches by
insisting Carfax was her only name.

Still, he had been glad when Medina told him that he was to
deal only with the girl or Medina himself. They had given him a
list of telephone and telex numbers. All of them laughed at
that, for the telephone system in Egypt hardly ever worked but,
as Medina pointed out, telexes from post-office bureaux
usually got through. They had given him two and a half
thousand dollars in clean bills, mixed denominations. (Ismail
had brought it through in an envelope made of hand-woven
rag paper — Medina's personal stationery, Chas guessed —

29

carried on a silver tray.) The two men had signed letters of intent concerning the Fisherman's Will, and Chas had signed a receipt. They had agreed that no announcements of any kind were to be made, at least until Henry Kircauldie and Jennifer St Clair had had the chance to carry out a preliminary inspection, and they agreed to keep in touch every few days although, except in the event of an emergency, they would not meet again until the private view and party for the Medina exhibition ten days from now. At the end, only one thing puzzled Chas Winterton. He had put the question directly.

"I think we're going to work together very well, Mr Medina, but will you tell me one thing? How do you know I'm genuine? For all you know this could be a — " he groped for the right American term — "scam or a sting. A way of making a quick twenty-five hundred dollars."

The old man smiled, and so, for the first time, did Carfax. He nodded to her and she went out to talk briefly with Ismail, returning with a small package.

"You're quite right, Dr Winterton. It could be a sting, but I knew that if you were who you said you were there was very little chance of that. You are a scholar, after all, and perhaps even a gentleman. All I had to do was to establish that you were really Charles Winterton, and there has never been any point in trusting Martin Foster."

Medina smiled again as Carfax handed him the envelope. He sliced it open with a fingernail, still speaking as he did so.

"I'm very glad to see that the Hotel Windsor still complies so exactly with police requirements. Your passport was passed to the police at eight this morning for registration. I took the liberty of instructing the Chief of Police to return it directly to me." He glanced at it briefly, and passed the battered blue document back to Chas, who winced again at the seven-year-old photograph taken in a booth at Victoria Coach Station. He hoped that Carfax had not looked at it.

Should he ask her to dinner? With what? Medina's money? She could get that directly. She made him wish he was richer and more powerful. She made him realize with sad certainty that, even with the kind of fame the Fisherman's Will would bring him, he could not have everything he wanted. Mad dons and Englishmen had their limitations.

The soft Egyptian night was already falling when he left. Medina's final warning still troubled him. "You're quite right to insist on confidentiality, Dr Winterton, as I expect you're sick of being told by Jones and Foster, but they have a vested interest. Like every other diplomat in Egypt, they have connections with the undercover services. You see, it isn't only the Catholic Church that won't take kindly to your discovery. There are powers who would do anything to prevent destabilization in Egypt."

What had he meant? Who had he meant?

As they stood talking in the hall, the wealthy silence of Zamalek, padded still further in the flat by the carpets on the walls, was broken by a single, flat thud.

"What was that?" asked Chas.

"That," said Carfax, who seemed to know about such things, "was a bomb."

"Be careful, Dr Winterton," Medina had added. "We can't afford to lose you now."

He sat up in bed and ran a hand through his hair. As he took a shower he tried to remember his plans for today, he tried to put her out of his mind. He would drive out to the monastery at Natroun. He had to persuade the Abbot to preserve confidentiality, for now at least. He was worried by the Coptic passion. They had been out of communion with the rest of Christianity since 451 AD, condemned at Chalcedon for heresy, but still believed they were the one true Church. He could imagine all too well how they would react at the opportunity to prove the fact, to their own satisfaction at least. Perhaps that was what Medina had meant. There were quite enough people claiming to have the One True Faith and look where it got you. War between Iran and Iraq. War within Lebanon. Civil War in Ireland and damn near the same in India. Was there any need to add another true faith to the pyre, with all the passions that went with it, in Egypt of all places? Wasn't there enough war round the world?

It was not his problem. He would try to get them to stay calm while the tests were done, but he would not hide the truth or hide from fame. Was that it? Was he just too greedy now success was in his grasp? Success after years of being scorned as a man wasting his and everyone else's time? The hell with that. Other people would do what they wanted, whatever decisions he might make. He wanted a bit of what David Medina had. He wanted Carfax.

Damn! he thought, as he went down to breakfast. *Damn the woman.*

He had arranged for ITI to send telegrams on his behalf to Henry Kircauldie and Jenny St Clair. After nearly fifteen years he still could not get used to her married name. Was she still married? Probably. Computers he had been in. One of those stable, sensible bastards. Minting it.

He ordered French coffee and one of the sweet Egyptian croissants. Whatever happened he had to keep the Copts out of touch with Rome or the Western Desert would be swarming with black-frocked priests screaming, "Liar! Fake!" And whatever Medina said he had better keep in touch with Jones at the British Council. There was no way he would get a knighthood unless he played the Establishment line. He could go to Alexandria tomorrow. Indulge himself a little. He was spending Medina's money now. He had changed five hundred dollars with a black-market dealer in Sharia Champollion the previous night, close to the Thomas Cook offices. Yes, Alexandria. Stay at the Metropole. Get a decent shave, a haircut, a woman. All the services of the Alexandrian barbershop. How long was it since he had even touched a woman? Weeks? *Months?* It was the one daft disadvantage of the work and place he had chosen. She had green eyes and chestnut hair. What did she look like naked? He could imagine. He could imagine. She was magnificent.

The hell with it, he thought. The hell with waiting. Was Ibrahim on duty? He was. He called him over, unfolding a banknote.

"Ibrahim," he murmured. *"Une femme. Jeune. Nette. Vite."*

Afterwards, feeling calmer, he had the hotel book a phone-call through to Carfax. He might as well use some of Medina's muscle, he thought. Miraculously, the call got put through.

Her voice was gentler on the telephone than he remembered. She sounded softer than she looked. He steadied himself. He had no business being sentimental.

She was surprised to hear him. "I thought you'd have set off for the desert by now."

"I had some business to finish in Cairo."

"Oh, yes? Was she worth it?" He hesitated. She laughed. "It must be the effect of wildernesses. David's the same when he gets back from the fur-farms."

David? The same? Mistress.

"I'm off to Natroun now. I have to get to Alexandria tomorrow. Can you get hold of Ewen Jones at the Council and tell him I'll meet him in the bar at the Cecil tomorrow at four?"

"At four, fine."

"And can you book me a room with a bath at the Metropole?"

"The Metropole. I'm impressed. I thought you'd be spending David's money at places like the Sheraton."

"Too far out. And I'm too old a dog to learn new tricks now. The Metropole's all right."

"I know, we've used it. Nice restaurant round the corner."

"Come again."

"Pardon?"

"Why don't you join me?" He was appalled at his own nerve. She paused before answering.

"No, thank you, Dr Winterton. I don't encourage desert rats. One night at the Metropole?"

"One night. You'd better take advantage of it. I'll be back in the monastery after that."

She laughed. "You will have to learn, Dr Winterton, that we really only love you for your mind. What about Athens?"

"Any news from Professor Kircauldie?"

"Not so far."

He thought before answering. Was Henry going to be difficult? He ignored the thought. "Book me on the cheapest flight to Athens on the 20th, returning on the 22nd. I think Balkan run a service."

"David will be pleased. He's not used to people who want to travel cheaply."

"He should try employing a few more real researchers."

She did not answer at once, as though the remark had been aimed at her, then was businesslike. "OK, where do you want to collect the tickets?"

"You pick them up. We'll sort it out later."

"Fine. If any news comes in today I'll have it telexed to the Metropole tomorrow."

She rang off without saying goodbye. Chas settled his bill, tipping Ibrahim heavily, and prepared for the trip to Natroun.

There was no way round it. He would have to drive through the worst the city could offer to get out to Highway 11. Wadi El Natroun was only a little over two hundred kilometres away. Even taking things easy in the summer heat he could be there in less than three hours. But first he had to get out of the city. It was a long time since he had driven in Cairo, but he had known the country long enough to learn patience. He chose the easiest but busiest route, down Tal'at Harb and El Qasr El Aini, risking the traffic at Midan Tahrir, the city's most insane intersection, to the Giza Bridge and the Pyramid Road. It was about a six-kilometre journey out of town, and it took the best part of an hour. He almost thought it was worth it as he swung out on to the Giza Bridge. Even now, after all these years, the very sight of the Nile calmed him. He loved it as Egyptians loved it, this gentlest and most generous of big rivers, placid since the dam was built at Aswan, harnessing the floods, but preventing the precious silts from flowing through the country. For thousands of years Egyptians had called their country the Gift of the Nile, and now it had been tamed, and Egypt had become an importer of the fertilizers the river's floodtide once bore to it free.

He turned on to Highway 11, the Alexandria road, built through the desert during the First World War, at Giza. He hardly noticed the pyramids at all, half-invisible in the glare against the chalk white sky. It was years since he had visited them. Envy partly. Envy of the way the vast majority of funds still got diverted to Ancient Egyptology, but also a sense that they were built to dominate rather than console. They were too big, too simple, to be human. He had once called them a monumental waste of time.

34

Still, perhaps he ought to go back one day soon. Perhaps his boredom would change — as it had that first time, sixteen years ago with Jennifer — to astonishment, and awe. Or perhaps he would go out to Saqqara, to the Serapeum and the Step Pyramid, the oldest of them all, where international teams were spending hundreds of thousands excavating the complex, always knowing that once they had finished the winds and the sand would cover the ruins again as though they had never been.

Yes, he would go to Saqqara soon, on camel from Giza, by way of Abu Sir. It took about four hours, past palm groves and canals full of water rats and hoopoes, out into the desert and the implacable sands. When all this was over, and he was covered in glory.

And he would take Carfax with him.

A truck packed with angry chickens swerved in front of him and he had to brake sharply. Behind him an angry taxi-driver hooted. Well, sod him.

It was one of those flash new Toyota taxis someone rich had hired to drive him out to the monasteries, or even Alexandria. Silly bastard. Didn't he know there was a bus? Even the First-Class train to Alex only cost a few pounds. Still, they were everywhere nowadays, along with Japanese machinery. Even the buses were built by the little guys who had brought you Pearl Harbour and the Sony Walkman. Years before they had been built by Tata Industries of India, but that was before the days of Hirohito's Second Empire.

He would have to watch himself. He was getting sentimental. There was no nostalgia worse than Third World nostalgia. Egyptians welcomed these sorts of changes, because they made their lives simpler, better, richer, and it was their country to do as they wanted with.

His problems right now were simpler, and a great deal more important. Was he right about the letter he had discovered? And what was his downside risk? What had he better prepare for?

Outside him, the dusty desert road and the shifting dunes curled out to the horizon. Everything was white now in the afternoon sun. White as far as the eye could see, which might

35

be all eternity or only yards away for all the difference it made.

That bloody cab was still sitting on his tail. He accelerated away. What was wrong with the old Peugeots anyway? he thought. He had liked them ever since he had noticed the taximeters (never used) were made in Paris by a firm in rue la Condamine, up in the seventeenth arondissement, where he had lived one summer as a student, with a French girlfriend and all the time in the world. It had been 1968, the summer after the riots, and at Cambridge afterwards he had been able to share all the reflected glory of the Latin Quarter, with none of the dangers.

That had been a long time ago. A lot had gone wrong since then, but now he was putting it right. Now he had hit the jackpot.

What had Medina meant about powers not wanting Egypt destabilized? He had sounded like Bismarck, or was it Metternich? Chas did not know much about modern history. Anything after about 500 AD was kids' stuff, petty cash. Modern historians amused him. They had too much to read and not enough to think about. Still, what had Medina meant? What could possibly happen?

It was true the Roman Catholics would not be delighted. He had been brought up a Catholic himself; he knew all about that. If the letter was authentic, and it was, then it was the draft of Peter's last letter (Simon, he still called himself in it) to James the Just in Jerusalem; to Jesus's brother, the Patriarch. The last letter of a dying man, reviewing his life and his faith. It was damaged all right (as what wouldn't be after nineteen centuries?) but in good condition, and there was plenty enough internal evidence to show that he had died in Alexandria, as the Copts had always said, not Rome. All right, so the Catholic Church had always admitted (in private) that the oldest records named Babylon as the place Peter died, but hadn't they always claimed Babylon meant Rome? Hadn't they excavated St Peter's tomb under the Vatican a few years ago? Oh, no, they had not. They had got it wrong. A tomb, yes. Of a saint, yes. Perhaps an early Pope. But not St Peter. He was dust out here, long vanished, like Alexander. So much for the Pope being head of the Universal Church by right of descent from the

Apostle, by treading in the shoes of the Fisherman. Wrong! Nice try, chaps. Worked for quite a long time. What are you going to do for your next trick? What about the next nineteen centuries?

No, Rome wouldn't like it at all, but who else had Medina meant, and why would that taxi never leave itself a proper braking distance?

What could happen? What could go wrong? True, the Copts would be ecstatic. True, things would take a bit of time to settle down. But the Copts were barely an eighth of the population, what damage could they do, in Egypt, the calmest country in the Middle East?

He decelerated as it sank in.

Christ! he thought, punching the dashboard. *Christ!*

He had been naïve. The taxi behind him had to swerve as he slowed down. They were approaching the Guest House half-way to Alexandria where he would turn off for the Wadi. The taxi overtook him and sped off for Alexandria. Did he recognize the passenger? Or was his imagination proving too fertile? Had it been Ismail? Surely not. He buried the thought. He buried everything he had been thinking of as he turned towards the village.

The road was tarmac through the village in the valley and out to Deir Abou Bishoi, the grandest of the four monasteries, which all the tourists went to. The previous summer, an American woman had spent six weeks camped outside Bishoi, complaining about the fact that women were not allowed to visit the monasteries. The local people had ignored her, muttering "Maghnoun," and making the sign of the Evil Eye, but it had offended Chas deeply. There were still places where men could not go either, and quite right too. When would people learn that not everywhere was Disneyland?

Near here was the Syrian monastery where Curzon had discovered a priceless cache of manuscripts in the oil cellar, a hundred and fifty years before; but Chas's destination was the least accessible monastery of all, Deir el Baramus, across the sands to the north. In the past he had always walked it. He was glad of the Range Rover now. He parked beside the high arch

37

which held the single little black door in the monastery's curtain walls. Buildings and palm trees showed above the compound and he knew he would have been spotted by now, but he rang the bell out of politeness, and waited.

It was nearly five o'clock. The monks would be at their prayers before re-starting work in the gardens or at the olive press, in the granary or bakery, in the cool of the evening. He would have to wait till they were finished and Abbot Yacoubu had retired to the Library in the *kasr*, the fortified keep, where he would intone the ritual Thanksgiving for Visitors as Chas was allowed into the monastery.

He did not have to wait long. The door was opened by a black-clad novice, Esa. He was a cheerful youth, though as grimy and ignorant as many of the monks. Only a few were ordained priests, and only they were literate. The rest memorized their chants and responses, learnt the gospels by heart, and hundreds of prayers, hymns and homilies by rote. Like every other foreigner who had learnt Coptic, in an exact reversal of the position during the Dark Ages, Chas had learnt the language out in the world and brought it back with him to Deir el Baramus. It was the hardest language he had ever learnt, a direct descendant of the language of the Pharaohs, the oldest living language in the world.

It was cool in the compound. The walls, the *kasr*, the two churches, the refectory, the cells, the date and banana palms in the garden, all gave shade and relief from the relentless summer sun. He had been allocated a cell when he first arrived at the monastery, and dropped off his hold-all now. The cell was hardly more ornate than a monk's. Bed, stool, portable type-writer, suitcase, a few books. He had paid for his obsession. Esa returned, to say the abbot was ready for him now. They walked over to the *kasr* together, Esa chattering all the way. It disturbed Chas to discover the abbot had announced that, by the grace of God and the patience of their visitor, he would soon be able to announce a great joy, which would gladden the hearts of the just, and cast down the unbeliever. No wonder the monks stopped their work to hail him as he passed. He would have to act quickly if the abbot was getting religion.

As he was shown into the library (a proper medieval library, containing no more than three hundred books, most of them in manuscript, most of them chained to the shelves, including some works dating back to before the first Viking raids on England) Abbot Yacoubu was just finishing the Thanksgiving for Visitors. Chas joined in the final prayer politely.

"Give them abundance of blessing. Bring them home in safety. After long life transport them to the brightness of Paradise and the life of bliss, through the Prayers of Our Lady the Virgin, and of all our holy fathers. Amen."

The abbot held out his arms, pleased to see Chas again. He was a short man even for an Egyptian and still very slight beneath his robes. He had been badly scarred by smallpox in his youth, and his left eye was clouding over with a cataract now, but he left no doubt that this was his monastery. "You are welcome, Doctor," he announced gravely. "Did your journey go well?"

"Quite well, Holy Father. Quite well."

"Be seated." Abbot Yacoubu waved him to a stool, reserving the single high-backed chair for himself. Here, at least, there was no doubt as to hierarchy or status. Within these walls, the abbot stood only a little lower than the imprisoned Coptic Pope, and God. "You have been in search of alms."

"I went to seek funds, yes."

"And did you find a benefactor?"

"I think so, Holy Father."

Abbot Yacoubu smiled. He approved of rich men unburdening themselves for the benefit of his monastery and their souls. It occurred to Chas that, after so many years locked away from the world, the abbot might be surprised at how rich the rich man was, and how little he had had to unburden himself to address their problem. The abbot continued with his prepared train of reasoning.

"Then I can announce your discovery to a waiting world."

Chas tried not to show his dismay. The abbot had been pressing for an announcement ever since he had first been told of the Englishman's suspicions. It was as though he expected the announcement of the discovery of the Fisherman's Will alone to lead to a wave of conversions, to redeem the Coptic Church from the margins of history, and to advance the date of

39

the Second Coming. It was more important than ever now to slow him down, to buy time. Chas tried to let the abbot down gently.

"I do not think that would be wise just yet, Holy Father."

"Wise, Doctor? It is not a matter of wisdom but a matter for truth. We house here the basis of salvation and the justification of my people. Every moment we delay lets more souls slide into unbelief, sin and damnation. It is my duty to witness the truth, and to proclaim it to the world at large."

Chas did his best to be patient for, by his own lights, Abbot Yacoubu was quite right. "As you say, Holy Father, this is a question of truth. We must never let it be said that the Coptic Fathers were too proud to let the truth be settled before they spoke. Sometimes truth grows in silence and in darkness. I am mortal, Holy Father, and liable to error. . . ." Once again Chas felt a pang of gratitude to the Jesuits who had taught him, and almost felt guilty at undermining their faith. "Errors of omission and commission arising from pride, or haste, or even excess of faith. As I told you before, that was why I went to seek funds. That tests might be made to ensure that I had seen rightly, and that what I took to be truth was true, before you endangered your reputation, your Church's reputation, and your people's reputation by announcing it. The tests are yet to be, Holy Father, as are the results. It is said that wise men know things yet to come. I am not so very wise, Holy Father, but in your company I have at least learned patience. Be patient with me yet."

Chas could feel his heart racing. Would it work? It would have to. It was eloquent stuff, especially for a foreigner, but could it defeat the impatience of centuries of injured pride?

It had been a mistake to tell the abbot what he had guessed until he was certain; he could see that now, but he had needed to tell someone and he had almost felt sorry for the abbot's injured and long-suffering faith. Abbot Yacoubu hesitated. Chas pressed home his advantage.

"There is more, Holy Father. Our benefactor wishes the letter to be authenticated with all certainty and skill. If you will only wait until we are certain, and he is certain also, I believe that the benefits which will flow here will be very great. So great as to make the gifts of Cairo and Alexandria seem as the playthings of children, and the treasures of Deir es Suriani seem as a candle in the noonday sun."

He waited. Would that do the trick? A little inter-monastic rivalry? A suggestion that this, the most remote of the monasteries, would soon outshine its sister-foundations? It was true, as well, quite true. Just as he would outshine all his fellow palaeographers.

It worked. The abbot hesitated just too long, and was convinced. He sat down defeated. "Very well, Doctor. You persuade me once again. But have you any idea how we suffer?"

Chas looked up and was taken aback to see tears in the abbot's clouded eyes. He had always discounted Coptic tales of woe and suffering. Although a minority, they had always remained a rich, proud, powerful people. They were heavily represented in banking, commerce and industry. They were great landowners. They. . . .

Then he remembered what had occurred to him as he had driven here. *Perhaps it's true,* he thought. *Perhaps it's especially a powerful, successful people —however long they have been established, however many thousand of years, even in their native homes — which feels most vulnerable when in a religious minority.* Perhaps this was how Jews felt everywhere. Then he remembered the headline he had seen on this morning's paper: "COPTS ACCUSED OF CAIRO BOMBING."

But it was not just political suffering the abbot spoke of. "You are young, you peoples of the West," he said gruffly, "but we are old. We have lived along the Nile in the Upper and Lower Kingdoms for ten thousand years. We welcomed the Holy Family here at the time of the Massacre of Innocents. We were the first great community of the faithful, and we have remained faithful ever since. We are old, and we have learnt patience. We saw our country ruled by foreigners for over two and a half thousand years, and when the foreigners were driven out a generation ago we found ourselves at the mercy of a majority who had learnt the foreigner's language and religion. And it is one and a half thousand years since our fellow-Christians passed into error, since we have been able to pray in their company. Yes, we are old. Yes, we are patient. But we are

41

weary, Doctor. Weary to death, and very much alone. How much longer must we be despised, and live in quiet places, like criminals in hiding, instead of proclaiming what we are, what we know?"

Chas felt embarrassed on the abbot's behalf. What could he say? What could he be expected to say? It was the plea of little peoples throughout history, and suggested that if they ever came to power themselves they would make up for centuries of fear and suffering by imposing fear and suffering on others. *The only thing oppression teaches*, he thought, *is how to oppress others in turn.*

As Abbot Yacoubu composed himself, Chas prepared to announce his most important condition. He coughed before speaking, to get the abbot's attention.

"There is one further matter, Holy Father."

Yacoubu sighed, his scarred face creasing, the deep pocks darkening his face.

"I realize, Holy Father," Chas continued, "that your Church's relations with Rome have been uncertain and troubled. . . ."

"They have been hateful, Doctor."

"As you say. I know that for fifteen hundred years, Rome has laboured in darkness, ignorance and sin. I know they have led others astray and usurped the primacy of the Coptic Church, and I appreciate that you wish to use St Peter's Letter to enlighten them and free them from the errors of centuries, but I would remind you they are deep in iniquity and the devices of the world. . . ." He thought he was laying it on a bit thick, but Yacoubu seemed to lap it up. "They are also rich and powerful and deeply entrenched. I implore you to make no move against them until the tests are completed. In fact, I would ask you to have no dealings with them at all."

The abbot smiled. Outside the *kasr*, red-breasted African swallows were singing. They had nested in the monastery for time beyond recall. They masked the sound of the distant call of the village muezzin calling the faithful to prayer. Chas was sick of the faithful. He had had a bellyful of religion at home and at school, enough to last him a lifetime. It tried his patience almost beyond endurance that he had spent the best part of his adult life pandering to the whims of priests. He would be glad when all of this was over, but what the abbot, still smiling, said next, drove out any thought of gladness.

"That is impossible, Doctor."

"But I beg you, Holy Father. . . ."

"You are too late."

Too late? What the hell did he mean "too late"? What had they *done*? "I don't understand, Holy Father."

"I don't suppose you do or will, Doctor, but in this matter you must trust me."

Chas thought quickly. He had to know what the abbot had done. Who had they spoken to and what had they said? What level had they got to, and could speculation be killed until he could get Henry Kircauldie to Egypt? He put on his humble face again.

"I don't want to interfere in affairs of the Church, Holy Father, but the discovery of the Letter, at least, is my concern. Is it possible to ask who else knows of the Letter's existence?"

"It is permitted." Yacoubu moved to the archer's window cut into the deep walls of the *kasr*. In past times the whole community had taken refuge in this building, giving up the rest of the monastery to their enemies, and enduring sieges as long as the power of prayer would allow. What was he listening for now? What opponents? What army? "You would not, you could not, have expected me to keep the news from our own Pope, if only to lighten the burden of his imprisonment."

Oh, Jesus, thought Chas, so now the whole Egyptian Secret Service knew. What was Medina going to say? Would he look a fool in front of Carfax?

"His Holiness is denied writing materials. He asked me to write to the Anti-Christ in Rome on his behalf. I have done so."

No, thought Winterton, *please God, no*. For an instant a wild thought flashed through his mind. *It can't have been in Polish, surely, so perhaps they haven't even shown it to the Pope*. . . . But that was ridiculous. It didn't matter. The secret was out, in writing, in Rome. How long had they known?

"May I ask when this letter was sent?"

"Certainly. Eight days ago. We have already received a reply. It is most impressive."

43

Chas almost lost his temper. *Of course it's impressive,* he wanted to shout. *They are impressive, you silly, provincial bastard. They ate your kind up fifteen hundred years ago and they've been growing ever since. History teaches the only way to deal with Rome is to get them before they get you.* Somehow, however, he preserved his silence. It encouraged Abbot Yacoubu to go on.

"Would you like to see the correspondence?"

"Very much."

Yacoubu returned to his reading-desk and opened a heavy carved leather writing-case.

"Why didn't you tell me earlier?" Chas asked, as the abbot handed him two letters.

"It was none of your business. It is a private — almost a family — matter between ourselves and Rome. They are sending out one of their people to see the Letter."

I'll bet they are, Chas thought, as he began to read the letters. *Rome never misses a trick.*

The abbot's letter was much as he expected: formal, highhanded, grieving and We-told-you-so in tone. The first surprise about the letter from Rome, from the Secretariat of Southern Affairs, was that it was in fluent Coptic. The second was the gentleness of its tone. They sounded genuinely interested, with the dispassionate interest of scholars. The nature of his discovery seemed to trouble them not at all. The letter had the calm assurance of the immortal, the invincible — everything, in fact which Yacoubu's had lacked. They were imperturbable. The third shock was the most violent, because the least expected, doing away at once with all the fine impression the letter so artfully created. It was the name of their emissary.

He must have gasped, for the abbot looked troubled. "Is something the matter, Doctor?"

For a few seconds he could not speak, but jabbed at the letter. At last he managed a few words. "The man they're sending. . . ."

"Yes?" The abbot was puzzled. "Do you know him?"

A single murderous image ran through Chas Winterton's mind, called up with absolute clarity after long-lost years: of a priest speechless with rage being dragged from the body of the boy he had just beaten to death, whose corpse he would not cease from beating still.

"Oh, yes," he murmured, "I know Monsignor Paolozzi."

Wadi El Natroun/Alexandria

He could not bring himself to tell the Abbot about Paolozzi. It had all been a long time ago, when he was a schoolboy and his father had been posted to Italy for a year, but he was worried now; worried for the Fisherman's Will and for himself. As dusk fell he had persuaded Yacoubu that the Roman should at no stage be left alone with the Letter. He wanted something else as well, but felt it was not time to ask for it yet.

After a dinner of onions and unleavened bread in the shabby refectory, its single table piled high with drying fruits and sacks of salt, he approached the Abbot again. He wanted to see it again, before the final service of the day and sleep; partly out of delight in his own discovery and partly, if he was honest, out of anxiety. Even the thought of Carfax could not lift his spirits. He was haunted by a vision of the mad, unstoppable priest.

The two men walked over to the larger of the monastery's two churches, the Church of the Virgin. It was dark, and the cicadas who took sanctuary in the gardens were scratching to each other. Chas gave no thought to the Church's antique marble columns or its devotional crosses. The delicate carvings on the rood screen might as well have been Cairo traffic-lights for all the attention he paid them. He forgot even to whisper his usual ironic prayer to the relics of Saints Maximus and Domitius — "Go for it." His mind was elsewhere, beyond the walls of the greater Church, inside the lesser one attached to it; that of St George, Mari Girgis, fallen into disuse these many centuries, with its soft light and its small ornamental dome. It had been used as a granary for many centuries. Officially, part of it still was, but for over a month now it had been kept under lock and key. Abbot Yacoubu let them in.

As always, Chas had brought a flashlight with a pale red filter with him. Once again he blessed these deserted com-

46

munities' pressing need for food. It was the conversion of this little church for grain-storage untold centuries before which had preserved the monastery's unknown treasure. The very requirements for keeping grain — a steady temperature and the exclusion of light — had preserved the icon, and the greater importance of food had meant that no one had taken any notice of it. It had never been looted or defaced. People ignored it, and it survived.

Even after the most rudimentary cleaning (he had not dared risk any more; it was his dream that this, at least, should one day find a home in Cambridge), it was beautiful.

Icons were unusual at this date in Egypt, late fifth or early sixth century. The Syrian influence on Egyptian monks had made them despise all things Greek or Byzantine. Perhaps that was why it had been retired to this disused little church. How quickly people forgot, for once it had obviously been greatly treasured. The framing surface had been studded with semi-precious stones, and the icon itself was rich in gold leaf. Yet the overall effect was not heavy or oppressive, perhaps because of its unusual subject: St Peter with Christ on the road out of Rome (but not Rome, of course, as now they knew; out of an ancient sea-port vanished with the winds; Alexandria, lost heart of the world), gold leaves sprouting from his staff. Even now, after so many viewings, he wondered who had painted it. What lonely painter far from home, far from precious Byzantium in the early years of its empire?

It was painted on boards. Not one board but two, bound tightly together, back to back. He separated them as nervously now as he had the very first time while the abbot held the torch. Then it lay before them, the single leaf of papyrus which had once been the most precious possession of Coptic Christendom and would be again very soon. So precious that it had been mounted in boards of sandalwood and cedar of Lebanon studded with semi-precious stones. So valued that, in time, a great icon had been painted on the boards to make it a fitting reliquary until, one day, the icon itself became the object of veneration, and the papyrus it contained was forgotten, as the icon would be too, in its turn, and relinquished to a granary.

Chas could hear the abbot praying under his breath. He

himself could make out the text by heart. He began to recite the first few lines, translating mentally as he went:

"A sinner in the service of the King, I, Simon, called the Rock, send greetings to my brother the brother of the Lord, James, Patriarch in Jerusalem. . . ."

Over the ages the papyrus had fused to the lower board. The two men bound both boards together again with painful care. Once they had done so Chas took the abbot by the arm. The old man's face looked more like that of a planet than a man in the pale red light. Chas hoped he would endure as long.

"Holy Father, there is something I must ask you."

"I guessed it."

"Over the next few weeks, Holy Father, I shall be away from the monastery often. We cannot know when the Roman priest will come, and when he comes he will want to see the letter. I may not be here when that time comes. Once he has seen the letter, Holy Father, I want you to hide it. I will show you where and how. Will you do this for me, out of the trust there is between us?"

The old man nodded, his face impassive. He said simply, "You trust the Romans even less than I do."

Chas could not but smile a little at that.

"I know them better than you."

He set off for Alexandria early the following morning. He felt a little relieved after his conversation with the abbot the previous night, but only a little. The monks rose at dawn, and he rose with them. Leaving after their simple breakfast, he could cover the hundred and twenty kilometres to Alexandria in a little over an hour. Already, in the first bright light of day, the soda flats the Wadi was named after shone with a furious light. He kept his head down and bounced the Range Rover along the sands towards the made-up road through the village.

The village existed because of the monasteries. The Nile floods had never reached this far into the Western Desert and the people scratched a meagre living round the shallow wells. Tourism had benefited them, mainly from the sale of hideous craft objects and crude rugs, but this morning, in the off-season, the farmers were going out to turn their dry fields for the last time before the long baking fallow summer when nothing at all would grow. Years before, the village had lived off soda mining, but although the chimney of the old Egyptian Salt and Soda Company still dominated the endless desert skyline the trade had fallen steadily away. You hardly ever saw or heard now the cheerful shouting of the men dredging the salt lakes or pouring red-hot caustic soda into metal drums. The whole place felt weary, listless. He wanted to call out to the farmers, "Hang on. Better days are coming." But they would not understand how tourism might transform their lives. And to most of them what happened in the monasteries remained as much an irrelevant mystery as it had been for centuries.

He checked his watch as he pulled on to Highway 11. He would be in Alexandria by six-thirty. The great thing, he thought, about driving to Alex was that if you knew what you were doing you could come in across Mareotis. The new road ran part of the way beside the lake, bearing lorries to the smoky stinking hell of cotton-rendering factories and processing plants which made up the arse the city presented back out to Africa, but the old desert road ran across the lake itself. There was no better start to any day, he thought, than passing over Mariout, the still reed-lake so flat it seemed to curve over into the sky it reflected. The little fishing villages it supported remained as ignorant and careless of the rest of the world as they had through all recorded time. In the city behind them, conquerors, religions, came and went, but they knew little of that and cared even less. Every time he saw it, he thought, he felt the way God must have done on the very first morning when he looked out over Creation. He preserved a healthy disrespect for all those travelling dons or visitors to the city who sighed at the mention of the lake, thinking of poems and magic, but who were never prepared to risk the complicated walk out to see it for themselves.

This morning, however, he had more pressing troubles than dons and visitors. He would have to telex Medina to warn him that Rome already knew about the Letter. Perhaps that would not prove so important, provided Kircauldie acted quickly enough, but remembering Paolozzi with a shudder he doubted it. Right now, however, what he wanted to know was who exactly worked for whom. They would have to work on the principle the Egyptian authorities knew something about the Letter, but how dangerous were Jones and Foster? He knew, of course, that Egypt was crawling with funnies. Ever since '79, and more so since Beirut became a nightmare, Egypt had once again become the espionage capital of the Middle East. The Russians had never got used to being kicked out as principal advisers (as atheists they had never been popular) and had maintained as big an unofficial presence as they could manage ever since. Then there were the Bulgarians, the Russians' hit-men, the Israelis, the Libyans, the French, the British and, most of all, the CIA. But Jones? The sad-eyed bugger who had been drawn to Alexandria by its poets and been disappointed to discover that, although his needs could still be serviced, the city was no longer the legendary paradise of boys? And Foster? Show-off, lecher, piss-artist, yes. But *spy*?

He would have to check with Jones. Jones was the weak link, if any. He had all the faults of the melancholy Welshman, with none of the virtues. He couldn't even sing though, God knew, he kept on trying.

That headline in Cairo still nagged at the back of his mind. Why should the Copts be involved in a bombing? They had everything to lose, and what could they hope to gain? Was that what Medina had meant? Were there people who feared the Letter might become the rallying-point for reawakened Coptic nationalism?

But why? The Copts were Egyptians. They didn't want a new country of their own. They wanted to feel safe in the one they had. If anything, they were frightened of people like Jihad bombing them, in their churches, shops and homes. None of it made sense. It was all bloody mad. It was all God's fault. He bumped across the railway track at the little town of El Amariya. Kids ran behind the car and bumped up against its sides, yelling for baksheesh. He grinned and ignored them, as he could not ignore the goats and donkeys left to wander about the street by their owners, living off offal and refuse. Outside the town he turned on to the old desert road, out across Mareotis, and after that he thought of nothing at all again until

50

he entered the outskirts of the city on the fringes of the Mahmoudieh Canal.

It was the price the city had paid for coming back to life in the nineteenth century, a stinking, fetid scribble of water, full of rusting hulks and garbage, but beyond it lay El Iskandariya, the city of dreams.

To look at it was an ordinary, rather run-down, Mediterranean harbour town. It worked better than any other city in Egypt, because the local council had avoided tower blocks where possible. Instead they had repaired the city's old three-storey mud-brick houses and put in running water and electricity. It made more sense. People had been building like this round the Mediterranean for thousands of years, because it worked. It still worked here. Even so, the city was nothing much to people used to the richer towns of the European shore, but to Egyptians, it was a vision of paradise. Chas still remembered how, years before, he had met a young man down in Luxor, in the hundred-and-twenty-degree heat of summer, who had just been accepted by the University of Alexandria. He dreamed about the city; dreams full of cool air and sea-water, and the easy openness of the city which had long been Egypt's gateway to the outside world, filled in imagination with untold luxuries and unimaginable vices and unobtainable consumer goods. It wasn't quite like that, not any more, but for a man like Chas Winterton, whose whole life had been the past, it was something else, something more. It was a city full of ghosts.

He parked in Midan Masr in front of the railway station where the Cairo trains came in, and walked down the Nebi Daniel. A few yards to his right was the old church where it was said the prophet Daniel was buried. Further down on the left as he worked towards the sea was the quiet crossroads which had once been the site of the Tomb of Alexander the Great, the ancient crossroads of the world. Nothing marked the spot. The tomb itself had been destroyed over sixteen hundred years before. Alexander himself was so much dust in the rich earth of the Delta.

The whole city was like that. It was not so much what was there, though it was hard not to feel comfortable in the shabby

51

elegance of the city centre, but what had once been there. Everywhere you looked there were memories of greatness, but the palaces and poets, the conquerors and craftsmen, were long since gone. If you knew, however, as Chas knew, and listened, the ghosts rose up and whispered in your ears.

It was still early, but it was already hot and he was thirsty. He would not rush this morning. He was glad he had come up the desert road, avoiding the lush fringes of the Delta, for coming through the dust and haze made the city still seem like a mirage risen fresh from the sea. He was going to enjoy it with Gemayel.

He turned down El Hurriya and walked the short block down to Pastroudis. It was the last and best of the old Greek tea-rooms in the city and, as he walked through the door, a fat man in a fez rose with a cry of, "Ya Doctor!"

"Ya Gemayel!" Chas replied, and the two men hugged each other heartily.

How to explain Gemayel?

Chas could hardly have done so. He seemed to have existed for ever. It was as though he was a last survivor from the days and empire of the Pharaohs, the Ptolemies, the Romans. It seemed as though he had been here the day that Amr of Islam rose victorious out of the desert, the day Napoleon landed, the day that Nelson struck.

For many people, Chas included, Gemayel was the city, its tawdry, corrupt and all-too-human heart. Chas had no idea how old Gemayel was. No one did. Nor where he came from originally. Some said he was of an old Jewish family in Smyrna. Others claimed he was entirely Greek, the illegitimate spawning of a shipping merchant with a Salonikan whore. Yet others said he was the last unlikely creation of the Royal Harem in Istanbul, before its destruction by Kemal Ataturk; a child got on a royal concubine by an incompetently neutered eunuch as fat as his son was to be.

Gemayel was all those things and more. Part Egyptian he certainly was; and part-Levantine, part-Circassian, part-English, part-Greek, part-Turk, part-Nubian black, part-French. And entirely Alexandrian, straight through his crooked heart.

52

All the races which had passed through the city had left a little of themselves to flow through Gemayel's veins. He was the seed of numberless cultures, a remnant of the old port city before the Second War; even before the First.

No one ever questioned him. Everyone came to him for advice. For years past remembering this fat heavy man had sat in the window at Pastroudis, eating cake and drinking tea and zibib, the local pastis. With the possible, and much-disputed exception of Sophokles, the old Greek barber in the Nebi Daniel, no one knew more about everything in Alexandria.

There was not a brothel, not a clap-doctor, not a gaming-den in the city that could hope to do good business without Gemayel's approval, without paying him his cut. Chas had learnt that early. He had first gambled in the city at a casino recommended by the fat man, and spent his winnings in a brothel he patronized, and been cured of their best girl's gonorrhoea by one of Gemayel's pet specialists.

He had the same patience as the city itself. There was no folly, no perversity, he had not seen before. No situation he had not at some time had to deal with. So it was that people came to him for advice. Some he gave free; to his few friends, or those he took a fancy to, or to the poor. But there was little charity in that, for he made the rich ones pay.

The fat man sat down and ordered tea, and rose-water, and something a little stronger, for them both.

"Sophokles told me to expect you."

Chas raised a lazy eyebrow. Nothing about the two men's information service surprised him any more.

"Hakim of the Metropole was in there yesterday evening and said he'd taken a booking. From an English secretary. A woman. You are dealing with rich men now, Doctor, not monks? Or you are hiding a new mistress from me?"

"I always hide my mistresses from you, Gemayel. A man shows you his mistress and you steal her, every time."

Gemayel laughed, flattered, and rubbed his shiny face. "Not any more, Doctor. I am too old for that, but I take pleasure in seeing them."

He spoke in the old Alexandrian mix of English, French and Arabic. Chas replied in kind. "Do not frighten me, old one.

When an Alexandrian is tired of that, he is ready to die."

Gemayel slapped his knee appreciatively. It was true he had an immense and justified reputation as a fornicator. There was a famous Alexandrian story about how, asked once what he attributed his phenomenal success with women to, he had answered, "Age. Young men are strange. They buy flowers and chocolates. They climb walls and sing beautiful serenades. So much time, so much money, so much effort to get what they want from women they have forgotten by morning. But me, I walk up to the front door and ask. If one says no, I go next door. And like all old men — and I was born old — I remember to be grateful."

Chas stopped the joking by telling the old man what he wanted to know. "But this was not a mistress, Gemayel. This was business."

Gemayel looked serious and knocked back his glass of hot sweet tea. It was cool and dark under the high ceilings and slowly revolving fans of Pastroudis and they were alone, so the old man was direct. "With the monks?" he asked, his fat left cheek bulging as he investigated his teeth with his tongue.

Chas was cautious. "I thought you might tell me that."

Gemayel looked troubled. He sat looking out through the open shutters of the windows and then suddenly, impulsively, leant forward and, taking Chas by the arm, said, "Doctor, I like you. We have always been friends. You should be careful dealing with your priests."

This was what Chas had come to see Gemayel for. In summer, everyone who was anyone came up to the cool of Alexandria as often as they could. The richest ones had summer houses along the beach out by the old royal palace. And when they came to Alexandria, expansive men on holiday, they talked. And Gemayel would know whatever they talked about.

"Why, Gemayel? Why should I be careful?"

The fat man scowled and picked at his teeth with heavy fingers. "Ah, Doctor. . . . You know we have a saying in Alexandria. When God created the world he blew life into the clay. First he made Adam. Then he made Eve, to be a comfort to him. And then, with the little clay that was left, he made a

54

priest — not one thing or another and a torment to them both. You must never listen to a priest."

He sat back again, squinting. Chas said nothing. Even with someone as steeped in cunning as Gemayel he knew that silence was the best policy. Eventually he would speak again, if only to break the silence.

"You know me well, Doctor, and you know El Iskandariya. Here trade matters, baksheesh matters. Not religion. We are concerned with wallets, not souls. I can understand a wallet. I can count what is in it. But men's souls? Ah, that is different. There are people saying. . . ." He hesitated, wondering how much to reveal. He started all over again. "I can buy a man. I can buy a woman. But how do I buy a priest? That is why they are dangerous. It is not the Copts. They are people like us, all honorary Iskandarians. They buy us as quickly as we sell them. This is good. This is well understood. It is the ancient way. But the priests? What do they want? And how much will it cost?"

Chas sat back, keeping things light; a man discussing an article read in a newspaper. "Oh, come, Gemayel. You can't believe the Copts are behind these bombings? What do they have to gain?"

Gemayel shrugged, or rather his shoulder-blades shrugged beneath the unmoving fat. "Me, Doctor? I believe nothing and no one. I only listen. And these are important people."

Chas feigned disbelief. "And they really think the Copts are more dangerous than the Libyans or Iranians?"

The fat man smiled indulgently, like a parent with a wilful child. "Iran? What is Iran to us? What do our people know or care of Iran? Go. Ask them in the streets. They have not even heard of it."

Chas knew he was right. He had already asked the question of many Egyptians, to whom Iran was more distant than Mars.

"But you, Doctor?" the fat man continued. "The danger to you? It is not what the priests want or do not want which is dangerous. It is what others think they want or might want. There are some people who say it would be best if we hit them before they strike at us. To them these bombings are a blessing. Any excuse will do. All they want is one excuse. And they worry, Doctor. They wonder why a certain priest made a prison visit recently. They wonder what this Cambridge doctor is doing working in the desert."

So that was it. It almost made him want to laugh. What did they think he was doing at Baramus? Making bombs? But he did not laugh. This was Alexandria, where anything was possible.

"If you should meet such people, Gemayel, tell them, tell them the Englishman is a coward with weak eyes and unsteady hands. Tell them all he knows how to do is read books."

"And when they say books are more dangerous than bombs?"

Chas had no answer for that. Instead, he asked advice. "So what should I do, old friend?"

Gemayel looked sad. He turned away to look out through the windows again before speaking. "The old thing, Doctor. The safe thing. The same thing the one wise duck in Mariout, who lives to breed with all the widow ducks, does during the shooting season. Be silent. Be still."

They chatted of old friends and desirable women after that, as usual. They played a little backgammon which Gemayel won, as always. Chas promised to call in at least one more time before he left the city the following morning. Then he strolled down to the sea as the offices of the city opened for the morning.

He had booked into the Metropole not only because it was relatively cheap but also because foreigners rarely used it. Most stayed ouside the city now, at the Sheraton in the old Montazeh Palace, as Carfax had expected him to, or one of the other American style hotels. The few who preferred the city to the beach tended to stay at the grand old, faded old, Cecil Hotel, right on the Corniche across the square from the Metropole, but he liked the fact that the Metropole was the hotel Egyptian businessmen used; people who had real work to do, not seekers after sun and sensation.

There was a telex from Carfax waiting for him when he arrived:

ATTN. WINTERTON

CAMBRIDGE PARTY ARRIVING ATHENS ONE
DAY EARLY. PROF WILL SEE U 19TH.
UR BOOKED ON BALKAN FLIGHT 19TH 4AM
RIGHT AFTER PRIVATE VIEW. RETURN FLIGHT
OPEN.
CARFAX.

He scribbled her a reply agreeing the flight, and added his
doubts, as securely as he knew how:

ROME KNOWS. DEFINITE. BELIEVE CAIRO
KNOWS. SUGGESTIONS?

then he went up to his room. He had asked at the desk for one
at the back of the hotel, facing out on to the Midan Sa'ad
Zaghloul, with the Cecil to the left and, before him, a view of
the whole Corniche, the road round the natural harbour which
had been the cause of the city's original foundation, from the
site of the Pharos lighthouse on the left to the site of the Palace
of the Ptolemies on the right. It was still the most beautiful
seafront he knew, but it might have been a bigger version of
any southern French resort, for all the ancient wonders were
vanished. Ghosts. Everywhere ghosts.

He sent his suit off to be sponged, and washed his other
clothes in the handbasin. Hung up in the window they would
soon be dry and the hotel would iron his shirt. He took a
shower and stretched out naked on the bed, luxuriating in the
slight sea-breeze.

He was woken an hour later by the porter returning for a
second time. His suit already hung in the wardrobe. This time
the boy had come back with the shirt and had woken him for a
tip. Chas gave the boy a pound; too much, but he had a
headache from his brief sleep and could not be bothered to
count change. The boy looked at the pound, then back at Chas
naked on the bed, and screwed up his eyes. Then he pointed at
Chas's penis and, with a questioning look, shook his right
hand briskly, thumb and forefinger joined. Chas laughed. He
had forgotten this was Alexandria. He packed the puzzled lad
off with a few extra piastres for devotion to duty.

He dressed and strolled down to the Corniche for a brisk
walk before setting off back up the Nebi Daniel to Sophokles's

57

barber-shop. He decided to check on the Range Rover first.

It was not until he opened the door that he realized it had been broken into. It had been expertly done. That did not surprise him. There were plenty of lock-picks in the city. What surprised him was that it had been done at all. Everything in the car had been opened and gone through. Nothing was missing, but then there had been hardly anything to miss. In any other city he would have been angry. He would have thought about going to the police. Here, there was no point. Instead, he locked it up again and headed back to Sophokles's.

The deep shop, lined with marble, alabaster and high mirrors, was still busy from the morning rush. Barber-shops were still institutions here. Half the city's business was conducted in them. Traders spent hours in them, being shaved and barbered, discussing transactions, outlining contracts, preparing alliances, corrupting officials, ordering up drugs and whores, talking about everything but sport and the weather. They were decorated like little palaces and run more like cafés or private clubs than beauty salons, and their proprietors were amongst the most important people in the city's commercial and political life. Sophokles's was the oldest and longest established of them. His grandfather and father had run the shop before him, and by now he was a kind of cross between the Secretary of the Treasury, the Chairman of the Stock Exchange and the Chief Fence for the Mafia.

He was busy with a customer when Chas arrived, but waved him to a seat and snapped his fingers. Hot sweet tea was brought immediately, with yesterday's *France-Soir,* this morning's *Herald Tribune* and next month's *Penthouse,* uncensored, courtesy of the local Customs and Police.

A few minutes later Sophokles was ready for him, and Chas uncoiled in the long barber's couch smelling of old leather and stainless steel which the barber's father had imported from New York in the Twenties. Sophokles himself would work with no other couch, though his under-barbers used slightly more recent ones built to order in Chicago.

Chas beckoned Sophokles closer to him as an assistant applied steaming towels to soften his face. "I was with Gemayel this morning."

"I know." He still spoke all his seven languages with a heavy Greek accent.

"Before going to the Metropole."

"I know. One telex message. You replied. Cairo number in the name of Carfax. I am told she is very beautiful and works for David Medina."

That last comment struck Chas as openly offensive. What was Sophokles trying to prove? He managed to keep his temper even as he spoke. "Who are you working for, Sophokles?"

The old Greek barber shrugged as he brought soap to a lather in his favourite George V mug. "Myself, as always."

"No one else?"

Sophokles began lathering his face. The badger-hair brushes were still made for him in London. "This is Iskandariya. You know how it works. People come in. They ask me things. They give me money. I tell them things."

"What things, Sophokles?"

The barber was stropping his razor, its Sheffield steel blade mounted in a Chinese lacquer handle from Macao. "Slightly less than they pay me for."

After that Chas had to drop silent for a while. He was being shaved.

When Sophokles had finished, and steamed him and scented and powdered him, the shop had emptied. Sophokles pulled up a chair and reach for a pair of scissors. "Hair?" he asked, opening them. Chas nodded. The public telephone, one of the old Bell Company box types, by the front door of the shop, rang. An assistant took it, listened and called down to the Greek.

"London. ICI down four. House of Fraser down six. Marks and Spencers down seven." *Marks and Spencers!* Chas wondered.

"Sell House of Fraser," the barber grunted. "Hold the others."

"How do you do that?" Chas could not forbear from asking. "How do you get a phone line to London?"

"I don't," came the smug reply. "I have an account with Chase Manhattan in London. Their local office in Cairo keeps on open line."

"Aren't foreign accounts illegal?" Chas teased.

The barber was dour. "Everything is illegal." He silenced the Englishman again by forcing his head down into the sink to be shampooed. A few minutes later, sitting with his sopping hair wrapped in towels as the Greek inspected his scissors, Chas was able to ask another question.

"Do you know any more than Gemayel?"

"No one knows more than Gemayel."

"Will you tell me more than he did?" The barber remained impassive. "Who has been asking about me, Sophokles?"

"Half Iskandariya. All Cairo."

"Which of them broke into my car this morning?"

The barber looked at him in the gleaming mirror without ceasing to snip his hair. "At last you tell me something interesting. I have to make a living, too, Doctor. What kind of car? When? Where?"

"Green Range Rover, parked in Midan Masr. Some time between six-thirty and ten-thirty this morning."

Sophokles nodded. "I will find out. Expect a message at your hotel this afternoon." He snapped his fingers for more tea and whispered instructions to the servant who brought it. "Now," he said, smiling into the mirror, "to business. Hashish is eight Egyptian pounds an ounce. Everything else is available but expensive. Women remain unchanged."

There's no question, thought Chas, *Sophokles's is the best club in North Africa.* "An ounce of hashish rolled into cigarettes."

The barber looked up intently. "Fifteen Egyptian pounds. Still Camel Filters?"

"Still Camel filters. I'm paying in dollars."

The barber nodded swiftly. "All right. It's been too long. For you, ten dollars, but don't tell any other foreigners."

Chas blessed his long residence in Egypt.

"Anything else?" the barber checked.

"A woman."

"At your hotel?" Chas nodded. "When?"

"After lunch. Say two or two-thirty."

"Any special requirements?"

Chas looked sheepish as he rose from the couch. "Well, yes, actually. Can you find me a Catholic?"

The barber raised his eyes in puzzlement, but stopped as Chas unrolled his dollars. Once Chas had finished the Greek unrolled an extra bill from the sheaf. As he counted the dollars again he asked quietly, "If you're working for David Medina, why didn't you tell me?"

The porter showed her up to his room. The lad was grinning broadly. She came as a relief. An Alexandrian could understand a preference for either men or women, but a preference for neither made no sense at all. She looked young, quite fresh, and very Italian. She was already running to weight beneath her tight black dress lightened only by a crucifix pendant. As the porter disappeared with a tip as large as his smile, Chas pulled her to him and undid her zip.

He was late for his meeting with Ewen Jones.

So was Jones. Chas waited in the bar, with its view out on to the harbour. He hated what was being done to the old hotel. Till recently, this bar had preserved a certain tatty grandeur. It had been a wilderness of gilt-framed mirrors, reflecting each other and the drinkers to infinity. Recently, however, it had been redecorated in grey plastic and nylon. The whole hotel was being converted from ornate Mediterranean splendour to a standard formula transatlantic tourism palace, all modern conveniences and no character at all.

He looked down at the message from Sophokles in his hand, and the telex from Carfax. Both were equally brief. Sophokles's note said merely, "The gentlemen in khaki." The army. Chas took another pull at his whisky sour. What the hell was the Egyptian Army doing breaking into his car? And what had he got himself into? Where was Jones? Would he know?

The telex was just as short and equally alarming:

NEED MORE INFO. EXPECT UR ARRIVAL TO-MORROW PM LATEST.

He had hoped and half-expected that Medina at least would have some idea what was going on. What was the use of all that

61

money and power if, when the chips were down, you were as ignorant as everyone else? *Knowledge is power,* he thought ironically. *Except I've got all the wrong kinds of knowledge.*

He was interrupted by Jones's arrival. The little Welshman looked red and sweaty, as though he were baking in clothes several sizes too small for him. He stormed up to Chas and whispered angrily, "Just what do you think you've been playing at?"

"What?" was all Chas could manage in reply. It felt as feeble as it sounded.

"We can't talk here. You'd better come with me."

He seized Chas by the shoulder and jerked him out of his chair. He was stronger than he looked. It was only now that Chas realized Jones wasn't so much angry as embarrassed. What did he think that Chas had been saying?

He had no chance to ask as Jones bustled him into the square, half dragging him up towards Nebi Daniel.

"Look, what is this?" Chas demanded. "What the hell are you talking about? Will you stop for a second, for God's sake? Will you . . .? *SHIT!*"

He thought it rather than said it.

It was all he could manage as the bomb went off in their faces.

Part two:
THE CIRCULAR PROFESSION

Abu Kir

Adams sat in the café at the end of the long main street of Abu Kir enjoying the cool breeze of the early evening. Further round the corner on the long rocky beach Egyptian families were sunning themselves, splitting open sea-urchins and offering the delicacies around, enjoying their holiday. In the café he was surrounded by gnarled old men playing backgammon at phenomenal speed and big, reflective chess players. He had first come here twenty years before, when he had been appointed the Agency's Resident in Alexandria, as a tourist, to look out on the sea where Nelson broke Napoleon's Oriental ambitions, on the desert where the same Napoleon decided in battle that for a century and a half the future of Egypt would lie in European hands. He had stayed for the chess.

There were players in this little nothing café, old men, afternoon players, who would not have disgraced the New York Public Library's First Team. Players who, locked away in the creative isolation of a North African resort, had learnt none of the frightened defensiveness big money tournaments and the big Russian chess machine had imposed on players in the richer North. He could go down to defeat here with almost no sense of humiliation in his pleasure at their bold strategies of attack, attack, attack. The thought surprised him, for he knew that, although chess-players smile, shake hands after a game, there was nothing in the world more humiliating than losing a game of chess. Nothing? No, nothing. He had the fanatic's devotion. Losing meant you were just plain dumber than the other guy.

He drew on his narguileh, the long-stemmed water-pipe which was as much a symbol of masculine solidarity in the cafés of Egypt as pints of bitter were in England's pubs. The water cooled the smoke, delivering the full blast of nicotine without the heat and ash. Better than cocaine, he thought,

63

thinking of his younger colleagues, and tamping down the chips of charcoal in the pipe's flat bowl.

He looked down the long street, up which the 53 bus from Alexandria should be bouncing any time now. It was quiet. Few of the traders would open up for the evening session. Here, in summer, most of the trade got done in the morning as families arrived still needing things for the beach. Down on the right, a greengrocer was hacking up his last watermelons of the day, hoping for a late rush of hot sticky holidaymakers, and further on from that the little restaurant where he usually ate was starting up for business. As the breeze changed direction he could smell the cooking prawns the size of lobster tails for which the bay was famous. He would eat after Ali brought him news.

He did not have to wait much longer. A cloud of dust built up at the end of the long street and started coming closer. Somewhere within it was the beaten-up old Tata bus which plied the suburban route from the centre of the city. From his office in Midan Orabi he had an uninterrupted view of the whole Corniche. He also had the more dubious vision of the city's central tram and bus depot, filled with clanking, fumes and the yells of impatient passengers all day long. Here, the depot was a single concrete wall with a couple of concrete benches, round which the buses turned in the broad beaten-earth street.

The passengers spilled off the bus. In the midst of them he could see Ali, the big black Nubian who had long been his most useful assistant. *Better than any of those damn fool Christian Scientists they keep on sending out*, he thought bitterly. Ali loped over to the café with long swinging strides, his *galabiyeh*, his long robe, flapping. He was smiling, a shining gash of white teeth in his black watermelon-sized face.

He ordered more tea as the Nubian sat down. A few of the chess and backgammon players glanced up to check out the newcomer. If they felt any surprise at a Nubian calling on the Boston, as they had come to call him over the years, they did not show it. If their friendliness could sometimes be wearisome, and suspect to someone of his profession, the Egyptians still had an endless oriental politeness which delighted him

64

after the Can-Do half-wit monsters his superiors sent out to assist him.

He had to check himself whenever he thought like that. Was he finally going native, the big risk with long postings? The hell with it, he thought. No one could deny he always did his duty. He'd done a damn good job.

Ali was still smiling as he sat down. That meant very little. Ali had been smiling all the time for three years now, ever since his income from the Agency had allowed him to return from the Sudan one summer with a seventeen-year-old bride and, for the duration of the honeymoon, the bride's mother, four sisters, seven suitcases and six chickens.

Sometimes he thought that Africa was crazy as Alabama. Ordinary Egyptians still thought of Nubians as pretty second-class. After all, they were black. It would have cost Ali up to ten times as much in bride-price to marry a girl from Cairo anything up to the standard of his little Sudanese. She had come with a bigger cash settlement, too, as well as being, on the one occasion he had been allowed to meet her at Ali's home, as pretty as the Queen of Sheba.

The Nubian held up one hand, fingers outstretched. Five. Out of seven. Not bad, better than he could really have expected. It had been a long time since he had had to arrange a bombing.

"Names?" he asked casually.

Ali swallowed his glass of tea and called for another. As the players' attention was disturbed by the owner forcing his way out through the crowded chairs, he whispered swiftly; "Fahzawi, Mahmoud, Gazaleh, Auwal, Aziz." The owner poured him a fresh glass of sugared tea. He drank it off in one swig again and motioned for a refill. A sweet tooth in Africa.

The American sat back, puffing on his narguileh. It was all right. It wasn't bad. Two of the colonels. The three majors. Thank God for Alexandria in the summertime. There was always somewhere like it, he thought, everywhere you went. Somewhere the rich and the powerful gathered to plot and negotiate. All you had to do was find out where it was and strike at them there. It crippled their plans. It dented their confidence. It bought you what you needed most at times like this. It bought you yet more time.

He had to ask the hard question, the question he always hated. Even now, after twenty years, after thirty with the Agency, he could not manage the icy contempt for innocent people the Christian Scientist kids they sent him seemed to have bred into them. "You can't make an omelette without breaking eggs," they would say. "There are no innocent people." Jesus, he thought, between the civilian and military politicians and the Christian Scientist crazies what chance did ordinary people have? Had it always been like this? It had always been like this. He remembered old man Craft of the China desk saying years before, "Ours is a circular profession. If our people can't find someone else to stab in the back they stab themselves instead. Men like you and me are the few sane fixtures in a sea of schizophrenics."

He exhaled a column of pearl-grey smoke and, raising an eyebrow, asked, "Others?"

Ali never stopped smiling. "Four," he nodded. "Including Jones. Sixteen in hospital, including the Englishman."

Aaron Adams, CIA Resident in Alexandria these twenty years, closed his eyes, his face impassive, as though he were far away. He was no such thing. He never was. But he was thinking, and what he was thinking was: *Shit!*

That was the trouble with bombs. Like sawn-off shotguns but bigger, they were indiscriminate. They took out the man you were after, and everyone else besides. It was not enough to feel regret, but he felt it none the less, for all the unnecessarily lost and damaged lives. Even Jones. Squat, solid, ridiculous Jones, with his wild eyes, his drunken melancholy and his appalling voice. Why did he have to go like that? If the Agency had needed to get rid of him there were easier ways they could have done it. They could have flown him out to San Francisco. He would have come back with a beatific smile, a size-eleven asshole and the AIDS would have dropped him in a week. But they had not had to get rid of Jones. He was just another of the unplanned bonuses, the thirty-per-cent-free-with-voucher, you got when you placed a twelve-pound PX bomb in the corner of the bar of some place like the Metropole.

And the Englishman. Jones and the Englishman, who every-

66

one had been mentioning out of the corners of their mouths for three days now. Had it been his fault, jumping on Jones to make him lean on the Englishman? It had seemed such a minor matter at the time, like running Old Glory up a flagpole to see if anyone saluted. Or had it been just coincidence? Coincidences happened, though none of the goddam conspiracy theorists on the Senate Foreign Affairs Committee could understand that. Had someone just got unlucky? Or had it been Medina?

It was the first lesson he gave the Christian Scientists when they turned up in their crewcuts and polyester light-blue summer suits. This was not America. There was still something like a frontier town about the USA. However hard they played, however mean they thought they were, Americans had a crazy kind of honour. Once they had sold you their souls they remained your property for ever. Even the bad guys remained resolutely bad, and if in the end they sang to the District Attorney they still justified their squealing in terms of the criminal honour codes they knew and loved. It was true that his fellow citizens used the hard words of pragmatism: "A dollar is a dollar. A greenback is still green, whatever sewer you pick it out of. *Me. Me. Now. Now.*" But they didn't really believe them. Deep down, Americans wanted to be loved too much. They could not cope with merely being liked. Every kid had to be the main man on the block.

So what could these innocents do with old, old races who had seen empires come and go and knew how to look after themselves? Out here there had been Me Generations one after the other down thousands of years. It wasn't like that back home. Back home they were Me-Too Generations.

The Christian Scientists had to learn that men like Sophokles and Gemayel were good sources of information for every secret service in the Middle East. There was no one they would not talk to as long as the price was right. He had seen too many injured innocents forget that the price of dealing with them was having everything you talked about reported to anyone else who could afford the fare.

And the deepest-dyed in damnation of them all was Medina. Oh, sure, the Agency had used him lots of times. More often than Adams liked or had advised. The guy's an American billionaire. Billionaires are always clean, the Agency reasoned. But Adams knew they were wrong. Adams had seen Medina a thousand times in different guises: hucksrering merchants from the sea-fronts of Istanbul and Tripoli, from the markets of Bombay to the opium-dens of Hong Kong. Medina was all of them rolled into one. There was nothing he would not buy or sell. "The wild card in the Middle East," Aaron used to say, "is always David Medina."

He clapped Ali on the shoulder. "Come on. Let's eat."

Later, in his house overlooking the sea (an indulgence the Agency, which still half-expected its operatives to sleep on their desks, like Japanese bankers, had never really approved of), he went over what he knew; or rather what, this being Egypt, he thought he knew.

He was working, he had to work, on the assumption that the Englishman was a temporary irrelevance. Alexandria was a gossipy town, and Winterton was this week's special offer. Medina had fatter fish to fry than one quiet Englishman.

He was tired and had a migraine coming on. He always did when he was guilty, and tonight he could almost smell the wasted blood, on his hands, on his face, on his feet, as though he had been wading in death. There was no one he could tell. There never had been. Guilt went against the ethic of the Agency. Killing gooks was business, there was no point crying over other folks' spilt milk.

He looked around the sparsely furnished room: a couch, where he was sitting now with a fifth of Old Forester, a desk, a couple of chairs, some photographs. Aaron Adams on Graduation Day at Princeton, with his father, smiling-eyed Jack, who had named him after Aaron Burr, the last great American horse-trader. Aaron in the football team. Aaron on the day of his wedding to crazy Jane, who ran off with a corporate lawyer six years later — a lawyer who shot her, then himself, in a motel room in Pasadena the following weekend. Aaron at his daughter's wedding, to another lawyer; a lobbyist for the oil majors in Washington DC these days, and a lousy source of gossip from the capital. His idiot grandchildren, all braces and baseball and cheerleading. Still, she was happy. His daughter was happy. That was something. Little Emma, who had loved but never understood her father, an honest man sent abroad to lie, to kill, to bribe, for his country. Aaron with the Georgia President, all broken heart and wringing hands, the day he'd closed the secret information treaty between Israel and Egypt, covering internal security affairs only; the only thing the two would trust each other with.

Aaron sighed as he thought about the ignorance and stupidity of the governors of his country. He had never known a head of the Agency he would have crossed the street for as a private citizen. His presidents had been cowards, knaves or fools. And now, whisper it who dared — *Make sure no Christian Scientists are listening* — they had the first elected Muppet in the White House. And "only a heartbeat away", as *Time* magazine kept on saying, the original vacuum-pack man. His former boss. A man who had been appointed to every job he had ever had, and never stayed long enough in any of them for anyone to find out if he was any good.

But what the hell. Why should it worry him? It worried him because he hoped that somewhere, even now, someone in Washington was reading his last report. Someone with a brain. Someone with some knowledge.

He had never felt so distant from his bosses. The Agency had always had more than its share of psychotics, but always in the past he had felt that somewhere, in headquarters at Langley in Virginia, or in the State Department offices at Foggy Bottom, there were rational people who could be counted on, whatever the passing whims of government. That feeling had been fading recently.

The Alexandria residency had been created for him. His job was to listen to the gossip from the deserts, the markets, the sea-fronts of the Middle East; to stand aside from the operations of the major stations in Bahrein, Tel Aviv and, until a few years ago, Beirut and Tehran. They had ignored his warnings over Lebanon and about the Shah. They had ignored him about every damn thing. And now, for the first time ever, he was acting alone, without authority, his reports unread, his communiqués unanswered.

Now that Washington was full of Californian cattlemen

who thought that other countries could be herded into pens like cows, now that all the Mid-East Residencies were packed with crewcut Christian Scientists, who could he turn to? Now that the US had a government which only thought of guns and generals as friends, how could he be certain his own government was not behind the dangers he was fighting?

He might have killed nine people today against his government's will. He didn't know. They had cut him out of the information exchange. That was what frightened him. That was the only thing that frightened him.

The name of the game in Egypt now was control. A game he was playing alone against David Medina, who held all the cards, who had all the advantages. There had to be some way in. There had to be something Medina had miscalculated.

The Englishman, he thought as he drifted to sleep on the couch. *I have to go see the Englishman.*

Outside the sea rushed hissing up the beaches.

Alexandria

When he came round, everything was white. White walls, white windows, white light. He was drowning in it. Where was he? What was this? What was the white that bound him down?

He tried to turn, and pain shot through him from the shoulder to the groin. He lay there, sweating, his left hip throbbing. He wanted water. He wanted air, but tight blankets bound him to the high steel bed.

His head ached and his vision was cloudy. There was a noise somewhere to his left beyond his range of vision. He recognized but could not name it. His neck was stiff. He could not turn his head to see. The same sound again. What was it? *Door. Door. . . .*

He slept again.

He was woken by bright lights in his eyes, glaring, making them water. He tried to turn away, but his head would not move. Something was holding his face.

He could not put words to them, but images of prison movies, concentration camps, interrogation chambers deep underground swam through his mind.

Deep underground and buried. Dead and buried. Long corridors and the click of heels, the slur of rubber wheels. He was going blind. He could not see. White light, nothing but light. *Make them turn it off,* he wanted to say, but no words came. His dry tongue crawled over his lips. They were salty. They were wet. He was crying.

There was a noise again. A different noise. He could not make it out. What was it? Where were the words?

The light went out. That sound again. What was it? They were whispering. That was it. The rats were whispering. The rats in the white cell, there were rats. . . . *Who had put rats?*

Why were there rats? He didn't want them. *Make them go away.* He didn't. . . .

His neck was moving now. He was rocking his head left and right, with his eyes tight closed. *Make them, take them.* . . . He wanted to cry out, but only thin sounds came.

His face was wet and there were rats and he rocked from side to side not wanting to open his eyes, until a sharp pain came in his arm and he slept again, away from the white and the light and the corridors and whispering.

Afterwards, it was better. The light had gone. It was cooler, darker. He could hear again. He knew where he was this time. This was a hospital. They called them hospitals. The Knights Hospitallers. Of Malta. Of St John. This must be Malta. Was it Malta? Valetta, Valetta. . . .

No. It wasn't Malta. So this was what delirium was like. Nice word, delirium. Rolled around like a drunk at a party. Rilium delirium hum.

His name was John Charles Winterton, of Cambridge, England. Noted for its punts. And this was Alexandria, Egypt. Noted for its. . . ? No. Which hospital was he in? He liked this hospital, now it was dark, now all the white was gone.

The doctor returned. The noise had been the door. The noise without a name. He was young; looked Palestinian; spoke with an American accent; wore a white coat. *Take the white coat off.* No.

He stood there in his coat, checking Chas's pulse.

"Can you hear me?"

Chas nodded, his mouth still dry, his tongue still salty.

"You're going to be all right. You're badly bruised. Some contusions. And concussion. But nothing serious."

Chas tried to speak. A hissing noise came out of his mouth.

"You must rest."

Chas closed his eyes and tensed himself, raising his head a half-inch from the pillow, concentrated, managed to croak, "What happened?"

"There was a bomb." The doctor forced his head back to the pillow. Chas strained against his hand till it was done; then

72

relaxed so suddenly he almost lurched into sleep.

"Jones?" Chas whispered.

"The other Englishman?"

Welshman, Chas wanted to say, but the effort was too great. He nodded instead.

"Dead. I'm sorry. Killed instantly."

Chas felt nothing now, not in his head. There was only a dull white ache all over his body. "Who? Who did. . . ?" He could manage no more.

"They're blaming the Copts."

His face was wet again. He cried silently, without noticing, without effort. "No," he croaked, "can't be."

The doctor shrugged, indifferent, with the slow sullen patience of a dispossessed people used to being blamed for everything. "You must sleep. I will give you something."

There was the sharp pain in his arm again, and he slept.

He awoke next morning, himself again. He still hurt all over and turning to his right was almost intolerable, but his mind was working at something closer to its normal speed. He could drink a little water. He could speak. The doctor called in with the orderly who brought him breakfast. He asked for French coffee and the doctor nodded approval.

"You can have anything you want now we know you're being paid for. Your employers are sending someone up from Cairo this afternoon."

His employers? That must be Medina. How had he known so soon? Was it so soon? "How long have I been in here, Doctor?"

"A day. Two nights."

"What day is this?"

"Saturday. I should be at home praying. Letting infidels like you die." He smiled sadly. "Someone else called too, a couple of times. American. I told him to come back late this morning. If that's all right? You don't have to see him."

"Did he leave a name?"

The doctor nodded. "Aaron Adams."

It meant nothing to Chas either, but he was intrigued, and safely out of it all. "OK," he agreed, almost chirpily. "But

73

don't let him stay too long."

He liked the boredom of the hospital. He had grown used to boredom in Egypt; waiting for third-class trains in dusty stations south of Asyut; waiting for officials to stamp a piece of paper; waiting for train and aeroplane tickets; waiting for permits, authorities and grants. He felt comfortable with it, at home with it. And the hospital boredom was clean and quiet and Medina was paying for a private room. He lay stretched out in bed, the covers loosened, his tender arms behind his aching head, trying to stretch the corkscrew out of his spine, thinking of nothing, watching the ceiling and examining the walls.

He thought of Jones and wondered if the little Welshman would be allowed into heaven if he promised not to sing. But then the reality of death and the closeness of his escape came back to him and he retreated into boredom, thinking of nothing at all. Stray images floated into his mind from his childhood; of boating holidays with his family on the Norfolk Broads, of the times he toasted crumpets on the electric fire at school, by hand, so his fingertips burnt as well, before he learnt to pin them up with paperclips or make a toasting-fork out of a wire coat-hanger; of his curiosity about the little girls in full-length skirts the nuns used to bring to Mass and wondering if females had legs; they must have, he supposed; he knew his mother did; and always, as always, of the priests.

He had always hated them, because they made him afraid. It was ironic that, in the end, he should find himself spending his life with others of their kind. At least the monks had never made him feel afraid. Alien and clumsy sometimes, even ignorant, but never afraid. What he had hated about his Catholic childhood was the fear; fear of God, fear of the Devil, fear of Hell and eternal damnation; fear of Protestants, unorthodoxy, contamination and sex. Most of all fear of sex. When all was said and done, their celibacy disturbed him. "Not one thing or another and a torment to both," Gemayel had said and, having become half-Alexandrian himself, he could only agree. Oh, there were fine men, good men, among them, but in the end the fact they denied themselves the pleasure of the flesh suggested

74

something was rotten deep inside them, something which had to be controlled by taboos and rosaries and guilt. What kind of religion was it that thought people should only exist from the waist up? Much more than any of the mortal sinners they condemned he found them quite literally perverse.

And then there had been Paolozzi. His father had spent a wasted year mineral-prospecting deep in southern Italy. A geologist, his father's greatest passion had been rocks. Perhaps that was why Chas himself had chosen to spend a lifetime in sand. ("This is the death of stone," his father had once said to him, filtering sand through his fingers on Huntercombe beach). The rest of the family had stayed in comfortable England, but Chas, who had been going through his stroppy phase, decided he fancied a year at school in Italy.

It had been a strange place, trying desperately to ape the grander manners of church schools up in Milan, Turin and Rome, full of the sons of seedy aristocrats and gangsters not good enough for Chicago. Paolozzi had been spending a year there as some kind of penance, an act of discipline imposed on him by the Superior of his Order. He had made the boys suffer as he suffered. He took his contrition out on their backs and arses. Chas had been spared most of the beatings as a foreigner, but one lad brought the worst out in the priest.

A puny boy, the runt of a minor gangster's litter, he had been the lasting object of Paolozzi's scorn; for his weakness, his asthma, his father's unsavoury trade, and his own thick Sicilian accent which made him sound even more stupid, more stolid, more slow, than he was. He had been beaten remorselessly. Then it happened.

Paolozzi just went mad. There was no other explanation. There had been no other explanation. It had been covered up, as the Church still could, in Southern Italy, in a school. Paolozzi was withdrawn to Rome. The incident had been forgotten. Except, occasionally, in nightmares or delirium by men like Chas who as children watched it happen, and whose sleep was still disturbed sometimes by the sight of the pale asthmatic body bleeding on the flagstones.

Where had they caged him up since then? And why had they bothered? Why hadn't they dismissed him from the priesthood? What had they been saving him up for?

He woke up in a cold sweat. He must not allow himself to be frightened. Medina would sort it all out. Medina had the money and the power. It was what men like Medina existed for.

Then he thought of Carfax and tried to build up a picture of her against the blank ceiling. He could not do it. Like a police photo-fit the separate parts would not add up to the living person. He wanted her here. He wanted her now. He remembered his childhood training.

The Jesuits used to say that if you wanted something from God you had to be prepared to give up something in return. They had taught him to make himself suffer, to make an act of will, to make himself worthy of the gifts of God. If he did it now, if he made an act of will, would Carfax come? he wondered. Could he raise the stakes with God? Would the room fill with Carfax's presence and her hands and mouth console him? He rolled deliberately on his right side and the sweat sprang from him at once. The pain took over. The whipcords in his arms, neck, thighs, stood out. He made himself endure it. He willed himself to suffer. He became a wall of pain.

There came a knocking on the door. He fell back gasping, speechless. God won. It was Aaron Adams.

He might have been any age from thirty-five to sixty, though Chas guessed he was nearer the latter. The only thing that aged him was his left foot. He dragged it a little as he walked steadily towards the chair and sat down. Only then did he seem to take any note of Chas at all.

"Are you all right, Dr Winterton? Is there anything I can get you?"

Chas shook his head, still wheezing slightly. "Don't worry, Mr Adams. It is Mr Adams?" His visitor nodded. "I was just trying to recapture my childhood."

Adams made no reply. He just sat there, blinking slowly, as though he were waiting for something to happen. He was tall and good-looking in a dated sort of way. Chas thought he had seen younger versions of the face in photographs of the Roaring Twenties. Like Scott Fitzgerald, but older and scarred. It started in his right eyebrow, ran across the bridge of his nose and down his left cheek, then under his chin and about half an inch down his neck. It looked as though someone very skilled had taken a single scalpel stroke across his face and throat, or a single whiplash had once cut him open. Oddly, on him it did not look sinister, as scars usually do. Rather it imparted a strange look of nobility to his head. He looked like a man who had fought hard in the service of his country. Chas asked him what he wanted. His reply was spoken with a precise rather dry accent. Chas thought he sounded Bostonian.

"I hoped you might be able to give me a little information."

Chas was ironic. "I see. I suppose you're with the FBI?"

Adams ignored the sarcasm. "Oh, no," he answered simply. "I'm with the CIA."

It was Chas's turn to blink, more rapidly than his visitor had done. *I'm still concussed*, he thought. *I'm hearing things.* Adams reached very slowly into his inside jacket pocket and, as though he expected Chas to be suspicious of guns, used his right hand to hold the jacket wide open so everything he did was on plain view. He pulled out an expensive-looking wallet and withdrew some plastic-coated cards. He handed them over to Chas.

"My credentials."

Chas looked at them uncomprehendingly. "I wouldn't know a CIA badge from the Golden Gate bridge, Mr Adams."

Adams just sat there, unamused, unmoved. Chas tried again. "You don't look much like a spy to me, Mr Adams. You see, where I come from, to be a spy, you really have to be brilliant, homosexual, go to Cambridge, and betray your country. Where did you go wrong?"

This time Adams did smile wryly. "We're a very unsophisticated country, Dr Winterton. We don't aspire to match England's sense of theatre." He returned the cards to his wallet and put it back inside his jacket. "I appreciate your uncertainty, Dr Winterton. It isn't very pleasant being bombed, and it must be unnerving to have a stranger walk in afterwards and tell you that he's CIA. Both Gemayel and Sophokles will confirm that last fact for you, by the way." Chas began to take more interest. "And I know the Agency doesn't have the best reputation in the world, but I can promise you I'm not going to hand you an exploding cigar or a poisoned bathmat. All I want is some information."

Chas thought about it long and hard before replying. Finally he decided on impulse. "All right, Mr Adams. I'll hear you out. But first I want to know what you can tell me about these bloody bombs."

Afterwards, both of them would know how little of the truth they had told each other, but now Chas felt more reassured than at any time since he had discovered St Peter's Will. They lied fluently to each other, revealing only as much as seemed in their own interests. Chas would not have put it quite like that. All he knew was that Adams, though clearly not an honest man (his was not a job where honesty was prized), was in his own muddled way an honourable one. Not even his enemies would have denied him that. His explanation of the bombs had been simple and cogent enough, even though, when he stopped to think about it, it made the blood run cold in Chas's still bruised temples.

"I don't suppose there's much harm in telling you the little we know," the American had said. "Most of it's pieced together from gossip at diplomatic levels, and between military attachés." He had stopped there, looking Chas over, wondering how much information to trust him with. Chas could not fault his judgement. "It doesn't take much to work out that the Mubarak government has its enemies. You've been in Egypt long enough to know the signs." Chas nodded his agreement. "As far as we can work out, the power struggle is being fought within the army. Most of it is completely loyal. To be honest that surprises me, but it's true. What matters, though, is that there are two anti-government groups slugging it out in the army. One's always around, wherever armies matter, including the States. It's the War Party."

More than anything else Adams said, that was what reassured Chas. At least the man was prepared to admit there were people in the Pentagon who weren't so far off crazy.

"The War Party accepts," Adams continued, "that war with Israel is no longer really feasible. What they want instead is

78

war with Libya. They're the people who've been pushing the anti-Gaddafi line."

Chas stopped him there, as much out of vanity as anything else, to prove he had not been entirely cut off in his years in the desert. "That ought to please you, oughtn't it?" he asked. "The US is hardly keen on Gaddafi."

"You're right," Adams replied. "What I'm not so keen on is that I'm pretty sure some of the bombs the Libyans have been blamed for have been placed by the War Party in the army."

"You said there was another faction."

Something happened to Adams's face. It seemed to redden, or perhaps his scar went very pale instead, but it stood out, a single diagonal in his square reliable face.

"Yes," he said at last, "and they put the fear of God in me."

Chas said nothing, forcing him to continue.

"After Sadat was murdered, not all of Jihad, the group that did it, could be routed out of the army. Its support was too deep and too widespread. You know and I know that Egypt is the sanest Islamic country in the world, but there are fundamentalists here as well."

Chas was bitter. "You have them in the States as well, except there they get tax relief and campaign for the President."

Adams conceded the point with a shrug. "Anyway, as far as we can work out, they're behind the bomb campaign, the main one, the one that's being blamed on the Copts."

Chas understood at once and shuddered. It made a kind of lunatic sense. If people could be persuaded the Copts were behind the bomb campaign, it might just provoke the kind of Islamic fundamentalist backlash Jihad were working for. Was that what Medina and the others had meant? It had to be. It was the same sick revelation he had sensed for an instant in the car while driving to the monastery. And the worst part was, it looked as though he was implicated. If Egypt blew, what price scholarly research? A friend of the Copts was a friend of the Copts. No wonder they were checking his car.

Then, in a sudden wave of nausea, he felt guilty. He felt guilty about forgetting Jones. What had the little angry Welshman done to deserve being shipped home in pieces?

"So it was Jihad that set the bomb which got Jones and me?"

79

Adams shook his head sadly. "I wish it were that simple. The bomb in the Metropole was intended for and got some of the most senior Jihad men in the army. I don't know who placed it, but I'm very glad they did. Sorry about Jones and all that."

Something about his honesty, his ironic dismissal of Jones, reassured Chas and diminished his sense of cruelty. He dismissed the Welshman too. "I hardly knew him."

Adams got up and walked over to the window. "Can I open this?"

"Go ahead."

The sounds of traffic and bargaining drifted in. Chas wondered which way the room faced, how high up it was. Adams leaned against the windowsill and crossed his arms. "You can check out everything I've said with Gemayel. Tell him to put it on the Agency's account. Unless you can persuade him to put it on the KGB's, that is." He put his hands in his pockets, relaxing. "And if you ever quote me on any of it, the Agency will deny all knowledge of you, and I will personally nail you to a wall." He smiled then, briefly, and it lit up his damaged face like fairy-lights at Christmas.

"OK," he said, clapping his hands, and the smile was gone, "Business. Before I ask you what I want to know, answer me one question. You've lived in Egypt ten. . . ?"

"Just over."

"Ten years. Fine. Tell me, what's the most important thing that's happened in the Middle East in the last two years?"

"Easy," said Chas, who thought it was. "After the PLO was expelled from Beirut, Arafat flew here first. Met Mubarak in Cairo."

Suddenly, uncharacteristically, Adams bent at the knees and raised his clenched fists in a football coach's victory salute, crying, "*Yowza!* He's my *main* man!" Chas looked on in concern at this strange demonstration as Adams raised two fingers crying, "OK, here's your second question on the End Of The World Cash Prizes Quiz: *Why?*"

"Because it means that Arab unity is broken. You can't run an effective opposition to Israel without Egypt. Big country, Egypt. Lots of people. Lots of army. After Camp David the other Arabs were saying to Egypt, Lay off the Jew-loving.

Remember the Palestinians. Once Arafat turned up in Cairo that argument didn't work any more. Add *that* to OPEC falling apart, Iraq-Iran, and Hussein of Jordan being foxy, and bang goes Arab solidarity."

Adams rose, looking stately, like an examiner, and applauded politely. "Dr Winterton, you ever want a job in State or Langley, Virginia, sunshine home of the CIA, you just let me know. You just explained every damn thing I've been trying to get those assholes to understand these last two years." His demeanour changed suddenly. "So tell me, how come, if you're so smart, you're fucking around with David Medina?"

Chas tried to show no surprise at Adams's sudden turn of temper. "I don't see what that has to do with you." Even to himself he sounded frightfully Cambridge. He feared the tone of voice would seem merely ridiculous to the American; another whining Englishman. But Adams merely smiled and unfolded.

"You're very good. Most people crumble. And you're quite right. It probably isn't any of my business. But let me tell you why I ask. What matters in Egypt today is control. In any situation as unstable as this the power goes to the people who exert control. In the end I don't care what the government of Egypt looks like as long as the whole country doesn't fall apart during a changeover. I think you'll find Medina feels the same. The only difference between us is that we have different interests to protect. Right now, both of us are about equally in control, and that's OK. But in the past few days you've turned up on the scene."

He moved back to the chair by Chas's bed and leaned over the back of it. "Suddenly you're spending a day with Medina. He's picking up the bill. Suddenly everyone's whispering Copt. Suddenly everyone knows you're the man from the monastery. Then yesterday the Coptic Patriarchate announces that it's closing all its monasteries to outside visitors. So perhaps you'd like to tell me what you're doing, just in case I end up losing my control."

He sat down as he made his implied threat and placed his hands out on his thighs, for all the world as motionless as an ancient Egyptian statue. Chas played it as cool as he knew how. He didn't care about the power games that Adams and Medina might be playing. It was enough to know they existed and that he had to avoid them. The worrying thing was Medina. Was he proposing to use the Letter as a means of holding the balance of power, by controlling the timing of its disclosure? Was that the reason for his insistence on secrecy? He couldn't believe it. As soon as he saw Henry Kircauldie the secret would be out. Within weeks the Letter would be head-line news worldwide and, far from trying to slow him down, Medina was paying to make the process possible. It made no sense, and he could guess the reasons for the closing of the monasteries. He mentioned half of them.

"You can hardly blame the Copts for closing up the monas-teries. They're being accused of a wave of bombings and the monasteries are the biggest targets they've got. No wonder they're frightened of retaliation."

Adams nodded. "You're quite right, of course, and I'm working on the same assumption. I assume it was an assump-tion since you were stuck in here delirious when the announce-ment was made?"

That did make the Englishman smile. "That's right. I'm sorry to disappoint you, but I have no access to Coptic think-ing. They don't put their trust in foreigners."

Adams was curt. "And you? What's your game?"

"No game. I have discovered a Coptic icon. Rare find. Very valuable. It takes time and money to have things like that authenticated. I asked Medina to get his Foundation to foot the bill and he agreed. To be honest, I think he wants to buy the icon once it's verified."

He watched, wondering if Adams would buy it. He had suppressed all mention of St Peter's Will and Paolozzi. How did it sound?

Adams looked troubled, unconvinced. "All right," he said at last in a quiet voice. "I can't make you talk, not here, and I'd hoped you just might care enough about what's going to happen to the Copts to tell me something like the truth. If you don't, you don't. But let me tell you something. Medina is a harder man than I am. There aren't many of those. And he *always* ditches his people once he's used them. One day you're going to need some help. When that time comes I'm going to be the only good guy on the block. So you take this card." He handed it out and Chas took it without looking at it. "It's got my whereabouts in Alexandria and Cairo on it. When you find you need me, you just yell, and I'll consider how I feel about it."

He turned to go, but at the door, like any actor, he turned to say, "Meantime I guess I'll see you at Medina's party. So long, sucker."

But even so, his visit made Chas feel easier in spirit. He felt at last that he knew what all the fuss was about. Let Adams and Medina play their necessary games. He did not have to be involved. All he had to do was to get by till he went to Athens, when eveything would be put in Henry Kircauldie's hands. Only four days to go. And if the worst came to the worst, he knew, now. He could play Medina off against Adams and Adams against Medina until he drove them both to a standstill. The main thing was that the monasteries were secure. The letter remained safe in its boards of cedar and sandalwood. The burnished gold of the icon glowed in Mari Girgis. The single door of Deir el Baramus stood barred against the outside world. Paolozzi and Rome were far away.

Poor Jones.

He dreamed of the Saint. He dreamed of the big fisherman, who had not wanted the hard life his master thrust on him. He dreamed of Peter whose own dreams had been filled with images of Galilee, the big lake blue against the amber morning hills as the fishing-skiffs returned, the heavy bellies of their nets being drawn to let their catch slide silver, green and wriggling to the decks. Who had dreamed of going home all his life, to his wife and children, his neighbours, family, friends, in the bustle and safety of Capernaum New Town. Who had been trapped in greatness, hardship, travelling, pain by his all-too-human loyalties and nostalgia. Poor Peter, who was never very clever, and only wanted to do what was right, to do the best that he could. Whose misfortune it had been to be called up by a moral absolutist who had insisted he — yes, even he — could be better than any man had any business being, if only he would try. Poor Peter. No wonder Rome had wanted him for their own from the earliest times. In all the stuffed-shirt dummies of the legend, he alone was a man among men. He alone was one of us.

He had lain alone dying here in Alexandria, far away from home, far from clever Paul, who was changing the world in Rome, amongst a clever foreign people who jabbered in clever Greek or the dangerous tongue of Israel's masters in a long-ago time of exile. Let me go, he had cried in his delirium, and no one could tell if he was thinking of the Pharaohs long ago, or of his master, whose memory and honour had dragged him round the Middle Sea for a lifetime, spat on, imprisoned, defiled.

At the end, all he had had left was a scribe who had taken down his letter to James the Just in a foreign alphabet the old man could not read. He could only just read at all. The scriptures he knew by heart; he read only enough to give him his starting point. And he read enough for proclamations, notices, tax demands. But this boy, this clever scribe, hardly knew his language. He feared the alphabet he did not know would carry his message full of errors back to Jerusalem, the golden city where he almost wished that it had ended.

It never carried the message at all, and, even in his sleep, Chas smiled as his mind worked through the errors in the letter, the errors a Greek of Alexandria would only make while taking down dictation, which any forger would, mistakenly, have corrected. The errors which had made, still made, each nerve-end in his body tingle as he murmured, It is the thing itself. The legends did not lie.

But none of that would have been any consolation to the old man centuries before, as he lay dying in the city built between the water and the water with all of Africa and the endless sands behind him; a stranger in a strange land, dying far from the carp of Galilee. He had felt, as others would do after him, here in the careless city where worlds of East and West, of past and present, met, as though the heavens lay upon the earth, and he between the two, breathing as though through a needle's eye.

It was darker when he woke again. The cool of early evening had settled in. The shadows lengthened and the pain began to ebb. As the effects of the bomb-blast lessened, his sense of security grew. It would be all right. He was not destined to die here like Peter in exile. He was not destined for obscurity longer and darker and more final than St Peter's Will. He sensed, rather than saw, that there was someone in the room. Someone in the chair. He turned. God had relented. Carfax was smiling in the darkness.

She stood up as he awoke and bent over him, kissing his forehead lightly, her heavy hair falling over his face, almost black in the dusk. She smelt of money, he thought foolishly. She smelt of wild silk and expensive perfume, of air-conditioned apartments and chauffeur-driven cars, of the clean fields of Hampshire and private beaches in the South of France.

She began to roll back the covers and as he murmured wonderingly she whispered with gentle amusement, "Don't fuss. I've made sure no one will disturb us."

He turned a little to his right and waited for the stab of pain which would persuade him he was awake. He gasped a little as it surged and she placed a long cool hand on his shoulder to lay him back on the bed. Then she bent down and slipped the long silk shirt over her shoulders, the dark hair tumbling down as she did so. Her green eyes glinted in the darkness, and she was smiling still, pleased with herself, perhaps for him. She took his hand in hers and placed it between her full warm breasts, helping him unfasten her. The bra fell open and her breasts swung forward a little, the pale nipples pink against the blue-veined skin. He reached for her, but she placed her hands between them, pushing him back to the bed with a murmur of "Hush. Be patient." Then she reached forwards again and stripped off the long silk pants with simple broad movements.

Her shoes, he found himself wondering idly, *where are her shoes?* Even in the darkness he could see her dark brown hair beneath the little triangle of lace. She slipped her thumbs into the hollows of her hips where her belly swept down to her sex, pushed down, stepped out, and stood before him naked.

He reached for her again and this time she did not resist him, climbing above him, her thighs pressed to his haunches. Then she reached down between her legs, her breasts against his

85

face, the clear skin soft against his two days' growth of stubble, and began to roll up the hospital robe he was wearing. He tensed at the hips, raising his knees to help her, his erection urgent against the fabric, but she only continued to murmur hush as she unpeeled him, kissing his forehead, his ears, his eyes. She adjusted herself a little as the robe rolled up to his buttocks. As she swept it past them, and the pain jabbed into him, he thrust himself upward, aiming, blind and hopeless, to connect, but she forced him down again and, with a single tangled sweep of heavy cotton, he was naked too. They lay together, breathing softly. Then she began to kiss him again, kissed every inch of his face, pausing for long deep kisses as one hand unscrambled and smoothed the knotted muscles of his neck, the other still between her legs stroked the wet head of his sex. She kissed his neck, his chest, his nipples, his arms. She licked his stomach and raised herself, letting her hair fall forward, stroking him with it till all his muscles strained.

She bent further down, and nuzzled the creases of his hips and thighs where the hairs began to coarsen. She kissed the softer skin between his thighs and the soft pouch between his legs. And then she began to lick slowly upwards, up the shaft of his sex, till at last she took it in her mouth as gently as she might hold a wounded sparrow in the palm of her hand, and stroked him up and down until he almost came.

At last she stretched forward again, her hands beside his head, her hair in his face. Through the mass of hair he could still see her smiling down at him. Then she lowered herself. He was too far gone in pleasure and desire to notice she was still dry, not ready for him. There was a brief stab of discomfort as she took him within her tight, unexcited flesh, but then there was nothing but the straining flood that built up in his groin, reaching, breaching the barriers of his self.

He took her by the hips and bucked upwards, trying to master her to his rhythm, his will, but she took his hands in hers and forced them back against the pillows, riding him as steadily as a lady out for a canter in Hyde Park, using her youthful muscles to control him, in a steady, unrelenting tempo, refusing to accelerate to meet the urgency of his desire.

86

He almost blacked out as he came, and seemed to come forever.

She lay against him, cool against his sweat, and as his mind returned, as the room returned, she kissed him once again and whispered, "Hush, Doctor, hush. I'm going to look after you."

Abu Kir

Adams took the chair by the window, looking out over his little scrub of shingled beach to the rock-pools and the sea beyond. The windows stood open and the soft crash of the waves was borne in by the breeze. Sometimes on days like this he wondered why he did the job he did, and who he did it for. It made no sense to say he worked to keep beaches like this free for democracy. The sea would still be here, the stones of the sea-shore would still be here, whatever he or Gorki of the KGB's Cairo station might do or say. And the people out on the beach today? Egyptian civil servants, soldiers, businessmen, out for the day with their families, what did they care for the posturings of super-powers or the anarchic struggles of empires? They had their empire long ago. They had been part of other people's empires twelve times longer than the United States had even existed. No, for them, the dream was still the same as Nasser's had been. Egypt for the Egyptians. But which Egyptians? And what would they do with the country when it was theirs?

No, it was no use questioning his duty. Men did what they did without ever really knowing why, and everything he had ever learnt or been had brought him to this, here, now. Whatever else his work had brought him, it had brought him here, to the old, ironic, unforgetting sea. He turned to the hatchet-faced young man on the couch. *Young?* he asked himself? Yes, young. Thirty-three, thirty-four. A couple of years younger than that damn fool Winterton. Twenty years younger than he was, and a way-of-life more ignorant.

"Nothing from DC or Bahrein?"

"No, sir," the young man answered formally.

His name was Kirk. It seemed appropriate. Kirk Stanshall. Adams knew he was getting old; he was having difficulty understanding the young. This Stanshall was a baby-boomer. He'd done a tour in Vietnam, with Military Intelligence. Adams knew what Militint had been like in 'Nam. They had sat in their air-conditioned offices in the cities talking to all the high-placed hard men who most needed American defence. While the Agency had gone into the hills and villages and reported the war unwinnable (Adams had gone before the Church Committee in '75 on that, when it was the only good thing the old hands of the Agency could report) these men had met in bars and restaurants in Saigon and reported back what they heard as the Real Gen, the feeling in the country. They didn't know that the only gossip that mattered was gossip from the forest. But like the other old-time heroes of the Army the kid had gone back home believing he had been stabbed in the back by cowards and losers. They believed in country, family, and God, this hardened generation, in that order, and they had passed on what they knew to all the sullen kids behind them. He did not understand it. Hard-eyed kids who snorted coke, got laid, and dreamed of the old-time virtues. He could not trust them. The only truths he knew were the truths of the old-time vices.

The first law of the road, he thought to himself, is Never get in bed with anyone crazier than yourself. That applied to everything. Always. Kirk Stanshall, he feared, like all the new boys in the Agency, was crazy as they come.

He was worried by the absence of news from the States or Bahrein. He never expected too much from Cairo. They had only had a full-strength team there since Camp David, and most of them were genuine military attachés. But Bahrein was the parent station for the Middle East. They, at least, should have had some comment on the line of action he had set in motion, even if everyone in Langley and down at Foggy Bottom had filed his reports in the Pending tray.

"All right," he said at last, looking out to sea, and thinking of the hard-headed Englishman who had won his battle out there the way he always did: on his own terms, before anyone had noticed. "I'm assuming no messages means no objections. I'm going to continue with the course of action we've set up already. We've bought ourselves some time. Jihad will need some time to reorganize."

Kirk Stanshall nodded vigorously. This was action. "OK, sir. I agree. But what are the Egyptians doing? Why haven't they kicked some ass since all this trouble started? Do we have to fight all the wars round here? Why aren't we getting our people to lean on the government?"

Aaron sighed. What to do with such unsophisticates? "Do you know why the Egyptians kicked all the Russian advisers out, Kirk?"

Stanshall frowned. It was the kind of question which troubled him. Questions about the past. Deep questions about attitude and motivation. What Stanshall cared about was now. Act, Do, Be, were his mottoes. If everyone spent all their time looking at the past to understand the present, the present would have passed before they could do anything. Still, he humoured the old man. He tried to remember his briefings with the Pol Sci (he thought of it like that: Pole-sigh, Political Science) Bureau before he had been sent out here, here where you couldn't get Sanka, where the only decent drink was Coke, where you would not see a blonde in months, where half the people couldn't understand you.

"Well, in my understanding of the situation," he replied at last, "it was the weapons budget, wasn't it? The Russians were screwing them through the floor for out-of-date hardware that fell apart whenever it saw an Israeli."

Aaron blinked rapidly. He was tired and frustrated. Tired of teaching people the knowledge which was the basic matter of their craft. Frustrated that they never seemed to learn.

"No, Kirk. No, I don't think it was really that." How to explain, he wondered, how to make him understand? "You might bear in mind," he said at last, "the way the world looks from a line drawn south of Houston. It looks the same whether we're talking about Russians or Americans. It looks like rich white men dumping on poor not-white ones. Sometimes people just get sick of that. That's when white atheist Russians get the boot. That's when Khe Sanhs happen."

Kirk kept his cool. He always kept his cool. Being cool was part of the Eighties ethos. He conceptualized himself as cool. But inside he had had enough of the old man dumping on

90

America. Like a lot of Vietnam Vets, he could not hear the names of America's defeats without feeling someone was criticizing him, someone who hadn't been there, one of the back-room phonies. He had no time for memory or the past. He was not interested in the wars, the quiet dirty wars. Adams might have fought for his country, whose scars he still bore, in his spirit as well as his face. He only knew what he was told at briefings. He left the hard men back in Langley, the proud men, to sort out what was important for his country. He just kept shut and did his duty, whatever the hard men decided his duty might be.

The guy's gone soft, he thought. *Adams is soft, after too long out amongst gooks.* Aaron Adams. Maybe there was some soft whiny Brooklyn Jew mixed in there a little ways back.

Adams kept right on talking. "The one thing I can't afford, we can't afford, America can't afford, is to ever give the impression we think we've got, or even want, the government in our pocket. It isn't my intention to sort out Egyptian politics. I'm only here to make sure America's enemies don't get too far ahead of the game."

The old man got up to fetch himself an apple. Soft fruit on a soft summer day by the sound of the soft sea-shore.

"But that isn't why I called you here," Adams went on. "I want you to do something for me. David Medina is up to something that I can't pin down, and the dumbest thing you can do in the Middle East is to fail to find out what Medina's up to. I couldn't shake anything out of the Englishman, and frankly I don't want to. The chances are he's a straight civilian, and covering up that kind of thing takes too much time and energy. It's cleaner if we keep our wars confined amongst our own kind." It was the kind of talk Kirk understood least. He did not know why Adams was so keen on keeping all his operations clean, especially after his experiment with dynamite a few days back. Adams was as bad as the rest of them. He just did not like to admit it. And what did it matter anyway? You could not dig a cabbage patch without stepping on some bugs.

Adams continued being nice to insects. "The British are no use to us. Their little man Jones is dead and gone, and Cairo's too compromised by Martin Foster. . . ."

Stanshall looked surprised.

"You didn't know?" Aaron asked. Kirk shook his head. "It was in my last report. Foster's been in Medina's pay for years. I wouldn't mind if it was the British Chiefs of Residency who always got corrupted. They never know a thing. But it's the useful men, the Deputies, who always dive into the honey-pot."

"I guess I must've missed that one," Kirk responded without apology or shame.

"It may be nothing at all, but I want to know. I'm leaving Smith in charge here in Alexandria and going down to Cairo." Kirk scowled inside his head. He would need to get some Acting Head of Station experience soon, to go down as a credit on his service record. "I'm going to spend a few days sniffing around before Medina's party. There's something else I want you to do, and I don't want the others to know about it. I want deniability."

It was the kind of talk Kirk Stanshall did understand. He approved of it as he had approved of bombing the Metropole Hotel. It meant doing, acting, being. It meant getting his hands dirty in the service of his country. It meant planting the cabbage patch and stepping on some bugs. "What is it, sir?"

"It's Foster. He's one of our kind and he's led enough time on both sides of the fence. I want him brought in and I want him broken. I want everything he knows about Medina and Charles Winterton. I want Medina taught a lesson. And I want Foster left alive. I want to deliver him back to Medina myself. And when we've finished with him I'm going to let the British clean out their own manure."

It was the small change of his profession, he thought, as the young veteran left. Once in a while the small private armies of the secret services took out a little lesson on their enemies' hides. And Kirk would do it well. There was something murderous about that man, he thought. Something lifeless in and about the eyes. He did not smoke. He did not drink. Aaron could not even be certain he went to the bathroom. But he did like hurting people, very much indeed, and he brought a

92

certain artistry to that necessary practical skill.

Aaron felt a little happier now that the interview was over. Kirk would do his job well, that was certain. He might have no imagination or insight, but he knew how to follow his orders. He could breathe a little easier now. Perhaps one bomb would prove to have been enough. He was back in charge. He was asserting control.

But Aaron might not have felt so certain about that if he had returned with Stanshall to Alexandria, and known about the cable the young man sent that afternoon from their office in Midan Orabi to Beirut, whose Head of Station had passed the message back to Langley. A pre-arranged message which simply read:

OLD EAGLE IS WILD. INSTRUCT.

Cairo

Chas wondered sometimes if he had been dreaming. It was three days now since their return from Alexandria and she had never, by so much as a gesture, shown that she remembered what had taken place between them. It was as though it had never happened, except that he could not forget.

Was she just being careful? He had been convalescing in Medina's flat on Zamalek since their return. Was she afraid of being watched or overheard? Was she fearful of electronic surveillance? But why then nothing at all? Why no smile in the eyes? Why not the furtive pressure of a hand in his?

She was attentive, she was thoughtful, she was the kind of nurse Englishmen dream about and look for in their wives, but there was not the slightest indication of anything further, any more. He had learnt since their return not to question her, learnt it painfully, and had learnt the answer to his most anxious question about David Medina. No, he thought ruefully, rubbing his temples as he remembered. She was not David Medina's mistress.

It had happened the previous morning when she brought in his breakfast. The jealousy and uncertainty of the previous forty-eight hours rose up in him and rebelled.

"Is it Medina?" he had snapped. It was the only time he saw her even slightly taken aback.

"Is what Medina?"

"You're his mistress, aren't you? You're. . . ."

Then she had started to laugh, heartily, like an English schoolgirl amused by some jape or antic. "Don't be ridiculous," she had managed at last, "I'm nothing of the kind."

"Then what? Just what do you do here for all the money he spends on you? Darn socks?"

She had looked at him, amused, as though she finally under-

94

stood what he was talking about and found it too ridiculous for words. He was too angry to go on, and finally she answered him, very gently. She made it sound like something she did not like talking about. "I'm David Medina's bodyguard."

Chas was bitterly sarcastic. "Oh, for God's sake, what do you take. . . ?" Then the pain began. He had hardly seen her move. The pain shot through his head and he saw, as though it was happening to someone else, as though they did not belong to him, his legs jerking about uncontrollably, feet flying into the air. Then she pulled her thumbs out of his temples and he fell back on the bed, catching his breath and almost sobbing with relief.

"If you ever laugh at me again," she had told him unhappily, "don't expect to walk away."

Afterwards he saw how much sense it made from Medina's point of view. Where other men surrounded themselves with guards who looked like the Kariba Dam, he made sure that he did not look like a man with any worries at all. She made him look like a man with no enemies and no fears, for who would think twice about a pretty girl who never strayed away from a rich man's side? He understood now why, at his first meeting with Medina, Ismail had asked if Carfax should join them. He had been an unknown quantity. They could not know if he was potentially dangerous. And he realized how close Martin Foster had come to being seriously hurt. No wonder she had kept her eyes on him all that first afternoon. And he remembered with a start the other man who always used female guards: Muammar Gaddafi.

But why, then, why? Why had this inexplicable woman climbed into his bed? And why did she now ignore him, as though they had never held each other in their arms?

He could not understand her, and she would do nothing to explain herself. He hoped, ridiculously he knew, that somehow he could get her away. Away from Medina and her curious work. Away somewhere where she might notice him again, where they might once again be lovers. He wanted her with the same simple, irrational power he had wanted toys or chocolates in childhood. It was indefensible, obsessive. He knew he could not imagine her amongst dowdy faculty wives.

95

He knew how the more glamorous women academics would react with loathing to her presence, to the mere thought of such competition.

None of it mattered. He wanted her. That was all. She was the kind of woman nothing and no one could buy. Not even the Fisherman's Will. All he could do now was hope.

It was the afternoon before Medina's private view. Chas was summoned into his presence. He felt easier about the old man. They had not talked about the Letter since his return from Alexandria. Ismail had told him not to worry about Rome or Cairo. Everthing was being dealt with. Carfax had given Chas his airline ticket to Athens. Everything was above-board and orderly. Everything was working out as Chas had planned. The two took tea together alone. Chas was surprised, almost unnerved, to see how tired Medina looked. He almost looked his age.

"I'm sorry to have been such a bad host, Dr Winterton," he had begun. "I hope you are recovered?" Chas reassured him on the point and waved away his apologies. The old man stretched out in the bright afternoon light, revelling in the simple pleasure, before explaining his failure to call on Chas. "We've been a little busy, as you can imagine, with setting up the exhibition, and there are always people I have to see. It's one of the more tiresome effects of serious riches."

Chas had never heard rich people talking openly about their money before. The few he had met had always complained about taxes, salaries, costs. He raised his eyebrows accordingly.

Medina smiled. "I know, I know. It's impolite to talk about money, isn't it? But there isn't any point in hiding it. There's no point denying I am unimaginably rich." He smiled disarmingly. Chas almost liked him, in spite of Carfax.

The old man reached forward for a sandwich and explained a little more. "The really delightful thing isn't just the money, you see? It does mean that I can buy almost anything I want, it's true, but what really counts is the deference. It's the way that people put themselves in your power, the way they will do anything for you, in the hope that a little of your riches will rub off. The great thing about being seriously rich is that you never ever have to give a damn."

Medina sat back triumphant with his sandwich. His little speech seemed to have cheered him up. He looked himself, or at least the self he always presented to the world, again. Chas had found it faintly alarming, like a schoolyard bully delighting in the fear that he was held in. Perhaps there was not so very much difference. Perhaps what Medina's money bought him was only what all children wanted, and got trained out of them by parents, teachers, the machinery of the world. He was simply used to getting his own way. Chas wondered what was wanted of him. He did not have to wait long to find out.

"Carfax will drive you to the airport in the morning, Dr Winterton. I'm sorry your flight's so early."

"Please don't worry about it, Mr Medina. I asked for it. Unlike you, I'm used to travelling cheaply."

That made Medina smile. "I'd noticed, and I can't say I'm displeased. But tell me, is it true that being poor makes you as free as being very rich? Because you have too little to worry about anything?"

Chas hardly knew whether to be amused or offended. "I can't say that I've ever thought about it; but on balance, no. It's the kind of thing rich journalists come up with as they sit in air-conditioned hotels getting pissed on their expenses. I think I'd rather be you, or even me, than one of the share-cropping fellahin dust-cropping out above Aswan."

Medina smiled shrewdly. "Point taken, Dr Winterton, but forgive me for wasting your time with chatter. Good luck in Athens, and give my regards to Henry Kircauldie. Tell him I look forward to seeing him again soon, but please don't tell him what I'm about to tell you." He stopped at that, deliberately intriguing Chas, leading him into speculation, the way cats tease their prey to self-destruction.

"It isn't any secret, Doctor, that I am, at heart, a collector. It's what I do best. It's what I enjoy most."

Damn right, thought Chas. Isn't that how you think of the companies you acquire and the people you manipulate? Objects in your personal collection, to be arranged, displayed or disposed of as you see fit? Isn't everything a game of auctions as far as you're concerned, with you as the highest bidder?

The old man's eyes glittered green as summer in the afternoon light. He at least was enjoying himself hugely. What he said next he said quietly, as something not intended for transmission. "I hope your meeting with Kircauldie goes well, Dr Winterton. I really do. You've spent a long, uncomfortable time in the desert and you deserve a little glory. Unfortunately, as you know, academic reputation can take a long time building, and you've been out of circulation, and out of print, for a long time now. We both know that what you want, the process of authentication, could take a very long time. All I want you to know is that, whatever happens, as a collector, I want St Peter's Will."

He paused to pour them both more tea. Chas knew he was right. What he dreaded most, what he had been trying to avoid, was the smear of doubt, the agonized decades of evaluation, which would follow the announcement of his discovery. It was what he had been trying to minimize or avoid by getting Henry Kircauldie's agreement. But what, he wondered, was Medina proposing? He must know very well that the Coptic authorities would never sell St Peter's Will. Even he, who had banked ten years of trust with the Copts, had failed in his requests to have the letter removed from Deir el Baramus, let alone from Egypt, to be tested in laboratories abroad. He could hardly blame them. It was their only weapon. It was their greatest relic. And they saw it as the focus of an eternity of pilgrimages.

As if answering his thoughts, Medina politely slapped him down. "I don't have to answer to anybody, Dr Winterton. I can take my time. I'm afraid that little things like laws don't matter too much to people like me. We are the people laws are made for, not against. If the worst comes to the worst, I'll take St Peter's Will on any terms I have to, any way I can, and sort out the consequences later. You will appreciate that that might not bring you fame, but there are better things than fame, Dr Winterton. There is money."

Chas thought it sounded as much a warning as an offer, and what was Medina offering anyway? For an instant he speculated about millions salted away in Switzerland, the chairmanship of the Medina Foundation, unlimited funds for his own research projects, but he checked himself in time. This is how Medina works, he thought. He doesn't have to say anything. He only has to let people know he's interested and the smell of money he gives off does the rest. We're all like drunks in a bar with him. Just by being there he releases our own dreams, our fantasies. And he's the bloody brewery.

"That's interesting, Mr Medina," he answered at last. "But I don't quite see how it applies to me. It's interesting to know, and I'll bear it in mind, but my only priority now is Henry Kircauldie, and publication."

Medina inclined his head, a man accepting defeat gracefully, and changed the subject entirely. "I hope you enjoy my little party this evening, Dr Winterton. *Le tout Caïre* will be there to look at the legendary monster."

It's attractive, Chas thought, *and very English,* the irony at his own expense. *Does he change himself deliberately to match the people he's with? There must be an American manner and accent on tap as well, surely? Or is it just me, or all of us? Are we so desperate to get a little of the glamour that goes with power and wealth like his that we latch on to any similarities we can find?* But he never got the chance to ask the question, even if he had cared to, for Medina was bringing the interview to a close with a final magnanimous gesture.

"It's a formal affair, of course, Dr Winterton, and you haven't had the opportunity to prepare, so I hope you will forgive me. . . ." As though on cue, Ismail led in a valet who was carrying a white dinner-jacket, dress shirt and trousers and shoes and black bow tie. "I think you'll find they're your size."

Chas was ushered gently from the presence before he could babble his thanks or get over his surprise.

Medina had booked (*Or would "bought" be a better word?* Chas asked himself) the Cairo Sporting Club on the southern tip of Zamalek for the party after the private view of his exhibition. There was probably no more snob place in the city, with its long view down a Nile framed on either side by the Sheraton on the West Bank and the much reconstructed Shepheard's on the East. Chas hated it.

He had had an unsuccessful afternoon. Once again Carfax had seemed to be avoiding him. In the end, to get some exercise after days of forced idleness, he had had Ismail arrange him a car to the great Khan El Kalili market. He had always loved the big market with its winding collection of specialist *souks*, the biggest working medieval complex left anywhere in the world, all built from the limestone cladding which had once made the Pyramids smooth as ski-slopes. He had wandered through its narrow crowded streets, stopping here and there for a drink, a trial run at bargaining, chat with merchants who ranged from smooth-faced late-adolescents puffy with milk-puddings to leather-brown grandfathers extravagantly gnarled by time, any one of whom could have left a computerized New York or London money broker standing.

It was the place he loved above all others in the capital, with the single exception of what he still believed was the most beautiful church building in the world, the first mosque of Cairo, the Ibn Tulun. Cairo might change and grow, swelling to unimaginable millions (already no one knew how many citizens it had, how many fresh recruits from the countryside daily engorged the slums built off the ash-pits and garbage dumps which fringed it) but this remained the same. Full of life and ancient vigour, full of an openness to the world which grew, as much as anything, from its numberless great and lesser mosques and ancient Islamic University, in the days before Islam turned back in on itself, full of merchants and customers wheeling and dealing on an easy open basis, not as clients of the impassable giants, the likes of David Medina.

It smelt. It was dirty. It was noisy. It was disgraceful. It was alive, as a suite of corporate offices could never be. Yet it was the starting-point from which the likes of Medina had grown. It had been the original of the covered market in the *Tales of a Thousand and One Nights*, and Medina was like the endlessly brilliant financier who sat in the heart of the market in those tales, one of the arbiters of last resort. But where, then, was the other one, the good lord Haroun el Raschid?

He bought a filigree silver bracelet for Carfax with some of Medina's money, bargaining briefly for forty minutes. It lay now in the pocket of his dinner jacket. He had not had the chance to speak to her alone.

The guests were drifting in, greeting Medina, crossing the room from the door to do so, clients pledging loyalty to their potentate; those who had failed to do so earlier complimenting him on the exhibition.

Medina had been right. All Cairo (an ugly phrase, he thought, discounting as it did the hungry millions in the city outside, all working, hoping, for a little of the luxury their dark-eyed children gazed at through the rich world's plate-glass windows) was going to be here. Half of them must have come down from Alexandria specially. Already he had noticed Abdullah abd-Bari, the editor of *Al Ahram*, though he had probably just walked down from his house on the other side of Zamalek, Mohammed Heikal, who had been Nasser's closest friend and adviser, and Reza Pahlawi, the late Shah's son.

Chas felt as though he were here on false pretences. It was not that he objected to grandeur, luxury, indulgence. It was just that, after a decade, he could not rid himself of the itch of the dust and sand beneath the expensive clothes Medina had bought him. They must know it, he thought. They must see it, beneath all the showers and shaving and eau-de-Cologne, they must know an English desert bum when they see one, the squinting sand-blind scholar underneath the white tuxedo.

He noticed as he stood lonely over a glass of Krug champagne how impeccable Medina's organization was. Not only were all the bakemeats *halal*, in good Muslim fashion, but he had also laid on a good champagne for those who wanted it, a range of fifteen fruit-juices for those who wanted to be good Muslims, and discreet cocktails of fruit-juice and champagne for those who wanted to look as though they were good Muslims. Ismail stood in one corner of the vast room, his back to the picture-windows out on to the Nile, chatting idly to those who passed him by, and never once taking his eyes off the servants, the arrangements, the needs of the most particular guests, despatching quiet but firm instructions to ensure his master's bidding was well done, no additional perfection overlooked.

And Carfax? She never strayed from Medina's side, to the

101

delight of guests who furtively investigated her cleavage or openly congratulated the old man on his good fortune, not knowing she had been hired for pain rather than for pleasure.

Beneath the chandeliers and brilliant lights of the room Chas felt a shadow fall across him and then heard a dry Bostonian voice saying, "So he's added you to his string of tame camels."

"What does that make you, Mr Adams?" he replied, not turning to face the man from the CIA.

"I'm the worm who's munching all his silks until they're damaged goods."

The American moved round to look him in the face. His scar was pale against a face livid with heat and weariness. Dear God, thought Chas. Him too. What game was it that Adams and Medina were playing till one or the other of them dropped from exhaustion? On second thoughts, he didn't want to know.

Adams blinked his big eyes once, slowly, like a lizard. Big hooded eyes in a lizard's dry rubbery face. *I've eaten things that looked like you,* thought Chas. *Are you here to devour me now?*

"I wasn't sure I'd see you here, Mr Adams."

"You should have known better. Our host is careful to invite anyone who might be of some use to him one day, and it pleases him when they fall over themselves to show. He thinks it's a symbol of his power over others."

"Well, isn't it?"

"Oh, yes. It is. And in any case he likes to make his opposition feel small. He always invites them to come see how powerful he is, and I've known him too long to want to disappoint him when he's in the mood for little power games like that."

A younger man, about his own age, who Chas had noticed glancing over at them, cut his way out of the huddle he was in and made his way over towards them. He had the square set and straight back of a man who felt more comfortable in desert gear than suits, let alone formal clothes. Chas would have sympathized, were it not for the blank face and dead eyes beneath the crewcut. *It isn't desert gear he's used to,* he guessed suddenly. *It's combat fatigues.*

The grapefruit juice he was gripping like a club endeared

102

him no further to Chas, either. The young man cut in on Adams. His accent was broader. Kansas? Nebraska?

"This must be the Dr Winterton you were telling me about, sir. Pleased to make your acquaintance, Doctor."

He reached out a hand, but before Chas could take it, Adams whispered without malice, "Take a walk, Kirk."

Kirk blinked once, slowly, just as Adams had done, before nodding and saying "Sir," and taking his grapefruit somewhere else. His manner puzzled Chas, till he realized what it reminded him of. Kirk had omitted the click of heels and the crisp salute.

"And you expect me to trust a man who employs dead-heads like that?" Chas asked, watching Kirk move to stand unspeaking at the fringes of another group. Adams flicked his eyes to the side for an instant, a sly agreement and understanding. Then he was impassive again, and grave.

"Forget my goons, Doctor. You have bigger problems of your own. I know about the Letter you found. I know it all, and all I want to know is how soon you can announce it. Because believe me, the sooner you do it the safer you'll be."

Chas knew better than to ask him about his sources, and it seemed pointless now to deny the existence of the Letter. His flight to Athens left in seven hours' time. Soon he would be with Kircauldie and in the clear. But he was intrigued by the American's advice.

"You amaze me, Mr Adams. Everyone else who knows about it wants it kept as quiet as the tomb. I would have thought that you would too. I mean, you aren't looking for a holy war, are you?"

Adams threw the holy war back in his face, by using the Arabic word. "No, Doctor. *Jihad* is not high on my agenda. But what you've got is a great deal more dangerous hidden than revealed. You academic sons of bitches," he almost made it sound a compliment, "will get so tied up in a holy war of your own about the goddam Letter that no one else will get a chance to think about it."

There was an element of cynical truth in the remark which Chas could not deny. Adams did not give him the chance. He was sombre.

"Dr Winterton, you have no cause to trust me, or the Agency. I wouldn't trust me if I were you. And if I were on the outside looking in, I wouldn't trust the CIA with chickenshit. But listen anyway. Listen good." He sipped a little champagne and turned in towards Chas with a smile, looking for all the world as though they were talking about the Yankees' chances in the next World Series. "You are the last thing on our minds. We all have bigger brownies to bite on." He smiled ironically at the extravagant image, sending himself up a fraction. "But you are also the one thing we hate most. You're the tiny factor acting at random in a scenario where we're all only just keeping control. And that means all of us, Medina included. It would be easier for all our peace of mind if someone stamped you out, and quickly."

Chas returned Adams's cheerful public smile. "Then why haven't you done it already?"

Adams conceded the aptness of the question with a nod. "Because I have a Senate Committee back home to answer to."

"Is that all?"

"No. From where I sit, it's just possible that, when Medina takes you apart, as he will, that I might be able to use you. Your skin might just be worth saving if, when the time comes, you put yourself completely in my hands. I'm not a virtuous man, Doctor, but I keep to my bargains."

"Are we making a bargain?"

"I think we are." He slid a small manila envelope out of his jacket pocket, on the side nearest the wall, masked by their bodies, and slipped it into Chas's jacket. "When you're alone, you read that. God knows, I may be crazy, but this crazy man is just about your last best hope."

As Adams stared down Chas, his eyes divided by his dead white scar, the light about them thickened. Medina was upon them, smiling, before Chas was even aware of it.

"Aaron, Dr Winterton, so good of you to come. I hope you're enjoying our little party?"

Chas could feel his pulse race in his temples, uncertain which disturbed him more, the closeness of Medina or Carfax. She stood at the old man's shoulder, successfully impersonating a bored little good-time putting up with her paycheck's dreary

104

friends, except that her eyes were alert and kept patrolling everything about her. Aaron spoke for both of them, the ritual congratulations.

"It's delightful, David."

Did Medina and Carfax both tense up on the name, Chas asked himself, *or is it only me? Are they infecting me with their own insanity?*

But Aaron continued regardless. "It's particularly delightful to see you again, Miss Carfax." She acknowledged the salute with the faintest bow of the head, one professional rival to another. "I'm only sorry I had to miss the viewing."

Medina leant forward a little and patted the American on the back of his hand. "Don't mention it, Aaron. It'll be here a long time. I quite appreciate you must have been busy."

It was Aaron's turn to bow slightly, from the waist, before asking, "And did your merchandise arrive safely?"

Medina must have known what he was talking about, for he answered without a heartbeat's hesitation, "Oh, yes, indeed, Mr Adams. So very good of you, but you really shouldn't have bothered. When we unwrapped the parcel we discovered it was damaged goods."

"I am sorry," said Adams, sounding as though he meant it, "but I'm sure you'll find some method of disposal. Now, you must excuse me. I must be a good guest and circulate."

He took his drink away with him into the crowded room, where some guests were already seated with narguilehs. Knowing Ismail's attention to detail, Chas could not help wondering what they were smoking beneath the heavy fug of aromatic tobacco.

Medina took Chas by the arm to say, "You mustn't believe a thing that man says, Dr Winterton. He's CIA, you know." Chas feigned alarm and outrage. "They're the kind of people who plant bombs in the Metropole."

Then Medina and Carfax swept from him, leaving Chas alone and not knowing what to believe.

It was half-past one in the morning and Medina showed no sign of flagging. Chas did. He was slumped on a couch ignoring the conversations which passed on over his head. He began

105

to think it was all an obscure display of power on Medina's part, for there seemed to be an unspoken convention that no one should leave the party before the host. He soon found himself proved mistaken. There was a murmuring from the door, and a pattering like rain on corrugated iron which swelled until he recognized it as applause. Hosni Mubarak had arrived surrounded by military police. Chas would never know if the President stayed little or long, for after a brief speech of thanks to Medina he passed with his uglies to a private room where Medina joined him for a quarter of an hour or so. But Chas did not notice Medina's return, for by then Federigo Paolozzi had risen up in black before him.

"It's very impressive, Doctor." The priest's eyes were so black they shone yellow in the bright electric light. It was a detail of the nightmare Chas had mercifully forgotten.

"You've seen it, then?"

"Oh, yes."

"How did you manage that? The monasteries are closed."

"Not to me. Not to Rome."

"You must be disappointed."

"In a way. It's almost a pity it's a fake."

"The hell it is, Paolozzi."

"Oh, not a recent one, I agree. Nothing so crude as that. I'm not accusing you of any academic iniquity. Though others might. It's late fourth century, of course, as the tests will show. From the time the Copts were first constructing their ridiculous pretensions against Holy Mother Church."

"You're lying. I know the kind of stuff you mean. . . ."

"And so do I, Doctor. We have several others like it in the Secret Archives. Why don't you just surrender now? You can't beat Rome, you know."

"I'll see you in hell first."

"Then at least I shall have interesting company."

It was only a long time afterwards that Chas realized that they had spoken to each other in Coptic throughout.

He was too angry to be afraid, but he would have been afraid, if he had heard the conversation Paolozzi, Kirk Stanshall and David Medina had had before the night was done. But he was

106

in the air to Athens by then, and had more recent events on his mind.

It must have been a little after two that Chas had found himself at the picture windows looking out on to the Nile, with only a few lights glinting now on either bank, the feluccas moored, the children sleeping, and nothing but the sounds of revelry from Zamalek to disturb the soft black flow of the river, velvety as sex. A few guests were drifting away now, coming over to Medina by the window to pay their respects with a touch on the arm or shoulder, like people in the past touching kings in the hope that doing so would ward off disease. Carfax had taken Medina by the arm, surveying each arrival, but managing to look like a mistress past her bedtime.

Medina looked at his watch. "You'd better change, Dr Winterton, or you'll miss your flight. Did you bring your things with you?"

You know I did, Chas thought. *One of your people drove me here.* But he only nodded and idled out to the marble-lined men's room. When he emerged, feeling scruffy beside the diminishing ranks of guests, he waited by the doors of the ballroom. Medina and his minimum entourage of Carfax and Ismail drifted over to join him.

Carfax got to him first and murmured, with the first smile he had had from her for days, "I think it's time I took you to the airport, Dr Winterton." She made it sound like an endearment, but as she looked at him her eyes clouded as though she was concentrating intently.

Then suddenly she turned, with a cry of "Back!" and was pushing Medina back into the ballroom.

Then Chas heard it too, and Ismail, the gunning of the engine, the full-powered roar. They ran back in. The ballroom was a shout of questions. And then the splintering of wood and masonry, the crumbling of plaster and the shrieks of fear, as the big Mercedes slammed through the doors, the hall, and into the ballroom, spilling trolleys and tables and glasses with crash upon crash, its windscreen erupting, a tyre exploding, sparks flying as its belly ground along marble. Then the big bang as the petrol tank went up and everyone panicked as the room began to burn. Everyone except Medina and Carfax, from under whose sheltering body the old man crawled out. Suddenly Medina was in charge of them, pulling them behind him through the crowd to the side door. When they were out on the lawn, the acrid smoke blacker than the blackness of the sky, sparks showering upwards in black and orange plumes, he turned to his assistants.

"Carfax, stay, Ismail, get the doctor to the airport. . . ." For a second or two they all stood there, catching their breath; then Medina asked the question they were all forming in their minds.

"The driver? Did you see the driver?"

The others nodded, dumbly. He had spilt out through the shattered windscreen, very very dead; and all of them knew him. He had not died of impact or explosion. Nor had he gunned the car towards the club. He had been dead already.

Gemayel was burning, back there in the building, on an aged stretch Mercedes. He showed all the marks of a ritual Islamic killing. His left eye had been shot out. His face and tongue had gone black, his right eye starting from his head: the usual effects when a man has been expertly garotted with a length of single-gauge three-millimetre insulated wire.

Part three:
THE TREASON OF CLERKS
Athens

Even if Chas hadn't had other things on his mind, he would not have paid too much attention to the conditions of his flight. Eking out grants, he had travelled too often on Balkan, Bulgarian Airways, to be much disturbed by their aged Tupolev aircraft, many of them turbo-props still clearly based on wartime models. (At Sofia airport you could see the planes used for internal flights, with perspex bubbles in their backs and noses, just waiting to be fitted with machine-guns). The décor — imitation-Sixties Western psychedelic nylon — no longer depressed him, nor did the filthy coffee, plates of sausage and bearded muscular stewardesses. What had disheartened him was that the plane was crowded. He had forgotten how, each summer after the final desert harvest, the Balkan flights up from Khartoum were filled by politically-acceptable Sudanese (city-boy college students, he had always guessed) on their way to summer courses at the agricultural colleges round Sofia, where they would be feared and loathed for being black and paid for by the Communist Party of Bulgaria. The plane was full of them now, running up and down the aisle, showing off the consumer goods they had picked up at the airport.

He had wanted to think. He knew there was no point in asking who had killed Gemayel. Egypt, indeed the Middle East, was full of people who might feel they had cause to, from secret services to outraged husbands. In retrospect — though this had never occurred to him before — so great was Gemayel's legendary status, it was a miracle he had survived so long. No, what worried Chas was that the corpse had been delivered to Medina so publicly, in a blaze of attention. It offended his muddled notion of how these things were supposed to work. He guessed that such things were normally a matter for dark alleys and mean streets, not the bright lights of the Cairo Sporting Club. What was going on? And was even Medina losing control?

Perhaps that was what Aaron Adams had meant. Perhaps power wasn't so important, not all the power at David Medina's disposal. What mattered was control, being able to control the big events as they arose and turn them to your advantage.

Thinking of Adams made him remember the small manila envelope in his pocket. He took it out and opened it. There was a single flimsy sheet of paper in it, the kind used for taking carbon copies. It had been typed on using an old manual machine with a large typeface. Why had Adams typed it at home, away from the electronic comforts of his office? Who or what was he unsure of? The note was short, unsigned, giving no indication of where it came from, nor mentioning him by name. It read:

> When this goes up, the most you can hope for is your life. If the time comes when you need a hand with hoping for your life, the only message you need to get to me is: I WANT TO SEE MY LAWYER.
>
> However it comes to me, I will be at Saqqara in the ruins of the complex all night for each of the next three nights thereafter.
>
> It's the best that I can do. Tough luck, sucker.

He stuffed it back in his pocket, thinking: *I suppose I'd better get rid of it when we land.*

He felt something cold in his pocket, and drew it out. It was the bracelet he had bought for Carfax in the Khan El Kalili barely twelve hours before. Damn! He had had no time alone with her, but she had smiled at him before. . . .

It was ridiculous. He half wished he had been Medina, and been thrown back under her when those delicate, knowing, ears had first half-heard, half-sensed, the coming message in a car.

Was it the desert, was it his years alone amongst monks and nomads which had made him abnormally vulnerable? Or was he just right to trust to his instincts, his instinctive desire for Carfax and her chestnut hair, his instinctive trust of Aaron

110

Adams? Both of them radiated what he could only call a curious kind of honour, not necessarily to the outside world or in their dealings with it, but in themselves. They both gave off a sense that they knew what they wanted and believed in, and would compromise everything but that. The trouble was, he didn't really know what it was they honoured and what, therefore, they really planned for him. No, it was ridiculous.

The fast light of the mediterranean dawn was flashing through the windows over the starboard wing. They would be landing in Athens soon, the nightmare descent into the cliff-face, the threat of the mountains of coastal southern Greece. *It's true,* he thought. *Sand has its advantages.* The desert must be the longest safest runway in the world. He had his doubts about mountains.

Athens, as always, came as a shock. It was full of Greeks. Also English, French, Germans, Dutch and Swedes. It was so much another Mediterranean town that Chas always expected it to be more like Alexandria than it was. But Alexandria wasn't a haven of Western tourists, and it was summer, and the pack had come down from the north to hunt down undiscovered islands, mystically equipped already with four-star hotels, tavernas and desalinated swimming-pools.

A rangy Swede, clad in denim shorts and running shoes, came up to him hopefully in the Customs Area and yodelled something at him. Well, it hadn't been English, had it? Chas answered in his best Early Aramaic and the Swede loped puzzled away. *God knows,* thought Chas, *I don't begrudge the Greeks the money, and my people could do with more of it, but how many hikers and playmates can one poor country absorb?*

He took a cab from the airport, and even he winced in the early morning light. It was different from the light in Egypt, even in Alexandria. Everything left a vivid trace in the air in Athens, and the sky was sometimes even blue. Was he just being a romantic, a classical historian convinced by the prop-aganda of the past? Or was it true? The sense, at least, that there was always water here, while back in Egypt only the Nile under the flat white sky held back the enemies of life from far back in the hot heart of Africa.

111

Rubbish, he thought, checking that the file of papers and photographs, a duplicate of the one he had given Medina, was safe in his overnight bag, deep among the crumpled formal clothes, the whisky for Henry Kircauldie, the bottle of scent for Jenny St Clair.

Kircauldie was staying as always at the flat in the heart of the city leased by the British Council. Jennifer, he guessed, would be out at the conference hotel, a bankrupt shipping tycoon's retreat (he had kept his mistresses there) a little way out of the city, commandeered by the government as a base for premium cultural events.

He found a message waiting for him at the flat, inviting him to wait in the bar across the road. Kircauldie had been called to the Embassy and the Ministry of Culture and was likely to be some time. Chas could guess what all that was about. Someone would have been lined up to speak at the conference demanding the return of the Elgin Marbles. The Embassy would be trying to find some way that Henry, as Chairman of the conference, would not have to reply. The Ministry would want the opposite; just a sentence of acknowledgement, a mere half-line of hope.

Poor Henry. The perils of distinction. The thought made him start. Wasn't that what he was doing? Labouring in the backyard of nowhere for a decade in the hope that one day he might gain a Chair of Archaeology or Paleoanthropology at a decent university? To be Sir Charles and sit on committees and have to answer a lot of damn fool questions about stones which politicians had already decided among themselves? Was that why he had been doing it? It had been so long since he had spent any serious time in England that he no longer really knew how the system worked, or even if he was a part of it. He remembered his uncertainty at Medina's party. Would he ever be rid of the odour of sand? And did he want to be? And Carfax as Lady Winterton? The thought was as intriguing as it was silly. Was that why he had fallen amongst villains, spies, murder? Then he thought of Jones, of Gemayel, of bombs. He began to tremble uncontrollably. What was it that had happened to him? What was it the priests had done?

He sat in the bar drinking ouzo after ouzo, drowning his

112

doubts, sweating out the booze in the hot bright sun.

It was nearly noon before Kircauldie arrived. *He looks fit,* thought Chas. He must have got off his backside for a change and been out digging recently. Had he? It was the sort of thing Chas ought to know. He ought to be keeping up with journals, and the gossip and trade of the academic life, but how long had it been? How long since he had seen a scholarly paper? Henry looked happy on it, in a flustered kind of way. *It's a pose, of course,* thought Chas, who knew. *Ever since he moved to London, he plays the daft professor, but he loves it. He loves the politics, the committees, the matters of public concern. He wouldn't have got there if he didn't. And he's good at it.* Nice, sweet Henry Kircauldie, who wouldn't hurt a fly, was the hardest hard case in the discipline. No one had crossed him and survived. After he had finished with Sliefert in the Basra Runes affair, Sliefert had disappeared. The last time anyone heard, he had been teaching English as a Foreign Language in Burkina Faso.

Kircauldie sat down heavily, looking tetchy, and ordered a beer. Chas let him mutter for a while.

"Really, Charles, these diplomats. Such a frustration. And the gall of the Greek government. I sympathize, of course, but really. Making a political fairground out of an academic conference. It isn't good enough."

"Well, I suppose they are picking up a fair part of the bill." He knew at once he should not have said it. For a fraction of a second Kircauldie glared at him then looked away, as though he were below the level of a Professor's attention.

Chas reasoned that he had no cause himself to talk about academics travelling free. What had he been doing for the last ten years, for God's sake? Even so a part of him rebelled at the thought of someone as distinguished as Kircauldie refusing to recognize that somebody was paying for him, that academic independence had to be bought like anything else. But he controlled himself. Henry was the best hope that he had of a quick, authoritative authentication. He could not afford to antagonize him yet. He hoped that the fit had passed, and tried to explain his presence.

"Henry, I'm here to ask a favour. I've got some material with me I'd like you to look at. It's something big, and it needs to be independently examined before I announce it. Can we discuss it in private?"

What took him aback most was not the speed but the completeness of Kircauldie's rejection. The old eyes flickered once and then he said, coldly, as though he hardly knew Chas Winterton, as though Chas were some vermin off the street who had crawled into one of his supervisions, "I'm not interested, Charles. Not interested at all. Nothing you find could possibly interest me. At least you've been consistent. You've been the same for a decade."

Chas tried to stammer some reply, but Kircauldie gave him no chance, and the old-ingrained habit of deference broke out.

"We kept you going for ten years, Charles. We couldn't really afford it, and you never helped. You were never ready to put in time on team projects. You never would work with a research group. But we kept you going out of a sense of duty. Even if what you were doing was mindlessly dull we reasoned it was probably a good thing someone was doing it. And you kept bringing us your fantastic suspicions of unimaginable long-lost records. But what have you produced, Charles? What have you achieved?"

Chas tried to answer, but Kircauldie went relentlessly on. "It's true you've found some things, but nothing important, nothing really new, in a time when people in the Middle East have been falling over major finds. And that was the trouble. We needed all the help we could get. We don't have much money and we have to perform well if we're going to get our hands on more. But you weren't having any of that. Oh, no. You wanted to work alone."

He took another swig of his beer and, thus refreshed, launched into his attack again. "We kept you going as part of a political package, not that you could ever bother to be interested in that kind of thing, that kind of necessary thing if we're to pursue our work. We paid for you as a gesture, to make sure we were adequately represented on the digs at Pharaonic sites. But we don't have to do that now, not since we set up the EEC Combined Research Council. We can spread that kind of chore. We can cut our unnecessary costs. As I recall, the last time we met you were too busy laughing about free trips to Brussels restaurants to pay any attention to what we were trying to do. Well, that's your loss."

With shock, Chas realized what he was feeling most of all was embarrassment. Kircauldie could not stop.

"You haven't published a thing, since a letter to an editor, in three and a half years, and that was a revision of an earlier paper. The only thing we know after all the work you've done is that no imaginable person ever will want to look at what you've catalogued. You've saved the rest of us from wasting time. That's all. And we're sick of you playing the noble independent out in godforsaken deserts. Only you would send a telegram about anything except a matter of life and death. You are ridiculously histrionic and I'm sick of your silly little dramas. To be honest I only agreed to see you because I wanted to make sure you were surviving without a grant, that you weren't starving. I feel that much responsibility for you, which is more than you've ever done for anyone. I thought we might have lunch. But what I was dreading was that you'd ride out of the desert like something out of *Lawrence of Arabia* claiming another wonderful find. To be honest I wouldn't put it past you to fake one. And I'm not interested, Charles. Not any more. Not any longer."

He slapped money down on the table to cover the cost of his beer, got up and walked away.

Chas ached as the bus rattled out of the city, clutching his hold-all to his knees. He had telephoned Jennifer St Clair at her hotel. She had not sounded too pleased to hear him, but had invited him out to see her that afternoon anyway.

Jennifer will listen, he kept saying to himself, over and over again, *and she can convince Kircauldie.*

At the hotel desk they told him she was waiting for him in the bar. He felt grubby again, surrounded by the marble and palms of the ship-owner's villa. The desk-clerk's face told him how out of place he looked. She was sitting by herself at a table by the windows and stood up as he came in. The past thumped Chas across the back of the head; she was as pretty as he remembered. He felt hideously nervous as he walked across to greet her. *Am I still as unchanged?* he wondered.

She was wearing a white cotton dress printed with flowers and a broad pink band of a belt. It underlined the full breasts Chas remembered. She had always loved the loose light clothes of summer, as he had once had reason to be grateful for. She looked better at thirty-five than most women he had known did at eighteen. But still she wasn't Carfax. He noticed she still wore a crucifix at her throat.

He leaned forward to kiss her on the cheek, but she sat down swiftly, smoothing her skirt beneath her, leaving him mouthing at the open air like a fish out of water.

"Hello, love," he said, trying to sound bright.

"Hello, Chas."

"How are you these days?" She shrugged her broad shoulders, curling down her full lower lip in a gesture of unconcern that was part of his composite memory of her. If it had not been for the opulent breasts and the broad, child-bearing hips, there might have been something mannish about her. She had a square face with big clear features beneath short, dark-blonde hair. She had always been definite and positive. She had always got what she wanted. There was nothing she hated more than indecision and weakness. He had been busy remembering on the bus, and asked carefully, "How's Eric?" (*Eric!* he thought, as always with a hoot of derision).

"He's fine."

"Still computing?"

She nodded. "Head of Research and Development these days."

"He must be doing all right."

"We manage."

"And the children?"

"Sophie's fine. Theo's decided he doesn't like being nine and will be insufferable for another eight months yet. Gemini's just at the stage where she's finding boys impossible and little Castor's suffering a bit in consequence. But he's a good kid. He'll survive."

"Sophie must be getting quite a lady now. How old is. . . ?"

A look of contempt crossed Jennifer's face. "You never

116

bloody change, do you? You ought to know. You are meant to be her godfather. She's eleven, well past her First Communion. At least you might have sent a bloody card."

He felt embarrassed for the second time that day. He fingered the silver bracelet in his pocket, wondering if he should try to hand it over as a present for Jenny's elder daughter, but decided that in her present frame of mind she would only throw it back in his face.

"You always were a selfish sod," she continued, as though it were a matter of public consensus. She looked at him with her deep blue eyes and said, giving vent to an age of malice, "You just disappeared into your desert. You never wrote. Not even bread-and-butter letters when we put you up in England, when you seemed to think it was your right. You've always been the same. You've always had such an inflated opinion of yourself."

She paused, to look at him again, preparing her final blow: "Even at college, when we made love, you used to bang away with your eyes tight closed as though you were saying, 'This isn't for God, or love, or the begetting of children, this is for Me, Me, Me.' You even made your pleasures a war-cry against the rest of the world." She paused once more, before adding matter-of-factly, "Quite nice for me, of course, because you kept banging away so long, but never very flattering."

He looked down at the hold-all at his feet, in silence, shrugging his shoulders at last and saying, "I'm sorry."

"Screw you." Then suddenly she was businesslike: "Now what is it you wanted to see me about?"

At least she looked at the photographs and read the draft of his paper. She wore reading-glasses now. He liked it. He could imagine what she would be like when she was old. Still handsome. Still formidable. *It's almost a pity,* he thought. *I threw it all away.* But he clung on tight to the silver bracelet in his pocket and thought of Carfax and Alexandria.

She took her reading-glasses off with a crisp brisk movement and used them to tap his papers. "It reads very well. But then, you've always been too eloquent for your own good. It isn't my area, of course, but I assume that it's a fake."

117

"But why, Jenny?"

"Because all this kind of stuff has always been faked in the past. And, if I'm being honest," (*Go on,* he thought, *be honest; you always are*), "because it's you that found it."

He wished that she had lied.

"Even so," she continued, "it's a damn sight more interesting than anything you turned up in the past. Write it up properly and submit it to SSRC. It'll get considered as one of next year's projects. We might be able to afford a few tests."

She explained the *We* with a smile. "I'm a Fellow of Girton now, and I sit on the Review Committee."

He tried to make her understand. He tried to lift his own complete conviction, his enthusiasm, above the threshold of her disbelief. "You don't have to wait a year, Jenny. Nor do I. I have access to funds. I've got enough to fly us both, and Henry Kircauldie, over to Egypt as soon as you want. Today. Come and look at it. Then you'll understand why I'm certain."

She shook her head. She seemed to be trying to stop herself showing pity. "There isn't any chance of that. You'll have to put it through the proper channels. We're busy people, Chas. We have real lives to lead. Even the Second Coming would have to wait a year before Social Science Research funds were released to pay for authenticating God."

She got up to go. "You haven't made things any easier for yourself, either. Henry can hardly bring himself to speak about you. I don't know what you've been up to, but you ought to know better than to try pulling a fast one over David Medina."

He was stunned. "Medina?"

"Oh, yes," she went on innocently. "He telephoned Henry last night. Just after we got in. I was there when he took the call. The Council was giving a little party. It's why we came over early."

"But what did he say?" Chas asked, in a desperation of doubt.

"As far as I can make out," Jenny told him, "though Henry wasn't wildly communicative, Medina said you'd been running all over the Middle East, and even been in to see him — he'd agreed to see you because of Henry — trying to peddle some fakes."

118

Cairo and The Delta

He was angry. He was still angry; ten hours later. He had never in his life been mad for much more than two hours before. But now, ten hours later, it was still his intention to throw Carfax a kiss, Ismail a right hook, and Medina the worst thrashing of his miserable lifetime. Never mind that, deep down, he knew that Carfax could kill him in a twinkling of her sea-green eyes. He wanted an explanation and he planned to beat the old man shitless till he got it.

It was just past midnight and the maniac who drove the airport bus back to the terminal put in the kind of performance, three wheels in the air most of the way, which drew spontaneous applause from the other passengers in their relief at drawing to a halt. It suited Chas's mood.

The terminal itself was almost deserted, an institutional pale green beneath the bare electric lights. He waved his residency permit at the sullen bank clerks at the end of the corridor; it meant that, unlike other foreigners, he did not have to change money as soon as he landed. Thanking God he had no luggage, he broke out of the scrum and headed across the arrival hall to report to Immigration.

Even a residency permit could not get him past the slow silent appraisal all foreigners went through. The clerk sat in his cubicle, fingering the battered British passport, its pages thick with Arabic, rubber stamps, and stapled-in authorities and permits. He slapped each thick page back with his thumb, not looking at Chas at all, each click of a page echoing with boredom. When he had finished, the clerk held the closed passport vertically in his hand, weighing it, testing its cutting edge.

Still without looking up he said, "Wait here, please. You must wait." Then he turned to the door at the back of the

119

cubicle, opening it a fraction to mutter at the guard beyond and handing him the document. Chas knew better than to argue with Egyptian authority. Everything would be attended to in God's good time, and with about the same sense of urgency. The walls of Egypt's ancient monuments were covered with a single hieroglyphic phrase, repeated again and again: Millions of years, Millions of years. They had had bureaucracy even then.

The clerk waved Chas aside, for a queue of baggage-laden passengers was forming up beside him. Chas stepped away, remembering to mutter polite thanks in Arabic.

Ten minutes later, the guard who had taken his passport returned with three policemen. The clerk, with an un-Egyptian haste, turned from his current inspection and informed the police the Englishman spoke Arabic.

Stay calm, thought Chas. *Keep cool. This happens all the time, at every border in Africa. It isn't their fault. They're trying to do their job. And none of them is David Medina. Save it all up for him.*

One of the policemen took him by the arm and pulled him past the barrier, saying, "Come with me. Come."

Chas shook himself free but followed him all the same.

They led him across the terminal building to a door marked Tourist Police (in Arabic still) and took him through into an outer office furnished with a desk, some chairs, a bench, the customary photographs of Nasser and Mubarak, and a bare, 100-watt electric bulb. Chas began patiently to explain that he was an English scholar resident in Egypt and approved by the Ministry of the Interior. He reached for his passport to show the appropriate permissions, but the listless sergeant at the desk waved back his hand and began going through Chas's bag, taking a note of every item he found besides the whisky and perfume.

Chas asked the sergeant what was happening and if he was being detained, and if so why. He got no answer. Then the other policemen started going through his pockets, singing out each item as they came upon it. Chas gave thanks he had got rid of Adams's letter, which he would have been a long time explaining, but as one of the policemen fished out with a grin

120

the little silver bracelet and dangled it before him, his temper snapped.

He snatched for the bracelet and the next thing he knew he was on the concrete floor with three policemen on top of him kicking and punching. One caught the bomb bruise on his spine and he blanked out as he vomited.

By the time he came round he was in the inner office being dragged out of his jacket while one of them removed his shoes. There was a senior officer with them. He was leafing through Chas's passport with the same bored flick of every page.

At length he asked, "You are John Charles Winterton?"

"Yes, I am, and who are you, and what. . . ?"

"Be silent. Your home addresss is care of King's College, Cambridge?"

"Yes."

"Your poste restante addresses here in Egypt are the British Council, Cairo, and Deir es Baramus, Wadi el Natroun?"

"Yes, in the name of God, it's all in there."

"Very good, Mr Winterton . . . "

"Doctor."

The policeman paid no attention to the correction. All he said was, "I am charging you with the murder of your country-man Martin Edward Foster."

They moved him to an underground cell, one of three open-bar cages. He was the only occupant. They left him there for hours. He couldn't be certain how long. They had taken his watch with his other possessions. Eventually, the senior officer returned and stood outside the cage staring down at Chas. He was holding a file filled with flimsy papers with typing on them, most in Arabic, some in Roman characters. He was looking at one of the papers when he asked, "Why don't you just confess? It will be easier in the end."

"Get me the British Consulate," Chas said, not moving from the low wooden bed.

"Not yet. You don't need them till you've confessed."

"You're mad. I haven't seen Foster in days. I hardly know him. I was out of Egypt all yesterday. When's it supposed to have happened? How am I supposed to have done it?"

121

The policeman leaned against the bars, cooling his forehead against the iron. "You don't seem to understand. I have all the circumstantial evidence I could want. But you're a foreigner. I have to be careful. So why not just confess? Nothing much can happen to you. After a few months in prison, I expect you'll be deported to England." When Chas remained silent and un-moving, he shrugged and went away.

As the day wore on the cell began to throb with the summer heat. They had left him some stale water in a bottle. Chas took a swig of it, grateful even for its gritty, plastic flavour. He was trying to think. Foster dead? Yes. It hardly bothered him. Death grows boring too, and Chas was tired.

He must have slept. He could not say how long. But when he awoke he could sense the day was turning. The heat was at its most intense, and movement was a torment, but soon the heat would begin to ebb, degree by painful degree. Someone had brought him food in a tin tray. Tahina paste and pitta bread. A fly had got stuck in the paste and died. He ate it anyway, slowly, careful for his thirsty throat.

When the senior officer returned, he had himself let into the cage with Chas and sat down on the bed beside him, still holding the tatty file. His voice was gentle, patient, seductive. Chas found himself wanting to listen, to agree.

"You can stop this," he said quietly. "You can stop the heat and the thirst and the exhaustion. We could put you in your consulate's custody till the hearing. You could bathe, eat, sleep. In a clean bed. All you have to do is confess."

"I didn't do it."

The policeman looked pityingly at him. "You had motive. You had opportunity. That's usually enough. Enough for me to hold you here indefinitely."

Chas tried to explain again. "All right, he wasn't my favourite person, but I only met him a couple of times. I've got no motive. And as for time, I've hardly had any to myself in years."

He sat back on the bed, holding his bruised lower back away from the wall, resting only his aching head and shoulders. His neck felt like a rope pulled to full stretch. The policeman stood up.

"We found him yesterday, in his flat off the Khan el Kalili. You know what Egypt's like, in summer." Even he was blinking sweat out of his eyes, Chas noticed. "You know how fast meat rots. It isn't easy to tell anything about it once it's gone off. He was a mess. But we think he was killed in the afternoon of the previous day. We know you were in the area at the time. He'd been beaten to death. We know from other sources that you hated each other. He'd spent some time in every diplomats' bar in Cairo announcing the fact. I'm not saying you planned it. Perhaps it was self-defence. I don't care as long as I get to clear this up quickly. Foreign deaths are an embarrassment to me. Why did you do it? Why did you have your fight with him at Medina's?"

Chas looked at him for the first time, saying simply, "It's Medina, isn't it? He's put you up to this. I'm being falsely accused." He could not remember the Arabic for framed.

The policeman shook his head. "We don't do that to foreigners. Sometimes to our own. But not to foreigners. As for Medina, it took him by surprise when we called to question his personal staff."

Chas could not restrain his sarcasm. "Is that all you went to talk to him about? Nothing about a car in the Cairo Sporting Club? Nothing about Gemayel?"

The policeman looked away. "You are speaking of things which never happened." Then he had himself let out and went away.

Chas no longer knew what or whom to believe, but he was beginning to believe that Adams had been right. Was he marked down as some obscure corner of a Medina plot? Was that why the old man had got to Henry Kircauldie? Had someone got to Jennifer too? Or was that paranoia?

It hardly mattered. He would take no chances. He needed help. Any help he could get. This time he must stay awake. This time he must wait for one of the others to bring him food. Watching the door all the time, he took off his socks and removed the five twenty-dollar bills concealed in each, slimy with sweat and dirt, but money all the same, in the safest place he had found in fifteen years' travelling. No one took his socks off without his knowing, and the way he travelled most people

123

would rather eat shit than approach his feet. Two hundred dollars. The last of Medina's money. He waited.

He was grateful he was still at the airport. He had some idea what conditions were like in the city's central jail, not out of cruelty but carelessness. People got forgotten there, for years or till they died. Here at least he had a chance to get word to the outside world.

At last a guard returned with some water, and a bowl of the fellahin staple: rice, macaroni, noodles, lentils and a squirt of pepper sauce. It had saved him often enough for a few piastres.

Chas unpeeled one of the twenty-dollar bills as the guard approached. The Egyptian's eyes lit up. He looked furtively back at the door, then gazed at the note again. Chas held it up, before unfolding another bill. The Egyptian licked his lips.

"What?" he asked, whispering.

"A message."

"No messages." Another bill. "Who?"

"An American. He will give you more. I will give you more if you return with him."

The Egyptian shook his head and made as if to go.

"Wait." Another bill. "Garden City. Sharia Latin America."

"Too far." One more. That made a hundred dollars. *Christ, let him break quickly.*

"Ask for Adams at Number 15. Tell him I am here. Tell him I need to see my lawyer. But tell him I am here." It sounded legitimate. It didn't sound illegal. *Why shouldn't I get the man his lawyer?* Chas could see the Egyptian thinking. *But tell him I am here. He's no use to me stuck out at Saqqara.* "Tell him I am here. One hundred dollars. More when you bring him."

The guard nodded, and reached between the bars for the money. Reluctantly, Chas handed it over. All he could do was hope. Hope and wait.

He had given up thinking about time. He had closed as much of his mind down as he could. The senior police officer had not returned, nor had the guard. He was left alone, to put into practice his Egyptian training in boredom. It was cooler, into the evening, when he was disturbed by the grating of the door,

124

the sound of footsteps, the click of high steel-tipped heels. It was Carfax, in a pale summer frock. *It's party time,* he thought wildly. Then he did not know which he felt more: anger, distrust or relief. All his emotions confused by the stab of desire between his legs. She gave some money to the guard and motioned to the cell door. He opened it and she stepped in. The guard did not move. She handed him more money and he locked the cell door behind them and left.

Chas was already standing. When she crossed the cell and kissed him, relief flooded through his weariness and doubt. He held her closer to him and forced his dry, hungry tongue into her eager mouth. She pulled away from him, a little breathless, and ran her hand down his body, her long cool fingers stroking his erection, swiftly, once. Then she was businesslike, sweeping her long hair back from her eyes.

"We have to run," she said urgently. "Medina's gone mad. We have to get away. He'll have Ismail after us in under an hour. If I can get us out of here, can you get us out of the country? You're the only one I can turn to."

"I can do it."

She smiled with relief, her green eyes gleaming, and kissed him again as his strong hands kneaded her buttocks. She pushed him away. "Take my shoulders." He looked at her in bafflement. "Put your hands on my shoulders." He did as he was told. "When the guards come in, start shaking me around. Hit me a couple of times. Rough me up." She looked amused at his dismay. "Just do it."

Then she started screaming.

The guards tumbled into the room, one after another, as Chas began to knock her about, fearful to hit her too hard till she jabbed him in the stomach. The guards kept on yelling, fumbling with the keys, rattling the bars. As the cage door swung open she hit the first guard as she turned. The heel of her hand took him under the chin. He lifted off the ground. Chas heard the snap of breaking teeth. The second guard got her fingers in his eyes and went down like lead shot. The third backed to the wall. She hit him anyway, once, with her closed fist, in the throat.

She took Chas's hand. "Come on!"

They ran.

There were more guards tumbling through the door at the head of the stairs. She took the first one with straight fingers to the groin. Chas hit the second with the swinging door.

In the offices beyond them they sent tables, chairs and benches flying as the policemen stumbled after them. Then they were out into the airport concourse, Chas sliding and slipping in his socks.

"Shoes!" he cried as he fell.

"Fuck shoes!" She was struggling with something. Her handbag. He saw her throw it away as a policeman ran up. Then she was taking brisk clear aim. There was an explosion as the muzzle lifted.

She took the policeman where she wanted, in the shoulder. He went scarlet from the earlobe to the waist as his arm disintegrated. The impact threw him backwards across the marble floor, and a severed artery pumped blood out in a fountain. She took aim once more, and another policeman went down, his left leg jelly from below the knee. And again, one last one, at the hip, so his guts spilt out like luggage on the ground.

Then everything was screaming as she half-lifted Chas, half-dragged him, her floral frock bright red with blood, through the scattering passengers to the door, while the last police ran to their injured colleagues or tugged at the flaps of their futile holsters.

She had the Range Rover waiting outside the airport, its engine running and the driver's door open. She pushed Chas in first and followed headlong, turning to throw the gun into the hands of the startled man she had paid to watch the car, and slammed the door. Then she put her foot down.

"Christ!" he yelled, as they roared away from the airport. "Did you have to kill so many?"

"I didn't kill them," she said frowning, concentrating on the road and dodging the traffic. "If I had done you'd have known it. And there'll be no useful fingerprints by the time they get that gun."

"Are you out of your mind? Fingerprints? How many white markswomen are there in this country?"

126

She said nothing. For the first time Chas noticed it was already night. A couple of miles on, at the fringes of Heliopolis, she pulled off the road. They bounced behind some trees. There was a Peugeot 504 shooting-brake, with sand tyres, parked amongst them.

"Sorry about the delay in getting to you," she grinned. "The planning took a little time." Then she was squirming into the back of the Range Rover and unzipping a leather and canvas bag.

"What are you doing?" he asked plaintively, as she pulled her dress over her head, wriggled out of her slip, and kicked off her shoes. Her skin gleamed white in the darkness against her black lace underwear. *Christ*, he thought vaguely, *as soon as this is over. . . .*

Then she was pulling on khaki army-surplus clothes, a desert shirt and pants and desert boots. She pulled her hair behind her head, coiling it, and pinned it up, covering it with a man's panama hat.

She dragged him over to the Peugeot. As they got in Chas thought it wise to mention that he still had no shoes. "Sorry," she said, thinking. "Later. In the meantime, whoever in this country stopped a sand-bum travelling with his liberated lover?" She released the handbrake and pulled out into the night.

She looked intent, wrapped up in herself, as she drove. Chas suddenly felt protective, as though she needed protecting, gratitude mingling with desire. He sat watching her for a while, dwelling on details, the delicate shell of her ear, her long dark eyelashes, her long bare neck clouded by a few stray chestnut hairs, the curve of her breast beneath her army shirt, before asking gently, "What is it, Carfax? What can I do?"

She said nothing for some time, mulling over her reply. When it came, it seemed as though she almost had to drag it from herself, as though there were things she was still unwilling to betray. She sounded tired as she answered: "It's Medina. We need something to bargain with once we're out of here. Because he'll come after us wherever we go. It's been coming for a long, long time, I think, but he's finally gone insane."

Chas said nothing. He was thinking. At last he told her to

127

stop the car. She looked doubtful. "Just stop it," he ordered and, to her own surprise, she complied.

He got out of the car and walked round to the driver's door. "Move over." She moved.

"What are you doing? What are you up to?" she asked as he got into the driver's seat, rubbing his itchy feet against the gritty pedals. He did not speak at once, thinking before he released the handbrake.

"Well, whatever else we do," he said, "there isn't any point in heading back to Cairo. Even if no one recognized us we could lose hours in the traffic. What time is it?"

"Early. Barely nine o'clock."

He looked puzzled. "What time did you come for me?"

She laughed at that. "Less than half an hour ago."

His brow furrowed with concentration. It was as though he found thinking difficult. At last he sat back, decided. There was only one more thing he needed to know. "Are we really in this together?"

She laughed again, but sadly. "We have to be. If Medina catches me now, he'll kill me. And he's written you off as a dead man. We are the only friends we've got."

He shook his head. "Maybe not the only ones, but you're right about Medina. About our needing something to bargain with. We're going to Wadi Natroun. One way or another I have to get my hands on the Letter. We need the Fisherman's Will."

It was her turn to shake her head. "Medina's bound to have the Alexandria road covered. And if I know him he'll get someone up to the Wadi as well. Probably Ismail."

Chas had already thought of that. "The monasteries are closed. He might get to the village, but no further. But the monks know me, and anyway it's Baramus we're after. It's remote. We can come round on it from the north. As for the Alexandria road, screw that. I've lived here ten years, remember? He won't have the back roads covered. We can go north on Route 15, double back on 3, cut west on 19 and 6 and then, in this old tank, out into the desert."

Carfax thought about it. "It might work. And we need the Letter."

128

He interrupted her. "And if the monks don't play?"

She shrugged her shoulders. "Then I have an arsenal in the back of this old tank."

"All right, let's try it." He was about to put the car in gear, but she leant across and stopped him.

"How long will it take?"

He guessed intelligently. "It must be getting on for two-fifty kilometres. Back roads, the desert. Maybe four hours, maybe a little more, and we want to get there under cover of darkness. Once there we'd be safe for a while."

She smiled in the darkness, and put his hand between her legs. "You're right, we'd better go," she said, shifting her thighs. "But it's a pity."

"What is?"

She laughed again. "It doesn't matter. It's just that shooting always makes me horny."

He swore, and put the car in gear.

They cut back into the broad boulevards and green gardens of Heliopolis to pick up Route 15, keeping within the speed limit. They were taking no chances. "I like this place," Carfax said unexpectedly.

Chas grunted his agreement. "Nice suburb," he added, watching for his turning. "Hard to believe it's the oldest part of Cairo."

"It all looks too new."

"Yeah. It got built for the foreigners last century. Now it's where the rich who don't live on Zamalek live. But before that there was a city here, four and a half, maybe five thousand years ago. There's a well here where the Copts say the Holy Family parked on the Flight into Egypt."

She looked at him intently. "Do you like your women old as well?"

"Stick around for fifty years. I'll let you know." But he would, of course. He was just beginning to imagine the possibility of spending the rest of his life with her. He liked it. Better than deserts or priests or empire-builders.

It was because the Romans called this city Babylon that the Copts believed St Peter had died in Egypt. The ancient tales only said he died in Babylon, but not in which one. Rome had simply grabbed the honour, the way for centuries it grabbed everything else. He remembered at last who Medina reminded him of. He made Chas think of Caesar Augustus, first emperor of the Roman world.

The Copts had got it wrong, of course, muddling the traditions, the way priests always did. Yes, this was it. They were on the right road. It was Alexandria Peter had died in. He knew that now, whatever Henry Kircauldie said. It made so much sense, in retrospect. It explained so much. Alexandria and Rome had slugged it out, in the years before the rise of Constantinople, fighting for Eastern and Western traditions. No wonder, if Peter had died in Alexander's city, that Rome stamped on the city hard every time it could, throwing out the Jews, burning the libraries, destroying any place where the secret tradition might be preserved, where a record might be kept. Not that the Copts were any better. They had the only real, credible man in the story as their founder, and they ended up being kicked out by everyone else on Roman orders at Chalcedon because they denied the human part of Christ. He didn't understand it. What was wrong with being human? Why did you always have to choose between spirit-gods like Egypt's and the relentless institutions which all modelled themselves on Rome? What was wrong with men and women? Then he remembered Medina. That was what was wrong with men and women. They ended up wanting emperors.

"What are you thinking?" she asked as they approached Abu Zabal on the fringes of the green fields of the Delta.

"I was thinking about how much I hated priests and emperors. That's what you get when you hitch up with a crazy archaeologist."

"I don't mind, if you don't mind being rescued by a halfway doolally linguist." He looked at her in surprise. She nodded her head. "Not all us bodyguards are thick, you know. Not all of us are ugly." He was forced to agree. "Modern languages at Oxford. Hence the nickname. All roads go there but no traffic gets through. And Russian and Persian at London. Also the Sorbonne, Tehran and Leningrad."

"What *is* your real name, then?" he asked, bewildered. She

remained silent, pleased with herself. He put the car into a spin deliberately, screaming through a 180-degree turn, to shake up her self-possession, and put them on Route 3.

"That wasn't very clever."

"Well, you'll have to tell me at the altar." She just smiled.

"Oh, shit."

It must have been the only police car still on duty outside Cairo, the Ports and Alexandria. What was it doing here? There were almost never police on the quiet roads of the Delta. Police at stations in the towns and villages, but not out on the road. And he was carrying no papers, official or otherwise. Now it was pulling up behind them, preparing to overtake.

"It must be just bad luck," Carfax said, agreeing with his thoughts. "Keep going at a steady speed unless he pulls you in. Then leave everything to me. My bad Arabic's more use than your flash stuff in a case like this."

He slowed down as she suggested, warning her of his problem. "Even if they don't know who we are and haven't heard about the airport, I'm travelling illegally. No papers. As well as no shoes."

"Where might they be from?"

"Hard to say. I can't believe they have a police car back at Abu Zabal. A van or a truck, maybe. But not a car. Could be Shibin el Qanatir, north of here on the Ismailiya Canal. They have guards there. Or Qalyub on the main highway north. Or Cairo. Any way it's bad. If it's Qalyub, even if we give them the slip, they can radio ahead. It's about ten kilometres. They could close the road and cut us off." The police-car overtook them, flashing its headlights. They pulled to a halt.

Carfax got out of the car. "Sit tight," she whispered through the open window.

Two of them in one car? thought Chas. *At night, on a quiet Delta side-road? It isn't any accident. Is it?* He realized that Medina's power and his knack of second-guessing everyone (except Gemayel's murderer? Or was even that arranged?) were getting to him. What would Carfax say?

One of the policeman spoke to her. The other came up beside Chas's door and looked in with suspicion. Carfax pretended to be stupid, speaking a mix of cheap English, whore's

French and tourist's Arabic. It would have worked in Alexandria. She explained they were holidaymakers, they had met at his hotel that night. He was newly arrived and lonely; she had been there some days but had nothing better to do; so they had come out for a drive. They had got a little lost in the Delta and were heading back to Cairo. Sorry about that turn back there; he had been trying to impress her. She had her papers right here. His of course were still at the hotel, still being registered with the Tourist Police. Sorry if that caused any problems, but you know what it's like when people get lonely.

That was when Chas saw the policeman with Carfax reach for his gun. He shouted, and leaned on his own door hard, just as his policeman fired. The door ruined the policeman's aim and, as the windscreen shattered, his arm and gun came through the window at Chas's side. Chas hung on and pulled, shaking the gun loose as it fired, once, twice, deafening him, blinding him, choking him with cordite, blowing holes in the floor and the transmission. The next thing he knew was that the gun was in his lap and the arm had pulled away. He turned. Carfax had the policeman by the chin and the back of the head, from behind, her knee in his back. She pulled back and upwards, hard, and there was a breaking noise, and an anguished moan, and a bubbling sound as his blood came up through his mouth and nose as he slid down the Peugeot's side.

Chas almost fell out of the car, shaking, slipping on the policeman's corpse, stumbling round. The other policeman lay in front of the car, his gun still in his hand, without a mark on him, but just as dead.

Carfax was already up at the police car, tearing out its radio. Then she ran back to the Peugeot to pull the bag Chas dumbly assumed contained her arsenal out of the back.

"These two won't be radioing anyone," she said breathlessly. "Give me a hand to get them into the Peugeot. If we fire it with two bodies in it it'll buy us time. Come on!"

Five minutes later, the Peugeot was crackling and bursting with flames which Carfax fed from the spare gas tank. The bodies slumped over in the heat, the faces peeling from their skulls. Chas was pulling on a pair of policeman's boots. Then she was back with him, as the air the fire sucked in turned the inside of the car into a single orange rose. "Ever drive a police car?" she asked brightly.

As they pulled away, his foot down to the floor, he asked her how old she was. She understood the reason for the question.

"I'm twenty-six," she answered, "and I'd like to retire at thirty. If I live that long. So drive like hell and get us out of here."

He drove.

An hour later, safely past the crossing with Highway One, and well up Route 19, having skirted the Barrage at Qalyub where the river forked, he asked her the question which had been troubling him, which had ended in his arrest, what seemed days ago.

"Who killed Martin Foster?"

She looked across at him anxiously, gauging his mood, before answering. "You know what you said about emperors and priests?"

She did not have to say any more. He thought his heart would stop. "Paolozzi?" he asked, appalled at his belief, knowing it was true.

She nodded.

Christ! he thought. *I should have guessed. I should have known.* "Beaten to death," the policeman had said.

Cairo

The moment he got to the airport a lifetime's instincts warned Adams off. The main hall was a shambles. There were medics everywhere, the smear of hastily mopped blood still streaking the floor. The policeman who had brought him here bolted at once, not even waiting for the money he had been promised. What happened here? he asked himself. What kind of crazy battle? The lazy throb of blood along his scar told him to get out, go home, go somewhere else. This wasn't his affair. He had no responsibility for the Englishman. Winterton was not under his control and, whatever had happened here, it had not been planned or executed by or for the Agency.

The policeman who had come for Adams at the Alexandria Station's safe house in Cairo returned, jabbering to the superior he brought with him.

"Good evening, Inspector Sennari."

"Not really, Mr Adams. I have three men in hospital in intensive care. Two of them have lost legs and another's lost an arm. I've had a firefight take place in the airport. I've lost a man charged with murder. And I've got an unidentified psychotic gun-woman loose somewhere in the Cairo area. I've had better nights."

"I sympathize." The inspector looked at him keenly. Adams ignored it. "Why all the medics?"

"For innocent bystanders. Shock. Flying fragments. One pregnancy brought to term early by fear."

"Is the child all right?"

"She will survive." Sennari took Adams by the arm. "My man here tells me Dr Winterton told him to fetch you. What is your interest in the Englishman?"

That's it, thought Adams. *I was right. I should have walked back out of here the moment I saw the place looked like a*

134

weekend in Gomorrah. But he forced an innocent smile before saying, "Is that what all this carnage is about, Inspector?" Sennari remained silent. There was no getting out of it. "Can we go somewhere private, Inspector?"

Sennari led him to the tourist-police office. It had been partly restored since the events of earlier in the evening. Even so, Adams found himself wondering what shock-troops had been through here. The inspector explained.

"Shortly after midnight we arrested an Englishman returning from Athens and charged him with the murder of another Englishman, Martin Foster. We held him for questioning. About three hours ago, shortly after I'd gone off duty, he persuaded one of my men, I assume in the usual way, to go for you. About two hours ago, an unidentified young Englishwoman turned up and demanded to speak to my suspect. I assume she too used the traditional means of persuasion to get in. They used quite different means to get out. You've seen some of the results for yourself. Now, can you tell me what the head of the CIA station in Alexandria is doing in Cairo waiting to be called on by an English professor?"

He's good, thought Adams. *Very good. Clear, concise, to-the-point. We could do with more like him in the Agency. A few more like him and Egypt would get by just swell.* But for the moment he evaded the issue. "This Englishwoman, what did she look like?"

"One metre sixty-eight. Slim. Good figure. Cotton print dress. Dark brown hair. Green eyes. Very attractive. Very dangerous. But you're avoiding my question."

"No more than you are an identification, Sennari. You know who she is as well as I do, just from that description. Why don't you go ask David Medina?"

The inspector was patient. He pulled up chairs for them both and offered Adams a cigarette, menthol-tipped. Adams stayed with his Chesterfields, and they smoked their own, like good Americans. Once they had lit up, Sennari explained.

"You know as well as I do, Adams, that Medina comes at the top of the blue-book of people we are forbidden to investigate. I don't like it. No real Egyptian does. Most of them are foreigners. . . ."

"But not all."

Sennari ignored the interruption. "Most of them are foreigners, and I don't like the way we let people push Egyptian law around just because they're rich and powerful. If I were in charge, you wouldn't be here either, unless I could lock you in prison and lose the key."

Aaron admitted the justice of the inspector's complaint, to himself. But what was Medina up to? What was going on?

"I'll make a deal with you, Inspector. You tell me who killed Gemayel, and why, and why his body was delivered to Medina and I will tell you what I know."

The Egyptian's sad eyes filled with a weary, unspeakable contempt. "If I knew, which I don't and don't ever expect to, I would not tell you, Adams. As far as I am concerned at least, Egypt and her police are not up for sale, though if some people got their way everything else might be."

He was angry, but the vast ancient reserves of Egyptian hospitality and politeness prevented him from showing it or doing anything about it. But he was right. Aaron wondered if the Giza Pyramids and Sphinx would do better business than Caesar's Palace if they were flown out to Las Vegas, and rather suspected not. The inspector dismissed him. "I can see that you don't intend to be helpful, and as you have diplomatic immunity I can't hold you as I would like. You may go."

Aaron felt sorry for him. He also felt dissatisfied. It was a matter of policy with him not to antagonize honest public servants like Sennari unnecessarily. You could never tell when you might need an honest man.

"Look, Sennari, I can only tell you this much. The Englishman had got involved with some deal for Medina, something to do with a Coptic treasure. I don't think it was political, or at least I didn't think so. Anything to do with religion can be political in this region. As you know. I needed a handle on Medina. Because I know he's up to something big. I try not to overlook anything so I approached this Englishman. I told him to contact me if and when Medina double-crossed him, which is what I assume the Foster killing is. Foster was one of Medina's less reliable employees." *Please God,* he thought to himself, *don't let it have been Kirk. Let Kirk have followed*

136

orders. Some deaths were too embarrassing. "As for what's happened since, I'm as much in the dark as you are."

Sennari leaned back in his chair, looking a little more satisfied, though not much. "All right," he said at last, in a cloud of minty smoke. "Not everything you have told me has been true, and you haven't told me everything you know, or suspect, but you have told me some things I didn't know before. Thank you for that much at least. Now you may go. I hope we never meet again, or not in such circumstances."

Adams rose, but he had one thing left to say to the policeman. "Mohammed, forget Medina, forget the CIA. All this, Gemayel, Foster what happened here, they all mean the same thing. The balance is out between your people's factions. I don't know who's doing what. Nor do you. The President's men, the Generals, Jihad, maybe all of them. But I do know that if even one of them loses control, then what happened here will be nothing. You will have a bloodbath, and no law. Or none that you would recognize."

The Egyptian looked down at his shoes. He sagged inside his suit. Then he said, "God be my witness, Aaron, but I know it."

Outside, in the terminal, Adams bought himself a Coke. He knew he had some thinking to do. So Carfax had sprung the Englishman? On her own. My, but she was good. One option out of three and Winterton was a very lucky man.

For there were three options. He had known that at once. Either Carfax had simply been doing her regular job; collecting for Medina; bailing out one of Medina's people. In which case it would be folly to do what he had promised. It would prove to be a set-up. Or, a variant, she had been doing her duty by Medina, following his orders, but against Winterton's will. In which case the Aid-and-Succour message from the Englishman still applied. And if they got to him he might still prove useful, particularly if resentment at being worked over by Medina put some fire in his belly for the Agency's fight. But how to find him now they had a two-hour start? It was a matter for luck. It was out of his control. All he could do was warn Alexandria and the Embassy attachés to be ready for the call if any call came. And that he would be available at any time for Winter-

137

ton. He would have to do that anyway. All his training told him to cover the options. Or, finally, the jailbreak was for real. Carfax had cut loose from Medina and bailed Winterton out for her own account. In which case the Englishman had the best damn woman in the Middle East and both of them would need all the help they could get. And if they got it, Medina would be vulnerable. For the first time ever, one of his best people was in a position where she could be turned. If he could only nail Medina.

If he could do that, he would not feel a lifetime in the Agency and in the service of his country had been wasted, whatever mess the younger men might lead them into after he and his kind were gone. His fingers traced the long scar from his eyes across his nose, down his face and chin and throat. It was cold and springy as some plastics.

What made him decide in the end? Bloody-mindedness? Desperation? Professional curiosity? A strange sense of human responsibility? A kind of decency? He could not have said himself. He would not have thought in such terms. He was a pragmatic man, brought up on Executive Action. He knew he had to make sure everything possible was done and every angle covered. And there was only one thing out of them all he wanted to do himself. At least it was a kind of action. And there was no one else he would choose to trust with it.

So he finished his Coke and decided, against all his usual judgements. All his instincts opposed it. And, if he was honest, it made him afraid. But he would go out to Saqqara.

Wadi El Natroun

Soon after they turned West on Route 6 she made him stop and check the tyres. She was right to do so, as he admitted.

"They're OK," he told her, kicking them. "Sand tyres. They're good enough to see us to the Wadi."

She nodded her head and shifted into the driving seat. As he got in beside her he asked what she had proposed if the tyres proved to be inadequate.

"That's why I stopped you here," she admitted. "If we'd had to we could have headed back down 19 a way. I spotted a garage in that last village. We could have made ourselves very unpleasant."

He could believe it, and felt relieved. They were out of the Delta, out of the lush green fields where the Nile broke up at the end of its long slow journey to the sea, turning the area since the ancient past into one of the richest in the Middle East. Other places had oil. The Delta had food. Even so, he was glad to be out of it, glad to be away from the constant rushing sound of water in ducts and races which followed you everywhere in the Nile's slow death, away from the farms and villages and people, crowded round waters whose reflections remained black and white till well past sunrise when suddenly the outside world bleached out the black and flooded them with colour.

They were in the desert again where he belonged. "Keep going about fifteen kilometres," he told her, "then we turn north parallel to the desert road." *If we can get across that*, he thought, *we're home and dry*. They had run into no further trouble since Abu Zabal. Now that they were on their way, he asked her some of the things which had puzzled him. Like, "How did you get to work for David Medina?"

She started to laugh at that.

139

"What's so funny?" he asked, peeved.

"You might as well have come straight out with it," she explained. " 'What's a nice girl like you doing in a place like this?' "

He grinned back at her, defeated.

She concentrated on driving, logging the distance they had travelled. "It was the languages, really," she told him. "I learnt judo at school, and I took up other martial arts at Oxford. By the time I did my term at Leningrad I was really very good. The KGB tried to recruit me. When I turned them down they suggested me to Medina. He always says they thought I was too dangerous and wanted me kept out of any of the Western services. Which is flattering. Might even be true. But David wouldn't have taken me without the languages, tri-lingual is the minimum for his staff, and the fact that I could pass as his mistress."

After his experience of her thumbs, he thought it better not to ask. And anyway, that was a life ago, she was here now, with him, warm and very alive.

There were no lights out on this minor desert road, and he had warned her to keep her headlights dipped (out in the desert, full beams could be seen for miles, and left tracks on the sky in neat pearl lines) so they rolled through the velvet night, its silence so rich it was almost noise, caught only in their own pool of vision.

"Here?" she asked. He nodded. She pulled out on to the ever-shifting sand and, after a first whine of complaint, the tyres bit and the car picked up. Chas thanked God and the French under his breath for building desert-worthy cars.

"You said he's gone mad. What's he doing? What's he up to?

She bit her lower lip and looked at him warily. She had learnt silence and suspicion in Medina's service.

"I don't know all of it," she said at last. "No one around Medina does. And I've only been with a him a couple of years. But I know something about this operation, and he's nuts. How far?"

He checked the map inside his head. "About fifteen kilometres. Twenty to be on the safe side. Then we have to cut west again across the old desert road."

"And after that we're in the clear?"

"For the moment."

"Then what? How are you going to get us out of this?"

He was thinking. "Leave that to me."

"He'll have covered the airports and harbours, you know."

Chas nodded. "I'm almost counting on that. He has to do the obvious things. Egypt's a big country, and the people and his patrols are all bunched around the Nile." He looked at her, concerned, he realized, for her safety more than his. So this was what it was like. "The only thing I've got on Medina is ten years in this country. I think I know it better than any billionaire insulated from it and the people can. It's time I used that."

He leaned forward to stroke the back of her neck, tenderly, attentively. At first she shook her head in surprise, as though to wave him away, but then she leaned back, arching her neck against his hand. But he had to think, for both of them. She had already saved him. He had to do as much for her. And he needed information.

"You were telling me about Medina."

She stared into the little pool of light before the car, her sharp ears listening for any variation in the soft hiss of sand beneath the tyres, the steady drone of the engine. "Yes," she said, and then said nothing for some time.

"He doesn't have any political principles," she said as a start, and then the words came more easily. "He's only interested in maintaining his holdings in the region, and improving them if he can. He's always played both sides. That way whoever wins is always in his debt. I think he saw the fundamentalist, anti-foreign-power thing early, earlier than anyone else. And he likes unrest, political uncertainty. It makes it easier for him to get his way. He was behind the assassination of Sadat, you know?"

Chas stared at her. She nodded and went on. "I know everyone thinks it was Iran, but he has a hand in the ayatollahs too. He financed Jihad in Egypt. Smart move. Sadat wasn't very popular at the end. Too much an American. Like an American president, even."

Chas agreed. "I know. I was here at the time. I had started on my first big monastery project. I've been in them ever since.

141

When Sadat was killed the silence in the streets shouted at you. The total absence of mourning. Even the guests at the funeral were mainly foreign."

She looked at him curiously. "You were here?"

"Yes. Why are you smiling?"

"I was in London. Just finishing my second degree and third black belt."

He did a quick calculation in his head. "You took them young."

"Everything, Doctor."

He thought over what she had said. "What's his involvement in Iran?"

"He isn't a fool. He knows he represents almost everything they hate, but also guessed they'd go on needing to export oil. The war with Iraq was a godsend. They're so desperate for money they'll deal with anyone, and he's one of the few people who'll talk to them, at least on the scale they need. And he's careful not to offend people's principles, at least in public. I don't know much about it, but as far as I can work out ITI's about all that's keeping Kharg Island and the Iranian oil industry going."

He could see the benefits. "It'll have done him no harm with fundamentalists elsewhere, either."

"Precisely. Playing both sides again. He was a friend of the Shah, but he helped bankroll Khomeini in Paris. Hence Jihad. Hence Sadat."

"Do the Americans know all this?"

She shrugged. "Who knows? I doubt it. They're not very bright. And he makes big political contributions."

"But peace must be good for ITI."

She shook her head violently, dismissing his innocence. "No. It's in the weapons business, for one thing. For another, it's easier for Medina to control unstable situations. A little goes a lot further then, and people need him more."

"So what's happening now, and where do I fit in?"

She smiled to herself, with a look of knowing pity on her face. It looked oddly maternal. "You don't, not really. If anything you're a distraction, a bit of a nuisance. But Medina the collector couldn't resist you." He hardly knew whether to

142

be flattered, relieved or disappointed. "No, all he's trying to do is clear out a mess that's partly of his own making. Jihad is more a nuisance now than anything. All he's really interested in Egypt for is land, especially cotton-producing land, and strategic advantage. His geologists have told him not to waste time mining here. Unlike Iran, where he's picked up seventeen zones in the five-odd years of war."

She winced as the car's belly grated and bounced across a depression, but held on and got them across it. "He doesn't really care if the President or the Generals win. If anything, he'd rather have the Generals. War with Libya would be good business. He already sells arms to both sides through different subsidiaries. But he's careful. He wants to keep in with fanatics round the whole area. So he's financed the latest Jihad campaign. That makes him a good guy to the believers. And if he gets it right it gives the others a chance, an excuse, to stamp Jihad out for good."

Chas remained puzzled. "But then why are so many of the bombings being blamed on the Copts?"

"I didn't get that either. Part of it's good publicity by Jihad. Trying to stir up ordinary Egyptians against the Copts as a prelude to seizing power. That's Medina's least favourite solution. A Jihad government would almost certainly nationalize all arable land, which wouldn't do his cotton interests any good at all."

"But what does he need cotton for?"

"Uniforms. ITI manufactures them. Same with the sheep-farms in Australia. Anyway, I think Medina played along with Jihad about the Copts. To keep them sweet on him. And to give the other groups a double excuse for stamping down on all civil unrest."

"But I thought you said he liked unrest. It'll leave him without anything to play off."

"No, it won't. There's still the President and the generals, remember."

"What next?"

"Don't ask. The trouble is he's not the only player in the game any more. If he ever was. He's worried about something and he won't tell anyone what it is. Not even Ismail."

Chas didn't understand the inference. "Why should he tell Ismail?"

She looked at him in something like amazement. "You astonish me. You're not very observant for a scientist."

"I'm not a scientist. I dig up pots and old love-letters."

"Then you should still have noticed. Medina and Ismail are lovers."

Should he have guessed? Perhaps. But the news relieved him strangely. He laughed to himself. "So you and he were never lovers?"

"No. But not for that reason. Medina's non-gender-specific. It's just that, when you're dealing with Medina, you have to have something to bargain with, and that was the best card I had."

Before them they could see the pale lights of the desert road to Alexandria, strung out at long irregular distances. This was one of the few illuminated stretches, a snail's trail set against an octopus jet of night. The road was clear. Beyond it lay the Western Desert, and their way back down to Wadi el Natroun.

"Go for it," he told her.

She went.

Across it they were almost safe. He took over the driving now, getting as far from the road as possible. He set his mind's eye on the monastery.

He remembered something she had said. "'So who is it he's worried about? Do you have any idea? Any enemy of Medina's could be a friend of ours."

Once more she shook her head. "I have been thinking and I just don't know. It's been puzzling. He keeps talking about Latin America, but that might be a separate problem altogether. I really don't know."

"What about the priest, Paolozzi?"

"Your guess is as good as mine. What I do know is they both want this Letter of yours badly. They want you dead. I don't. So."

So you threw it all away. What did I do to deserve you? This was one he was determined not to blow. He would be faithful by her.

"So what is it he's planning now?" he asked at last.

She shuddered, crossing her arms beneath her breasts in the relative chill of the desert night.

"I told you not to ask. He is insane."

They coasted down into the depression of the Wadi, the nitrous valley below sea-level, and crawled towards the black mass of the monastery, blacker still against the blue-black sky.

"I'll have to go in first and wake the abbot. You'll have to wait outside for a few minutes. I have to get him to declare you a temporary man."

"What for?" She was genuinely baffled.

"It is a monastery, remember. They don't allow women inside. But I think we'll be OK after what you've told me about Medina. Fear has a marvellous way of overcoming discipline."

"Do they never allow women in?"

"Sometimes they claim the last woman on the site was Hypatia, the martyr. But I doubt that. She wasn't even Christian."

"How long ago was that?"

"About sixteen hundred years."

He pulled to a halt. They left the car in the Wadi, out of sight from the village, though not, as Chas was aware, from the top of the monastery wall. They set off on the last short climb up to Deir el Baramus. At the door Chas waved Carfax to one side and pulled the bell. The chain rattled and scraped and the bell chimed once, its blunt flat sound seeming to leak across the desert for mile upon mile. Beneath it Chas thought he heard another sound, cut off even more sharply, something like a hammer being dropped. Then he waited, till footsteps came, and the door inched open.

He announced himself and, as the door swung open, stepped inside. He was puzzled. Behind the black bulk of the porter he could make out figures moving silently. There was a monk lying misshapen, like a rag doll, on the ground. Then he recognized the porter. It was Ismail. He turned to shout a warning to Carfax. The last thing he saw as he went down was the back of her open hand flying at his throat.

When he came round, his throat constricted like a hot

145

squeezed flannel, he recognized dimly where he was. He was in the bigger of the churches, Mary the Virgin. He was tied to a chair, his arms behind his back, his legs bound to its legs. There were corpses everywhere. Monks in the attitudes of sudden death, thrown kneeling against the walls, their spines shot out, the shattered vertebrae standing up like fins, on their faces, by pillars, at the altar, in the aisles, their blood already black and tacky all about them. His chair was at the southern wall. Someone was standing beside him looking out of the thick silica window on the moving lamps beyond. There was the sound of running and whispered instructions outside. Carfax turned to face him. She looked happy. She was about to speak to him when Ismail came in.

"Well?" she asked the secretary.

"The charges have been laid beneath the keep and at the corners of the walls. Also in the side-chapels of the churches. We douse the central buildings with petrol at the end. Right now they're setting the detonators and the fuses. The bomb-truck's wired already."

"And the transport?"

"Back out in the desert as you suggested. They'll move back in when they see the first explosions."

"Don't wait too much with the petrol. This won't take long, and by the time we're finished exact timings won't matter."

This time she did turn to Chas.

"I hope you enjoyed the performance, Dr Winterton, while it lasted, but you see we wanted you here with as little fuss from you as possible, and to give you a few sharp examples of David Medina's power." She nodded to the secretary. "All right, Ismail, you can leave him to me."

The Palestinian scowled, but left.

Carfax squatted down beside Chas. She had got rid of her hat and her hair swung loose again. He wanted her and hated her at once. And he was afraid, with fear in his head and his stomach-muscles and in each prickly hair across his body.

"Why don't you tell me?" she asked softly, "It would be so much less painful for you." He noticed she adopted the same aggrieved reasonable tone as the Egyptian policeman had done, but hers carried the greater menace.

146

He could not answer at once, his head aching with self-loathing, at the ease of her deception, at his own gullibility. "I don't know what you mean."

She looked and sounded suddenly tetchy, like a nanny. "Don't be so stupid. You know I want the Letter. I have to have the Fisherman's Will."

"Yes, you do, don't you?" he replied, sullenly. "Or what will Medina do to you?"

She shook her head, preparing to disillusion him. "It won't do, Doctor. No bargaining points there. Medina will live with that. With you gone, no one knows where it is, so no one else can have it. He can live with that. But we do want it. It might even be useful. And I suggest you tell me before I make you."

With him gone no one else knew, she had said. He thought furiously. Yacoubu must have done as he had asked after showing Paolozzi the Letter. *Only he knew*. Did that mean they had killed the old abbot?

Carfax answered his thoughts. "In some ways you ought to be grateful it's me and not Ismail. He isn't very patient. And if he had his way, he'd bugger you and then kill you without asking any questions. It isn't very pretty, what he did to the abbot. It seems the old fool wanted to be a hero. You should see the price he paid. Ismail is very fond of broken bottles, and you know his inclinations."

If Chas could have prayed he would have done, for the old man and his torments, for his stubborn, absolute faith. He stared Carfax in her cool green eyes, his own filling with rage and desperation. "Why should I tell you? You're going to kill me anyway. Why should I give you the additional satisfaction?"

She stood up, looking out of the window again. "I don't know why you should, but I know you will. And if you're worried about your blessed Copts and their dead, heroic leader, don't bother. By the time we're finished tonight they'll be lucky to escape a massacre." She bent down over him and took his chin in one strong hand, pushing his head back as though she were about to kiss him. Then she squeezed, slightly, and he heard more than he felt his teeth grind against each other. His head jerked forward as she let him go. Her eyes were

147

shining. He remembered what she had said in the car, through the dull throb of the blood at his temples. *She's excited*, he thought. *She's hot.* He could almost feel the waves of pleasure coming off her, the rank odour of satisfaction.

"Two hours ago," she continued, "the Al-Azhar mosque in Cairo was hit by something over two thousand pounds of high explosive in four fire trucks. In about an hour's time we're going to blow this place into paradise. Another hour after that, and Jihad are going to claim responsibility, in retaliation for the Coptic strike on Al-Azhar. Whatever happens after that, and it won't be very pretty, Medina can hardly fail to come out on top. We're throwing the whole deck up in the air and shuffling to make sure we get the cards we want."

Chas's mind reeled. He could only guess at the consequences. He could have wept for Al-Azhar. The mosque stood at the heart of the oldest university in the world, beside the Khan El Kalili. It bore the goodwill and respect of the whole Islamic world. It was filled with the treasures of Arabic art and craftmanship. Its manuscript room was matchless. For many of even, of especially, the most moderate non-violent Muslims it was the mind and soul of Islam, as Mecca was the heart. He could not bear to think of what Cairo might be like by now.

He looked up at Carfax, straining against his bindings, the cords cutting into his chest and arms and wrists. "You're mad," he told her simply.

She merely laughed. "Perhaps. But if I am, you had better talk, before I teach you what pain can be."

A kind of furious resistance filled him. A desire to crush the lovely thing before him, to mangle Medina, Ismail and all their filthy kind. A kind of resolution. It was as though he was looking down on himself, willing himself on, to hold out against his adversaries. Somehow he knew he was no longer afraid of death.

"Go suck, Carfax."

But it was as though she knew everything he was thinking. It made him remember things he had read, about the curious intimacy of captor and captive, but he shook such nonsense out of his aching head. She stroked his temples as she spoke. "It

148

isn't death you have to be afraid of. It's what I'm going to do with you before I kill you. I give you one last chance, Doctor. We have the icon, but the old fool had ripped the back board from it and hidden it. Where is it?"

He did not say a word.

She walked to the doors and called something through to the men beyond in the compound. The noise-level had increased. There was battering, clanking and the sound of snapped orders now. How many of them were there? he wondered. It wouldn't take many with modern weapons against monks. A dozen? Twenty at the outside. Well within Medina's capabilities. With Jihad or without.

She was in front of him again. She stepped forward and straddled him, her thighs grazing his haunches, her breasts and hair and perfume in his face. Then she strained against the chair and pushed it right against the wall, his head snapping backwards and cracking the plaster. She still leaned against him, and only moved back slowly, smiling.

"You mustn't get excited, Doctor," she warned him, her eyes and lips bright as she teased him. "I have something hotter than sex in mind for you."

Ismail returned. He looked annoyed, angry at the waste of time he saw the whole charade with Chas as being. He was carrying an open steel tin, and a petrol-tank, and what looked like a book ripped from the library in the *kasr*, the few links of its chain still swinging from its spine.

"We're nearly ready," he announced, handing his burdens to Carfax. "They're just finishing wiring-up now. Will this take long?"

She shook her head. She looked knowing, proud, amused. "No time at all," she answered. "Get ready to blow, pull all the others out, then come for me. It'll be done by then."

Ismail left, half-trotting. It was the only time Chas had seen him hurry anywhere.

Carfax squatted on the ground again. There were flashes of light outside more often now, more shouting, more instructions. She opened the book. Chas recognized it. It was a Gospel, one of the Uncanonical Gospels of Egypt, illuminated and handwritten by a monk called Eusebius twelve hundred years before. It wasn't very beautiful. Its drawings were crude, but it was part of the Copts' inheritance. He hated her as she tore page after page from the binding. She crushed the pages into loose balls and dropped them into the open tin.

"Interesting how well this stuff burns after so many centuries, don't you think, Doctor?" she asked with a smile. "But I forgot, you're not a scientist. I am. In my way."

The tin was nearly full of crushed pages. She added a last one as she spoke. "I am a technician of pain." Then she poured petrol into the tin. "Have you guessed yet, Doctor?"

He did not move.

She stood up. "I always say the old ways are best, and the simple ones best of all." She jammed her foot between his thighs at the front of the chair and levered them further apart. Then she slid the tin beneath the seat, at the front, between his legs.

She squatted again and pulled a Zippo petrol-lighter from the pocket at her left breast, flicking back the lid with a clank.

"Now, Doctor, will you tell me where the Letter is?"

She struck the lighter and held it to the tin. He smelt and heard the faint whoosh of petrol vapour catching fire. Then she put the lighter back into her pocket and stood up, standing looking out of the window, her hands clasped behind her back.

It must have been thirty seconds, maybe more, while Chas sat sweating against the wall, before he smelt the heavy cotton of his desert trousers baking, on the turn, browning before they burned, before he felt the lick of flames up his calves, became aware of growing heat between his thighs. He thought of Yacoubu and concentrated. The flames licked backwards and he smelt the small hairs on the back of his hands burn. Then the flames flicked forward again, and the cloth burned. The wood of the chair was black and burning, the flames licked up and over, and stroked him in the groin and wooed him, and played, till the fire lost its patience, and the sweat turned to vapour as it sprang, and the salt left on his skin burned first, dragging more flames behind it. Then the heat struck him with all its force between his legs as his testicles drew up within him and began to wither. Then there was only pain, unending pain, beyond his darkest imagining, and Carfax, standing, unmoving, at the window.

Then more pain as all the black blood smashed in panic and defeat into his brain. With some poor tattered thing, some obscure part of himself which held on through the pain, the fire, the agony of burning flesh, he knew he must be shouting, wordlessly, banging his head back sideways against the wall, trying to beat himself unconscious, baying at her to stop, to stop, but no words came in all the screams. And then, for an instant, all of him was there, present in his mind. All conscious of every inch of death between his legs, at his hands, in his mind. And, conscious at that instant, he turned to yell some vileness at her, when all the world shook, once, and her lovely head, its fine bones, its powerful muscles, its delicate skin, its clear green eyes, turned into bloody pulp as a storm of broken glass and leading blasted through it.

It was dark. There were noises. There was pain. Most of all there was pain. Parts of the chair were still tied to him. He lay on his stomach and reached down to pull them away. His hand grazed his thigh, and the pain sang. He must have blacked out once again. The blasts which tore through the monastery, ignited by the first one at the *kasr*, blown out of time, too early, blasts in each other building, the burning of plants and trees, palms imploding in showers of sparks and fire, the burning of corpses, of dead livestock, came to him, if at all, as distant thunder in some other country of the mind.

After a time, he woke, and he remembered. He knew even in the darkness that the thing beside him in the rubble, the soft stiff body with the mush at its head, must be Carfax. And in the end he grieved a little. Something had gone wrong. Something had been blown. He began to crawl.

There were the bodies of men dressed as soldiers amongst all the other corpses, adding to the stink of burning flesh. It had gone sour. Only small fires were burning now, glowing in the embers. The great ones had been blown out by the force of each succeeding blast. Each fire succumbing to its brother fire. All he could think of was Yacoubu and the Letter. When he

151

stopped crawling he was outside.

It was strangely quiet outside the ruined shell of Deir el Baramus. There was no sign of Ismail's transports, nor of Ismail himself. He guessed from the condition of the sand in his face, between his fingers, that they had come in when the explosions started and fled again in panic. He could see there were lights in the other monasteries, lights in the village beyond. On the still air of the desert night, silent once more after the wind that had rushed in on the blasts and fire, he heard the voices of people, shouting and dismayed, crossing towards his sick-bed in the sand.

He thought of Yacoubu again, the dead defiled abbot, and, though his body screamed rebellion, he forced himself to stand, to stumble, out beyond the eastern edge of the curtain wall. Ten paces, that was all. Then he fell, and began scraping with his hands. It was safe outside the monastery. It had taken him two hours to persuade the abbot of that. The abbot had been one man on his own as well, and an old man at that. It was not buried deep. It would have moved with time, but what of that? How far could it move in the short time it was left? And if it had been left longer, what then? It would not have been Yacoubu or Chas who removed it. His dry fingers found it and he pulled it free. He did not even bother to pull back the sheets of plastic wrapping he had left with the abbot. He knew what they contained. He felt the weight of the cedar board within his damaged palm. It was enough. They had both survived.

He stumbled out into the Wadi, sliding, falling, the sand and the soda burning his wounds, but though he whimpered he did not cry out. He had to get away from all the people, all the questions, all the enemies. Words kept rolling through his empty, hurting mind. Ointments, unguents, medicine. In the car. He kept on walking till he crashed upon it. They had left it. They had not found it. He collapsed inside and blanked out for some seconds. Seconds filled with burning and with images of Saqqara.

Saqqara

He had been right about the ointments. The police car had had an emergency kit. The relief the liniment gave was slight and temporary, but it let him think. He drove into the desert, slowly, with the lights out, away from life and enemies. Then he slumped and slumbered a few hours.

Petrol was the problem. He realized it as soon as he came round, his head thick with weariness and pain, his eyes seeled with sleep, his dry tongue big in his barren mouth. There were water bottles in the back of the car. He fetched one. It took time. It took time to unpeel his burnt flesh from the plastic seat, already beginning to get hotter as the sun rose. It took time to put his feet down on the sand, keeping his legs apart, trying to avoid contact, trying to ignore the ruination in his groin, the feeling he had been smoked inside. It took time to walk. It took time to handle anything with his bleeding hands, three nails gone and the skin coming off in strips and tatters. Everything took time. When it was done, he slumped again, and tried to make himself think.

How far was it to Saqqara, and would Adams even be there? About eighty kilometres, and where else could he go? He had no one else to turn to. He had to hope in Adams.

He was running short of petrol. Desert-driving used up more, much more, then even the worst of the tarmac roads. There was a little left in the spare tank in the back, but even so he doubted the old police car would make it. He didn't want to be in a police car anyway. It made him noticeable, vulnerable. They would have found the Peugeot with the policemen in it by now. Medina, at least, would be warned and alert. He shuddered as he remembered Carfax's silent despatch of the two men. He shuddered for Carfax's death by glass.

How far could he get? He had to move soon. By eleven at the

latest he should be holed up somewhere. He should have found shade. This was the Western Desert, the fringe of the great emptiness. If he tried to move through the afternoon, in his present condition, he did not think he could survive.

Fifty kilometres? It sounded possible, achievable. If he started now, if the car engine gave out, he might be able to finish what was left on foot. He shook once more. He feared it was wishful thinking, the offspring of his growing fever.

There had to be a way. He turned in on the atlas in his mind, turning its pages in an agony of exhaustion. All he wanted was sleep, but he could not allow that again, not here. If he slept in the day he doubted he would ever wake. The roads were a tangle and a deception. The nearest ones led into Cairo. Medina would have them watched. There was no direct route out to Saqqara which did not bring him past the capital. And he did not have the petrol to cover all the distance. He thought again.

Saqqara. In the past he had always made it by camel from Giza or bus or truck from Cairo. Was there any other way? He thought, but nothing came.

Jenny. That first time here with Jenny. They had ridden to the site. But not come back that way. They had had too little time. They had hired a trap down into Memphis. Half an hour, the driver promised. It had taken five times that. And then the train from Memphis, third class only, never shown on the tourist schedules. A local train for the outlying towns and townships, filled and filthy with people and livestock. Another half-hour journey which had taken over two hours. But that had not been the frustration. It was the sitting at Memphis Station. She had joked it would have been quicker to ride back to Giza. Had it been a joke?

He tried to remember. He tried in desperation. They had waited in Memphis for something. Something he had checked on later. Something he had meant to try one day, out in the Western Desert. They had waited for a train.

A connecting train. It came in late. Third class and worse. Where from? From somewhere in the desert. From some oasis. Bahariya. Yes. The Bahariya Oasis. The small town of Bawiti. He had checked. He had meant to go there, some time he could

154

afford the time for the world's slowest form of travel, an African rural train.

What was it? How had it worked? He forced himself to stay awake. They had been delayed at Memphis, waiting for the connection. They had left at six. It was night when they got into Cairo, or nearly. It had been due at five. It had travelled slowly. Where did it run? What was the route from Bawiti? Along the old road, the military road, the hardly ever open road, down to Farafra, the southern HQ for the Libyan border. That was it. And another fork, a slightly better road, out to Siwa, the main depot against Gaddafi. Irrelevant.

The train skirted the road. But it pulled aside safely well before Giza. Because it crossed to Memphis, past Saqqara. If he drove south-south-east it would bring him to the train line. South-south-east was the shortest journey.

How far? Fifty kilometres?

And soldiers? Troop shipments from the desert. If there were soldiers on the line, what chance did he have? More chance than he had out here. It was the train line or the desert. And in the desert, he would die.

He made it, just. The car gave out five kilometres from the line. That far had only taken him an hour. The last five kilometres took him two. His watch was still with the police at the airport, or adorning a policeman more probably. He guessed it was about eleven o'clock. If he was right about the train, and if it travelled as slowly as most others, it ought to pass here some time around noon. If it passed this way at all.

If Carfax had told the truth, and for once he guessed she was not lying, then the army would be on full alert. And he was a foreigner, without papers, in burnt clothes. There was a good chance all trains were cancelled, and if they weren't, he could hardly fail to be arrested; a suspicious figure in the back of beyond. There was no point in worrying. If it came he would take his chances. If it did not, then his troubles would soon be over. He stumbled down into the defile between the road and the track. He had brought the remaining water bottles with him from the car. He finished one of them. Then he squirmed into the sand, face down, sheltering the Letter, and waited. He

155

thought about the monastery again. About what had happened. Something had gone wrong, unless Medina was more devious than he dared to imagine, and had sacrificed his bodyguard, his troops. Somehow the bombs had blown too early, before everything was prepared. Deliberately? Impossible to say. But the whole thing had gone off in their faces. In hers.

It was the only reason he was still alive.

Up on the road, army trucks passed, their canvas flapping. *Troop movements*, Chas thought. *It's begun. Medina's plans must be in motion.* The President? Or the Generals? He hardly cared. What he cared about was the heat and the dust and the sand. He could feel the infection building in his wounds. He drank more water, determined not to pass out, but he passed out anyway.

He was woken by distant drumming, a sound like an army marching many miles away. If his lips had not cracked open he would have smiled. It made him think of his childhood, of the *Boys' Own Paper*. You could always tell when a train was coming by laying your ear against the track. You would hear the vibration as it approached. Before it took your head off, he had always assumed. Out here, in the desert, you didn't need the track. Sound carried, endless miles, where it was not baffled and muted at once by rising air and dunes.

It was coming. But why were trains still running? He had almost hoped the trains had all been cancelled. The smallest movement seemed to require unimaginable effort, and if it came he would have to think. He forced himself to think.

Why were the trains still running? Had something gone wrong in the capital? In Medina's plans? It seemed too much to hope. Medina seemed to have out-thought them every inch of the way. He had what Adams had said was important. He had control.

But if it was running, wouldn't it be full of soldiers? Unless the army trucks had been going out to secure the bases. But what could keep the soldiers at their bases till the trucks arrived? It didn't matter. All they could do was shoot him then and there or take him in at least as far as Memphis, maybe Cairo. He would have to do the best he could, whichever circumstances arose. He staggered to his feet. He saw the

156

distant speck on the horizon.

It was nearly an hour before it passed him, travelling fast for hereabouts, a little above trotting pace. He had thought again as it approached, and hidden himself a little way down the defile. It was a single small steam locomotive and two carriages, all built in Swindon, nearly fifty years before. He waited till it passed and then, as the last carriage pulled by, launched himself upwards, all his muscles straining, running behind it, sliding in the sand and scrub, till he could jump aboard and climb on to the roof of the carriage with his last precious water bottle, and his package.

The sun was at its highest, beginning the baking which would take the temperature, even as far north as this, into the early hundreds, until they approached Saqqara and the river. After that, all he could think of was heat.

Some time later, as he lay on the roof, he felt something stroke his incinerated thighs with an infinity of tenderness, something grainy and moist. He turned, blinking in the glare of the flat desert light. An old fellah crouched above him, disgusting in his dusty robe, reaching into a leather pouch for leaves. He was grinding them in his mouth and, moist with spittle, applying them to Chas's devastated legs. He was grinning, with the interested amiability Chas had first opened to in Egyptians. His hands went on applying the filthy mixture to Chas's legs. The Englishman relaxed,. He knew from long experience that, in the desert, he was safer in the hands of a fakir than of any doctor. Then he passed out again, and dreamed of Carfax.

Was it true? Was it him? Was he so self-besotted that he could not judge himself or the world with any accuracy? He could not believe it. Arrogant, obsessive, yes. But with good cause. It had taken him years. It had taken Carter and Schliemann years. But he had found the Letter. Like the masters of his craft, he had sought, against all odds, for years. He had sought and, at the last, he had found. Unconsciously, he curled around his package. And Carfax? With her gentle voice and chestnut hair, her face in ruins in the rubble? He knew how she had been sent to Alexandria to entangle him. It had been foolish of him, but he did not know of any man who might have resisted. If he had not been so dehydrated he might have wept for what was past.

Later, the old man helped him down into the compartment. Chas slumped, amazed at the world and his own folly. The train was empty. The old man just shrugged and went on grinning. "*Maghnoun*," was all he said, and Chas agreed. Crazy.

It was Saturday. Most good Muslims would not be travelling. Not country Muslims anyway. But where were the bad Muslims, the Copts, the soldiers? The old man could tell him little. The train had left Bawiti a little after dawn. The army base was sealed up, he said. On the radio there had been news of shooting in the capital. That explained a great deal. They were careful people, the fellahin. They had very little; some land, their lives. They preferred not to risk either. And they could read the straws in the wind. When bases were closed, and there was shooting in the great city, they took no chances. They stayed at home. But the old man, with his brown flotsam face and his few yellow misshapen teeth, he went anywhere, when he wanted. He rode trains out of boredom, evading payment, skipping where he willed, in search of people and pleasure. Saturdays made no difference to such as him. There was a room prepared in hell already, he said, for him and all his kind, and the devil had the only key.

Shooting? thought Chas. Only shooting? Was it meant as some kind of new blockade? Telling the small hard facts and concealing the disaster until the situation was under control? He had had experience of news control before, all over the Middle East, but Al-Azhar? It seemed inconceivable they could hide it. However quickly the ban had been imposed, some foreign journalists or agencies would have got the news out of Egypt. And then it would be beamed back in by the BBC World Service. By now everyone would know. Everyone who wasn't caught in a tiny train back in the arse-end of nowhere.

Could it be that Medina had failed? It seemed impossible. He had to have news, so he could think and plan. He had to have information. He prayed that Adams would be waiting.

Still, he could take no chances. If the worst had happened there would be troops at all the rail-heads and junctions. There

158

would be soldiers at Memphis with instructions to shoot before they talked. He could not risk entry into the town till he knew better what was happening.

The afternoon was turning. The heat solidified. Soon it would melt. Already he could sense a change in the air as they pulled towards the big river. There was a ghost of blue in the sky at the horizon. There was hope in the shimmering distance. He thought hard.

The train ran south of Saqqara. It had to. He knew no track passed between the complex and Abu Sir or Giza. Everyone else came to the complex from the north or east. From Giza or Memphis. He would be approaching through the empty quarter. If anywhere would be safe it was this train line, between the river and the roads. If they expected him at all, they would not expect him from the desert. He gathered his things and waited. The fakir looked down on him with pity, at the ignorance of the foreigner. He led Chas by the hand to the end of the carriage.

There were toilets even in third-class carriages. Chas knew them well; stinking middens with holes in the floor and iron grilles to stand or squat on, filthy with flies, disease, and vermin, and the stench of faeces. He never used them. But he had forgotten the first thing the old fellah had looked for. He took Chas's water bottle and raised it to the ceiling and plunged it into a cistern still full in a train with so few passengers.

Chas nodded at the old man gratefully, and mouthed his thanks for the hospitality. It was rusty; it was germ-ridden; it was dirty, disgusting and dusty; it was almost certainly days old; but it was water. As the train chugged on the long bend south of Saqqara, the two men embraced and wished peace upon each other, then Chas took his bottle and package to the back of the train, and jumped, and was gone, his burns and muscles screaming as he skipped and slid down in the sand.

He knew why Adams had selected it, and approved. It was the oldest site of them all, the first pyramid, the Step Pyramid of Zoser, yet remarkably few visitors made it this far. It was just too remote, too much of a nuisance; not Giza's comfortable

159

half-hour taxi ride from Cairo. And in the summer even the great excavating parties closed down. They only dug in the winter and spring. Up there, about a mile away up the dunes, lay the second biggest complex in Lower Egypt, empty, safe.

He would wait, another hour or two. By then the sun would be almost mild, and even the guides, the dragomans, the fake antiquities sellers, would have left; the last occasional visitor departed, the tourist bar pitched in a great tent empty. He would walk up into safety with the dusk.

It took him longer than he thought. After the respite on the train the panel and bottle were bulkier than he remembered and, despite the old man's herbs and attention, the burns were still real, the infection still there.

He trudged slowly up towards the complex, stopping often. He had no way of knowing which way Adams would come, if he came at all. He guessed the best thing to do was track round the Pyramid and hide in the dunes beside the road. If the worst came to the worst he would take to the tombs. He blessed his training. At least he knew his way around Pharaonic tombs.

It took him well over an hour. By the time he was crouched down in the dunes the light was failing fast. Soon it would be even more dangerous on the site.

For it was dangerous. Here, more than on any other ancient site in Egypt, the sand moved. The excavators never knew from one season to the next what the wind would have uncovered, what precious workings it would have washed away. It was still barely one-third excavated, Saqqara, and the site was filled with unmarked and unexplored shafts and chambers which opened up in a night and the next night were gone. It was not unusual for tourists to go missing here and not to be found till two years later, shrivelled mummies in their paltry rags, as new parts of the complex were opened. Sometimes it took much longer. Sometimes it took centuries for the sea of sand to cast up its wrecks, its victims. Years before, he himself had walked here and stumbled over a human thigh-bone, brittle and dry and picked white by time. He had had it checked by one of the anthropologists on the site. "Female," she had told him, "under thirty. At a guess about a thousand years old." When he had asked if she could guess any more she had shrugged,

160

saying, "Who knows? Maybe would-be tomb robber come about three thousand years late. Maybe local villager, or member of a caravan, or a victim of crime. There's no way of telling. Hereabouts the sand just sucks them in and spits them out in its own good time. We've found more human remains here than we know what to do with, and we hardly know anything about them at all."

Sand. Sand and wind. And time. The enemies of man. Here he was again, amongst the monuments the emperors and priests had built against death and time, knowing the sand would erase them, knowing they would be the victims of time. Only the Step Pyramid endured, always, as a kind of symbol. Ironic, really. It had been built for Zoser, about whom almost nothing was known, by Imhotep, his chief minister, his chief scribe, whom the ancient world had turned into a god. Quite rightly. Medina should learn the lesson. When ITI lay broken, in some distant future, when politics were forgotten, bright kids would still learn at school how Winterton found the Petrine Letter.

I'm fantasizing, he thought. *Is this delirium again? What were those leaves? Or is it the burns? Am I hallucinating?*

But he was not hallucinating about the lights. There was a car coming, slowly, its headlights dipped, cruising towards the clumsy parking lot between the pyramid, the refreshments tent and the entry to the sunken Serapeum, the mysterious tomb of bulls. It was a Cadillac. Chas watched the tail-lights with relief but, taking no chances, waited. The big car sighed to a halt. There was the sound of a door opening, and a crunch of gravel, uncertain footsteps as eyes peered into the darkness. The footsteps turned to a grainy sliding noise as the man took to the sands. Then he started calling gently, in a broad American accent, "Dr Winterton. Dr Winterton, can you hear me? Are you there?"

Chas shrank back, disappointed; not knowing whether to come out or stay concealed. It sounded like Adams's assistant, met briefly at Medina's party, but how could he be sure?

The visitor settled that for him by speaking again, louder this time, "Dr Winterton, if you can hear me, this is Kirk Stanshall, Mr Adams's assistant. Mr Adams should be here already, in

161

the tomb of Sekhemkhet. To show you it's all right I'm going to go back to the car and turn the headlights on and stand in them for a minute. That way you'll be able to see it's me. After that I'll go over to the tomb. If you need help, please call out to me."

Chas remained silent, thinking. Even if it was straight, the man he wanted was Adams. He knew the tomb, the biggest recent discovery. If he moved now he could be there before Kirk Stanshall. If Adams was there all might be well. If not (and he had seen no vehicle or other evidence of Adams's arrival) then at least he would be in, and could be out before the young man had caught up with him. He turned and slipped across the sands.

As he approached the mouth of the tomb, the pyramid black and looming in the darkness, to one side and some way behind, he looked round briefly and saw a figure standing in the Cadillac's headlights.

He moved more slowly across now. The wind had done its work in the month since the dig had halted. Scree and shale and sand had tumbled back into the mouth of the tomb. He tried to ease himself down gently, but he slid with what seemed an endless rush and clatter down the last ten yards to the gate of the tomb.

Wooden battens had been nailed across the excavators' timber door-frame. Chas knew the kind. They warned in Arabic, and sometimes French and English, of the dangers of entering tombs where excavation was not complete. Where are the guardians? he asked himself, for the first time. Someone must have bribed them. Adams, he hoped. It had been happening since ancient times.

Some of the battens were already loose. He pulled them aside, and stepped over the lowest into the tomb.

Even a few feet from the door it was blacker than the blackest night outside. Chas wished he had a lamp of some kind, but on second thoughts decided he was better off without. He had seen how vulnerable light could be when Kirk stood in the headlights. He knew the format of these tombs anyway. It was almost a prototype of the more famous ones down at Thebes. There would be a long straight corridor, diving ever deeper underground and, at the end of it the main

162

burial chamber, surrounded by smaller chambers or storage-rooms. There might be storage-rooms off the corridor as well. He moved as quickly down it as he could, the floor shifting beneath him in the darkness.

He called out Adams's name, but there was no answer. All he could hear was a faint creaking sound. It was impossible to tell where it came from. He guessed the battens at the mouth of the tomb.

He continued forward and down, his left hand before him always, against the wall. He had left his water and the cedar board outside, stuck lightly into the sand. He heard the creaking sound again. His progress slowed a little. Then the fingers of his left hand came to the end of the wall. He bent them and his fingertips inched round the corner. It must be the end of the corridor, he thought. This must be the burial chamber.

"Adams?" he called louder than before, one last time, ready to break and run back up the corridor if no answer came.

I can outflank Stanshall, he thought, in a sudden rush of clarity. *With a little luck he may have left the motor running.* He moved forward one last fraction. What was that *smell*?

Then it fell upon him.

It was clammy, heavy, alive. It appeared to have no legs.

In his screaming as he struggled with that thing he did not hear the slide of shale and rubble as Kirk tumbled into the tomb. Then there was a single gunshot, roaring in the narrow tomb, its fire half-blinding him and, as he saw what was left of its face, he fell crawling into the burial chamber, groping blindly for safety and shelter, behind the sarcophagus. He did not know he was still screaming. He was aware of nothing but its face.

Kirk was laughing. He switched on a torch. Its bright light filled the mouth of the burial chamber, interrupted only by the body hanging from a steel cable pinned into the roof of the corridor, beaming out darkness as it revolved in the light. It was Adams.

He had been shot three times, the first time; in his throat, in his belly, and in his groin. The guts hung from him in tapes and coils like Christmas decorations. The steel cable had been fastened in a noose round the hole in his throat so it pulled the

163

flesh, revealing his papery windpipe and fragmented spine. His body-weight was slowly pulling his head off his shoulders. Kirk's latest shot had taken the lower part of his face off, leaving it a tangle of fibres and muscle and bone beneath the eyes.

"I don't want you to think I missed just then, Doctor," Kirk said, still with laughter in his voice, "I just promised to deliver you alive."

Another shot howled and roared through the darkness. Sparks showered from the steel cable as it severed. What was left of Adams slumped in a heap to the floor. The flying chips of stone thrown off by the ricochet came rattling to a halt as the echoes of the gunshot faded. Kirk stepped forward, a malignant black shape against the intense beam of his torch. Loose hair on his head lifted, glowing in the light. It looked as if he were on fire.

"I must admit I wouldn't have thought of it," the American went on. "It was the priest's idea. He's very good. I'd never have used a dead man as an alarm without his suggesting it."

The only thing which passed through Chas's mind was the thought: *I wish I were dead.* He had never meant it before, not as he meant it sitting in that tomb, with the slime of Adams's extinction still on him. Whatever it was that died inside him there, on behalf of all the lost and innocent victims of the past, he was never the same again.

Stanshall stepped into the burial chamber, over his dead chief's corpse, keeping his fingers clean. "Now, are you going to come out of here peaceful? This gun could take that sarcophagus to pieces, bit by bit, and you wouldn't look much healthier, neither."

Chas stood up slowly, blinking in the fierce light of the torch.

Kirk motioned him towards the wall. "Assume a position, Doctor." Chas stared at him, not understanding. "Hands against the wall, Doctor. Keep them high. Lean into it. Keep looking at the floor."

The American pulled his feet back and apart. Then he frisked him, quickly, with one hand, whistling at the state he was in. "She did a pretty good job on you, didn't she? Didn't

164

you give her a good enough time?"

That was enough for Chas. Only one thing would satisfy him now. There was something utterly cold about his resolve.

Stanshall motioned with his gun. "OK, let's get out of here. Enough sightseeing for one day." He nudged Chas with the gun's muzzle, inching him towards the door, towards the thing that lay there which had once been human, which had once offered him help. There was filth all over the floor.

Chas slipped in it, heavily, on to the body, whimpering, his fingers searching in the slop.

"Oh, no," Kirk said, as Chas turned on his side. "Get up!" Then he leaned forward.

Chas's arms flew up with a yard of small intestine between them and crossed over each other once behind Kirk's head as he pulled with all his might. The gun went off once, wildly, before Chris trapped Kirk's gunhand with his knee against the wall. The torch went flying with a crack. Everything went dark. All Chas knew was the pulling, and twisting, and smashing against the wall, till the thing he had caught was limp and sticky. Even then he kept on pulling, twisting, with a steady certainty of purpose, longer than he would ever know.

When it was over, he stripped the body, and carried the clothes and the gun out of the tomb into the still, clean, night air. There were stars in the sky, but they seemed to be different stars from any he had seen before. There was a faint glow in the distance, from the small lights of Memphis, but the thought of towns brought no consolation. He collected his bottle and the Letter from the sands. Then he set off with a steady step across the wastes of the ancient burial-ground to the car whose headlights still shone in the parking-lot, leaving Kirk Stanshall dead in the guts of the good soldier he and his officers, the desk-clerks at Langley, had so grievously betrayed.

Part four:
DEATH AMONGST KINGS

Memphis/Cairo

He used the water to sponge the clothes. The shirt and the trousers were spotty with blood, but wearable. As for the jacket, he threw the jacket away. He ransacked the glove-compartment of the car. As he had expected, it was wholesomely well equipped in the best American fashion. The travellers' bottle of cleaning fluid stank, but it cleaned him up still further. The cologne and paper tissues got the smell off him. Once into the clothes he could pass in the street without evoking undue attention. Best of all, he found papers, money, maps. A thousand dollars American, eight hundred Egyptian pounds, some credit cards. No small change. Of course not. That and a Cadillac. They paid these shits too much.

American passport, diplomatic papers. Could he pass as Kirk Stanshall? He doubted it. The photograph was the problem. Still, best hang on to the passport, and the papers. Somewhere, somehow, he would find a fool or a villain with a Polaroid camera. The gun. He knew nothing about guns. It was a revolver, six chambers, three full, heavy, with a long barrel. He made sure the safety-catch was on and laid it on the passenger seat beside him.

Maps. Where next? What did he have, what was he missing? Mainly, there were things he did not have. Allies, for one. Information, for another. He still had no idea what was going on in Cairo. He wasn't sure he cared, but he did want to know what he was up against, what his adversaries had planned, and he had no way of knowing.

So where? Where now? He sat in the car, still, silent, safe in the knowledge that, here at least, he would have no further visitors before dawn. But he knew where he would go. The airports and harbours were impossible. The Western Desert was mined and patrolled. He knew what he must do. He knew what refugees from the Upper and Lower Kingdoms had

167

always known. That the only way was Africa. The only certain escape was South.

How to go? He checked out the car. It was as he had guessed. City-boy driver. No sand tyres, no filters. Off the roads it would choke up and die within the hour. On the roads it was much too visible. The roads would be covered in any case; that much was certain and easy. Going south, the only roads that mattered ran on each bank of the river.

He thought about trains. Somehow the trains were still running. They had been yesterday. The stations, at least, would be covered, but the trains? In Egypt, even, there were surely too many. Especially the third-class trains the visitors avoided. With luck and judgement, if he got into Cairo by train he could get out again the same way on a train down to Aswan. It was risky, but it could work. It could work if he consistently did all the things no foreigner would do, if he used all the routes they assumed foreigners would avoid. "The only thing I have on Medina is ten years in this country," he had told her. The time had come to use it.

He worked at remembering. The third-class trains took seventeen hours to Luxor and another nine to Aswan. Sometimes you had to change at Luxor, sometimes you could go direct; but if you had to change at Luxor you could count on waiting up to a day for the next train south. Unless you already had a first- or second-class reservation. All tickets, all seats, on Egyptian trains had to be arranged a day or many days in advance. He would solve that problem when he came to it. What mattered now was getting south. There was a slow train at least as far as Luxor at eight. The air-conditioned first-class train left earlier, and only stopped at Asyut, just long enough to change driver and conductor. It was quicker, too. Eleven hours to Luxor, another five to Aswan. But how to get on it?

Enough. He would have to take his chances. The important thing now was getting in and out of Cairo. He knew there would be early morning trains from Memphis, for the labourers who commuted to the city, but would Memphis be safe? It was patrolled at the quietest of times. There would not be another train up on the branch line from Bawiti until the following evening. That would have got him into Memphis station all right, past any guards, but he could not afford the time. He had a car. He checked the maps.

It was worth a try. The engine coughed into life. He set off down the high new road to the river. Below him the Nile valley slept. He travelled slowly, keeping the engine as quiet as he could manage. The bridge to Memphis was the only one across the river between here and Cairo. He knew there were buses from the bridge. Was it worth risking? No. There he would be most visible even to the regular army patrols. It had to be the train. He was counting on the random behaviour of train-lines everywhere. Even if there was no cause, trains always seemed to stop outside a station and dawdle before they entered. There was a station a couple of miles north of Memphis, one of six or seven the slow trains stopped at on their laborious way to the capital. He would try to pick the train up there. Helwan? No, that served Memphis. He shook his head. It didn't matter.

Once on to the valley floor, no map could help him, and there were no signs. In the dark he could not even take his bearings from the rocky massif on which Saqqara stood. He steered by instinct, through a night sweet with water and the scent of ripened dates. He got there at last, surprised when he recognized the dim outline of the Memphis open-air museum, pallid against the deeper dark of its luxury of hedges and the sigh of palms. He had seen no one, not even on the bridge, its lights extinguished and its sentry-boxes empty. He had expected the lights to be out (it was never said, but it was meant as a defence against bombing raids, whether Libyan or Israeli), but not the absence of guards. Was everyone confined to barracks?

He ignored the turning to Helwan station. In less than a mile he was out amongst open fields again, the last of the unharvested cotton and corn high and hairy against the sky. Everything was silent except the occasional stamp and snuffle of a sleeping buffalo, and the thin trickle of water in the irrigation sluices.

Two miles on there was still no sign of a village, but on his right he noticed that a second train-line came in and merged with the main line into Cairo. There had to be points at such a junction. The train would have to slow. He would take his chances here. He drew to a halt with a hiss of soft rubber tyres. Then he reversed till he found a parting in the avenue of date palms. He backed the Cadillac into it. Let some farmer have it as an end-of-season present.

He put the money and papers into his pockets, reserving two hundred dollars for his socks. Once he was across the border, in Sudan, a handful of dollars would get him a long way. He kept the credit cards as well, though less certainly. He had never pulled a credit-card fraud before. Then he gathered up the Fisherman's Will, placed the gun within its wrapping, and walked over to where the train-lines met.

He guessed it was about four hours he waited. It was almost dawn before the first train rumbled steadily past and he pulled himself aboard. He even paid a dour conductor for a ticket. Paid too much, in fact, by feigning to be ignorant of Arabic, pretending to be a crazy traveller who had got lost out in the valley. It worked, and he settled in for the long slow haul to Cairo.

Even at this hour the train was full of sleepy villagers going in to work in the city or set up stall in the markets. Underneath all the filth of ages he guessed the paintwork had been olive-green or grey; stock bought from France or Italy decades ago, perhaps. As it was he decided safety was better than comfort and sat against a bare steel wall, rather than take one of the few remaining thin plastic-cushioned seats where he could count on being shat on by the scrawny chickens struggling in wicker baskets in the luggage racks. He would have climbed up into one of the racks himself, if the only space had not been filled already by a sleeping Egyptian who had had the idea before him. Like all first trains of a morning, this one was slower than those which would follow after. Its passengers, all of them regulars, seemed inured to its halting progress. It stopped for up to twenty minutes at every wayside station, dropping off staff and waiting for local latecomers. The drivers and station-masters knew their customers on lines such as this, and would not willingly let them miss a train.

It was well after six before the train came to a halt on the railway bridge across the Nile in the north of Cairo. It sat there for another half-hour. Chas waited, sweating already as the air thickened with the day, awaiting the dust and noise of Cairo as soon as they were off the bridge. The traffic would already be thick and loud around Ramses station by now, buses and taxis honking their way past trucks and donkey-carts and private cars, with people eating sweetmeats and snacks on the fore-court of the station, beggars or new arrivals being roused from their inadequate sleep on railway trolleys, wrapped in torn-up cardboard boxes, black-clad tribes of women following their menfolk into the concourse, shouting and laughing with the excitement of travel.

But there was danger in the station for Chas. There were always troops in the high vaulted ceremonial mosque of a terminus, and who knew how many more there might be today? He stood up and went to the open door which showed the usual preference for ease of access over comfort or safety. As far as he remembered, the local trains came in on the old side platforms of the station. There was a single arched gate-way and an underground passage between those platforms and the main station from which the long-distance services left. He had to assume both passages would be covered. But if he could get back far enough in the train, he could jump off before the train passed the long wall which divided the two sections of the station, and do it without being noticed. He began pushing his way down the train, jumping the sliding grilles which con-nected the compartments.

The train pulled off as he was moving backwards. He quickened his pace. In the last compartment but one he swung out of the door. The dividing wall was almost upon them. He jumped.

He stood against the last of the wall, letting the rest of the train rattle on beside him. He put his head around the corner and pulled it back again in a hurry. The early morning express to Ismailiya and Port Said roared out of the station past him. He closed his eyes and breathed in deeply, trying to quell the beating of his heart.

Once it had passed, that line should be clear, at least for ten minutes or so, until the points were changed and a fresh train was signalled in to the platform. He turned the corner and began walking briskly.

171

It was a long walk back into the heart of the station and, as soon as the long side platform started its rise from the beaten earth, he switched away from the dangers of the track. The station was taking shape before him now. There were people flowing through the access door from the adjacent platforms, probably passengers from the train he had just jumped off, and larger crowds in the concourse, briefly glimpsed between the rows of silver locomotives and the carriages of the long-distance services now boarding for departure. One of those would be for Luxor or Aswan.

The crowd was thickening on the platform before him, struggling to get on to the concourse, out of the station — farmers, traders, hawkers, workmen, students, bureaucrats, porters, soldiers. A porter and a soldier, pointing at him, and shouting.

He stopped, began to run back, realized that was no escape, and jumped on to the track, picking his way between the rails as the men got closer, shouting, as the early train from Alexandria pulled up almost on him, as he stumbled, jumped, stumbled, and was clear, the train hissing in behind him as he hit the emergency entry handle and climbed up into the train on the adjacent platform.

People pulled away from him in panic at his sudden entry, at his sudden exit through the door on to the platform. Across the platform, pushing, scattering people out of his way, leaving them floored and yelling. Into the next train and over to the other door. Open it. There another train. Another emergency handle. Into the carriage. There. What he was looking for. The white plaque by the door read "Luxor".

He pushed into the carriage, pushing aside the startled porter, forcing a way through the parting families, the fathers lifting luggage into the racks. Pushed deeper into the train, compartment by compartment, further from the concourse, from the porter, from the soldier, out of danger. He could hear things on the platform. He could hear voices lifting. Were they farewells that they were shouting? Were they orders?

And the families were getting off, the crowds were thinning. Was this paranoia? Was this fear? Or was the train about to leave?

172

He stopped and, speaking loudly, so the whole compartment could hear, he said in Arabic, "I want to go to Luxor. I have no ticket or reservation. I will pay five hundred US dollars for a seat."

He stood there, waiting. There were people looking at him as though he were mad, as though the sun had got to him. It was unimaginable money. He pulled the notes out of his pocket and began to count them, over his head, fifty dollars at a time. There was a hiss of hydraulic brakes; a shudder, a clank, as the engine strained. An old man got up and looked at Chas benignly.

"Sir, you are a foreigner?" he asked, as courteous as a shah.

Chas nodded.

"You are a visitor?"

Chas nodded again, adding, unnecessarily, "I'm British."

"You have little time?"

Chas nodded one last time, not knowing what else to do.

"You like my country?"

"I love your country." There was still shouting on the platform, the carriages were straining, they would leave at any moment.

"I am old," the old man told him, "I have the time to travel." He took a single fifty dollars from the wad in Chas's hand and with a little bow he passed across his ticket and reservation.

"I am glad you like my country."

He stepped down from the train just as it began to pull out of the station.

Zamalek

He had been at home, asleep, that lunchtime when they finally tracked him down. He had not slept in days, but he knew better than to refuse an invitation from the Under-Secretary, especially when they sent a car with it to ferry him from the suburbs to Zamalek. Sennari would never rise above the rank of inspector of police; he had antagonized too many politicians by trying to be honest; but he was not a fool. He had changed his shirt and said farewell to his wife and children and gone with the car. It was impossible to tell how long you might be gone once the Under-Secretary sent for you.

Whatever else he might have done, the Under-Secretary had survived. He had served Nasser, Sadat, and now Mubarak. Whatever changes came and went in governments, he always seemed to stay. Some said it was because he knew too much about almost everyone. Others said it was because he discreetly ensured he knew nothing at all. Ignorant men may prattle, but they cannot betray. Whichever theory was true, the Under-Secretary inspired one remarkable thing in his associates: trust. It was to him they confided their most sensitive business. It was to him they turned for covert advice. The price he almost absent-mindedly extracted was power. He could destroy a mere policeman at a whim or gesture. So when the Under-Secretary called, Inspector Sennari came.

It is power, too, Sennari thought, as they approached the bungalow in a quiet street on Zamalek, *not money he collects. He still lives in the same small house, while many of his contemporaries are in what could pass for palaces.* Still the same small house; but the Inspector did not know about the other small house, in Chiasso, Switzerland.

The Under-Secretary was waiting for him when he arrived. It troubled Sennari, who feared he might be punished for being

174

so elusive when the Under-Secretary wanted him. Little men like him were supposed to foresee a great man's needs. He worried in vain. He was offered tea and an amiable welcome.

It was not until they were chewing small sweet cakes from Groppi's *pâtisserie*, out in the garden alone, that the Under-Secretary explained the reason for his summons. When he had announced it the policeman wished he had been angry instead.

"I want the investigation into the Foster murder dropped, Inspector. It is to go the same way as the Gemayel inquiry."

It troubled Sennari, this kind of interference with police work. He tried to say so, politely. "That might be difficult, sir. I have had my chief suspect escape. I have three men in hospital. There are signs of gunfire throughout the airport arrival lounge."

The politician was understanding. "I suggest you mark the files as suspected Jihad atrocities. That should quell unnecessary speculation."

Sennari remained unhappy. "But my suspect, sir, and the woman who released him. They are clearly dangerous, and they are still at large. I have a duty to the public."

The Under-Secretary halted him by waving another pastry in the air. "You need not worry about the woman, Inspector. . . ."

Medina, thought Sennari. Friend Adams was right. He hated this kind of political interference, but what could one policeman do? He tried to register his disapproval discreetly. "Am I to understand these are political instructions, sir?"

The politician looked pained. "Don't preach, Inspector, however politely. Two nights ago we nearly lost the Al-Azhar mosque, and the police knew nothing about it. . . ."

They were true, then, the rumours. The army had acted well and quickly. The policeman found himself feeling pleased for them. But still he wondered how much it had been prearranged or exaggerated to try to minimize the effects of the Jihad attack on Deir el Baramus. He could understand Jihad's reasons, just, but an attack on the mosque seemed senseless. He wondered who was doing what to whom. He wondered how many soldiers were dying in the barracks and why.

But the Under-Secretary was still speaking. "It was left to the

175

politicians to uncover that plot, Inspector. The police failed us entirely."

Sennari felt like suggesting that it was perhaps because it took a politician to catch a politician, but he knew better than to interrupt the Under-Secretary, especially with comments like that.

The politician continued his whining. "And it would have been left to us to sort out the catastrophe if the plan had succeeded."

He relaxed a little after his complaint and offered the inspector another cake. Sennari declined. The politician munched another, its juices thick on his jowls as he talked.

"I called for you, Inspector, because you understand our occasional special requirements."

What is it? Sennari asked himself. *What is it this time?*

"We received our information," the Under-Secretary explained, "from an unusual source."

Medina, thought Sennari, *always Medina. That's why he wants the Foster enquiry dropped.*

"And, as always in these cases, there is an unusual price to be paid. It involves the Englishman Charles Winterton."

He wants me to get him out of the country, Sennari thought. *He wants me to clear up his mess.*

The Under-Secretary surprised him:

"It is possible, indeed probable, that you will have to cover over, and yourself ignore, the murder of the Englishman. You will not be required to help with the killing."

Sennari did not bother to ask the Under-Secretary what he was doing conniving in murder. It would not have been the first time.

"I am putting you in charge of a special force to be placed at the disposal of our source. It is to be based at Luxor. However, your instructions do not end there. Unfortunately our source's requirements conflict with those of a long-established friend, who you must also assist. Help them both, but do not let them know you are helping both of them. It is a private affair between our source and our friend. You are not to take sides. Once the matter is over between them you are merely to dispose of any evidence which may be left."

176

The politician wiped the sugar from his mouth with a Thai silk handkerchief. Sennari, a puritan in such matters, would have preferred it to be Egyptian cotton, which was why he would never rise above inspector.

"There is a military aircraft awaiting you at Cairo airport. Our friend, of course, is David Medina."

Sennari visibly preened. He had been right. But the source? If not Medina, who?

The Under-Secretary passed him a dossier, opening it as he did so. Clipped to the cover were the inspector's various letters of authority. The dossier itself gave him the details of the source. Sennari's surprise was hidden, even from himself, by the Under-Secretary's parting comment.

"By the way, Inspector, our source also informs me there are two dead Americans in the tomb of Sekhemhet at Saqqara. Please deal with the appropriate authorities. The Coroner's Report should read 'Accidental Death' in both cases. Have the corpses returned to the American Embassy for transhipment and cremation with full military honours."

Luxor/Thebes/Qurna

He was travelling first class. He had not travelled first class in more years than he could remember. It was comfortable, quiet, air-conditioned. Tea was constantly available, and meals whenever appropriate. It unnerved him. He kept expecting them to stop at every tinpot station to let on hawkers selling glasses of sweet tea, mixed nuts and dried fruits, or soft-drinks bottles carried in galvanized-iron buckets filled with ice. That was what he was used to.

There had been no trouble since the train pulled out of Cairo. His ticket and reservation was valid. He obviously had money. He was a foreigner of consequence, if clearly somewhat crazy. He almost wondered if he had imagined it all, all the recent days, but touching the Letter and gun beneath their wraps reminded him of reality.

The train had swept through Beni Suef, and stopped briefly at Asyut just as he finished the light lunch served to him in his chair. He had forgotten what leg-room on a train was like. Now, however, caution asserted itself once more. It was mid afternoon. They would arrive in Luxor in about four hours. Then the steady calm progression of the Nile at one side and, on the other, the cliffs of the Saharan plateau, would cease, and he would be in a world of trouble once more. Medina's world.

If he had not imagined the scene at the station, Medina would know by now. Even if he had been overly-suspicious, news of the fracas was likely to spread. Cairo was a gossipy city, and Englishmen did not jump tracks every day. No, he had to assume Medina knew. And if even Medina could not make the telephone system work, there were radios, there were aeroplanes.

Because he knew the difficulty of getting on scheduled flights he had forgotten about private aeroplanes. He cursed

178

himself beneath his breath. They could be in Luxor already, waiting for him. And now that they had passed Asyut there was nothing he could do about it. It was what they were bound to have done. But why no checks at Asyut? They could not know he would not get off there. He might have tried one of the ferries; a local would get him to Abydos at least. It was as though they were letting him run, as though they had fore-thought him. Something was wrong, something he could not place, and there was nothing he could do. He could only wait for Luxor. If he got through there he knew what he must do. He would turn to the criminal classes.

Ever since the days of the thieves in the Pharaohs' tombs, Thebes had been the centre of organized crime in Upper Egypt. Even now, he knew the currency black-market and the smuggling from Sudan and the smaller Red Sea ports were run from the ancient city. Here, crime was a major business, open and tolerated, so the *chef de tout Karnak* could hold court outside the temple every afternoon, reading *France-Soir*, for the pin-ups and the exchange rates, accepting the homage of all his clients from the gharry-drivers to the merchants. What Chas would have to buy from them was protection and a passage, by felucca, by trading sail-boat, up to Aswan and Sudan.

He turned to talk to the other passengers. What they told him brought him hope. He picked on the richest looking citizen as a good source of information.

"What has been happening in Cairo? I heard reports of shooting." The eyes swelled in the big brown face, clearly wondering what this crazy man was doing asking about the city he had just come from. Chas explained. "I was not staying in the city. I have just arrived. I have been away from news."

The rich man nodded, unbuttoning his jacket, glad the Englishman was sane, glad of someone to talk to. "Rumours," he said, spreading his palms. "You know how it is. Some good, some bad. You like my country?"

He asked with the same eagerness as the old man in Cairo. Chas smiled with relief. He had been in danger of forgetting the most obvious thing about Egyptians. They loved their country, and they wanted other people to like it. If you did, then nothing seemed too much for them. He hid his impatience and answered with animation: "I love your country. I think Egypt is a very fine country, very beautiful, very nice people."

"What do you like about my country?"

In his early years he had prepared a routine to match these standard questions. "I like the weather, the heat. In my country it rains often, too often. Always wet and cold."

"Good for farmers?"

"Sometimes. Sometimes not so good. You know." He acted out an Egyptian fatalism.

"You live in London?"

"Yes, in London." He knew better than to confuse the man with Cambridge. Most Egyptians had only just heard of London, let alone any other town.

"Nice place, London?"

"Yes, very nice," he answered, half-truthfully. "But not as nice as Cairo. Cairo is beautiful. I like Cairo almost as much as Alexandria."

The man beamed, but stood for civic pride. "Alexandria is beautiful, very beautiful, but Cairo is better."

"Yes," Chas agreed, happily, back on the subject at last. "Cairo is better. You were telling me about Cairo, about the shooting."

The old man dismissed it with a wave of the hand, but his eyes were serious. He tapped Chas on the chest and beckoned him closer. "Very bad. They keep it quiet. Not to frighten people. But we know. We merchants know. Bad fighting, bad shooting, at night, in the Khan El Kalili. You know the Khan El Kalili?"

Chas nodded vigorously, not wanting to distract the man from the subject, not wanting him to stray.

"Many dead," the merchant said. "Twenty, thirty, maybe more. Our army killed them. Foreigners with explosives. Libyans, Iranians, who knows? All kind of stories. But I don't believe it. I think they were Russians. Atheists." It was obvious that if he had not been travelling first class he would have spat at the thought. Chas was only relieved that he had not mentioned Copts. "Must be atheists," the Egyptian continued. "You know what they say in Cairo?" Chas dutifully shook his head. "They say they were trying to put a bomb in Al-Azhar."

180

Chas sat back relieved, scarcely able to believe it. Had Medina failed? Or was there something he was missing? He remembered to turn his face into a picture of outrage and astonishment.

The merchant beckoned him closer again. "Atheists everywhere," he said, "even in the highest places. Yesterday, it was terrible, there was a bomb at Wadi Natroun, at the Copts' holy places, many holy men died. This is terrible, to murder priests." Chas could have wept for Egypt's tolerance, but the merchant had not finished. "The worst is that Jihad, you know Jihad?" Chas nodded, looking as secretive as the Egyptian expected when talking of such dangerous things. "Jihad has claimed responsibility. It is madness. They are crazy, but they are Muslims, this is what we always thought. But to murder holy men, even of the Copts, this is atheism. Who would have thought it? Atheists in Jihad?"

Chad knew better than to reduce it to sense. For now he accepted the merchant's view of the world and pressed on. "I heard the barracks were closed, out in the west where I came from."

The merchant nodded gravely. "Everywhere. Never have I seen so few soldiers on the streets of Cairo. All of them picked men, officers or sergeants. There has been shooting in the Cairo barracks. Many sealed trains going out to the countryside." He leaned forward, a conspirator again, "I think it will be good. I think the President, some Generals, have some problems. I think they are being solved, by shootings in the barracks. I think that that is why everything is so quiet, so few soldiers on the streets. You will see. It will be good. Jihad, the foreigners, I know you are a foreigner — " Chas waved it aside — "the atheists, these must be stopped."

"It is true," Chas agreed, "Egypt for the Egyptians. Like Nasser." The merchant nodded and sat back. Then he shook his head with a sigh.

"I am going home, for one day only, and it may be a wasted journey. My youngest son, he is in the army, on the border with Libya. One week's leave a year. This is why I return home from Cairo, in the summer when I should be going to Alexandria. Four days' journey it takes him, by train and truck from the

181

desert. One meal, we shall have together, in the house of my wives. Then he must leave in the morning, as must I. One meal we eat together, each year for three years. Then he must return to base. Always he arrives two days late. Always they dock his one week's pay. Four Egyptian pounds. And this time he may not even come. This time there is shooting in the barracks."

The merchant pulled out a fat wallet and extracted a grimy black-and-white photograph, passport size. It showed a young man in uniform, indistinguishable from the thousands of others gathered in by the army each year. Chas hoped the lad got home, and told the merchant so.

All the time, however, he was trying to piece together what he had learnt with what he knew or thought he knew already.

Had Medina failed? Had he really meant to blow up Al-Azhar? Or had even Carfax been betrayed, or cut out from his planning? If the Egyptian was telling the truth, and Chas had no reason to doubt it, then the heart of his plan had been accomplished. Jihad would be eliminated, on a wave of pro-Coptic sympathy, but, though the country itself was stable, the President and the Generals had been left to slug out their own differences. The perfect solution for Medina. But what about the Letter? What about the Fisherman's Will? He touched the parcel once more, in an almost superstitious fear that Medina might have found some way of spiriting it away. Had he been a side issue, as Carfax had suggested? It seemed probable, but Medina had made it plain he wanted the Letter, and did not care too greatly how he got it. She had said it might even be useful. Was that it? Was the Letter Medina's reserve position, available the next time he wanted to make trouble? Or was it just the collector's passion? Chas had seen it before; a disease of the mind as dangerous to some as drug addiction or compulsive gambling.

Whatever had been going on, Medina had been prepared to engineer murder, kidnap and torture to get his hands on the Will. And now Chas was a murderer, too, and guilty of the death of Adams. He looked out of the windows, from side to side. In the middle distance, shifting from palest sandstone to ochre to purple, stood the bluffs of the desert plateau, the place of dust which had made him what he was. A murderer? Yes, a

182

murderer. Now he had done it once, he knew he could kill again. It had not been so before, in the dark tomb at Saqqara, but now he could kill as casually as the desert itself had done, since before there were men, since the birth of the Nile. The deep blue waters of the river on his left hardly seemed to move at all. He saw the peppercorn heads of children swimming, and a single felucca big-sailed on the water, bobbing on the waters which were running slowly out of the hot hell towards which he had set his face. He touched the bulk of the gun beneath its wrappings, for power, for reassurance.

He was on his own. He knew that now. He did not understand exactly what had happened. He did not understand the CIA or Rome's involvement. But he knew he was at the mercy of Medina. He was the one outstanding piece of business the old man had in Egypt. There were no more distractions.

He needed help, any help he could get. He would cross the river to Qurna.

If there were older living villages in the world, Chas had never heard of them. For five thousand years the governors of Egypt had attempted to undermine it, but though they could burn down houses, tear up roads, no Pharaoh or General could destroy the fabric of Qurna. How do you demolish mountains?

The villagers lived in caves in the cliff-face of the desert, tangled networks of passages and chambers which, though roads ran to the cliff itself, could only be approached in the final stages by narrow winding paths, part of the intricate system cut into the cliffs of Western Thebes in the days of the great tomb builders and preserved ever since by these villagers who had never farmed, never laboured, never fished, for they were thieves.

They robbed tombs. They had always robbed tombs. It was the villagers' ancestors who had swept clean the funerary treasure-houses of the kings, and now, though the materials they still had left to steal, to hold, to dribble on to the market, were slighter than in the days of the empire, they were, if anything, more valuable. Though none would admit it, there had been no archaeologist in the valley-system at Thebes who could have done any effective work at all without the villagers of Qurna, who provided labourers for the price of a steady loss

183

of minor artefacts and who, in emergencies, could make large sums of money available for further excavation, simply by selling a large find like a mummy or a wall painting. They controlled the antiquities market out of Egypt. They always had done, even when the antiquities had been new. And Chas was one of their own kind now, for what else was the Fisherman's Will?

He had toyed with the idea of appealing to the academics based in Luxor, but the Chicago House, the Oriental Institute of Chicago University, would be closed for the summer by now, its members back home or elsewhere in the Middle East on holiday, and the Luxor Museum was answerable to the authorities; authorities who might even now be being paid off by Medina. No, he would have to turn to Qurna, to the hard men of the mountains. He would have to call on Abdel Amr.

They had met only once, years before. Every scholar in Egypt was introduced to Amr in the end. Some of them were in his pay. Many other villagers had partly succumbed to the latest government persuasion, the latest plot to destroy the village. They had moved into the modern village built by the government on the El Fadliya Canal through Thebes, a village full of rural amenities: breeze-block houses roofed with palm leaves and river mud, electric light, diesel-powered pumps, televisions run off two car-batteries wired together in series. But all of them preserved a base up in the caves. And the hard men, the controlling families, had made no compromise at all. They had seen governments come and governments go and they had never trusted any of them. They would not come down from the mountain.

It was time he paid his respects again to Abdel Amr of the Mountain. If they would let him. The idea roused him from his thinking. He had immediate problems. They would be in Luxor soon. Would Medina or his people be waiting at the station? It seemed likely. How long could they go on playing with him? How long could they let him run? He guessed Medina was enjoying it. He was the old man's cat's-paw.

People were standing, gathering their luggage, tipping the porters, happy to have arrived. They were pulling into Luxor. Chas would have to take his chances. He felt for the gun

184

beneath the wrapping. The merchant at his side across the aisle buttoned up his jacket and leaned over to wish Chas well, adding, "I am glad you like my country." *Not all the time,* thought Chas. *Not always.*

Chas climbed down from the train, slowly, his burns still tearing at him underneath his clothes, or Kirk's. It had been better, he thought, in the shade of the platform, in the clothes left tattered by the explosions. Nothing to rub against his wounds, and the air could get to them. He tried to keep in the centre of the pack of travellers spilling into the station's single hall, empty save for a few disconsolate back-packers waiting days for trains they could afford. Canadians, he noticed from their rucksacks, and Swedes. But no soldiers, no police.

The crowd moved out through the high doors of the station, the windows still blazing with the summer desert light. He moved with the others, suspicious. The scene in front of the station was as ordinary as ever. A broad square, like something out of a Western, sided by low-rise bars where young visitors sat, spending too much on Cokes and saying, "Yeah, I did the Valley of the Kings, one day last week. It was OK. Now I want to get to Nairobi." Nothing special, in fact, at all.

The *fiacre*-drivers were touting for business, offering horse-and-trap rides to the visitors' hotels. Chas, still glancing about uneasily, intended to walk. He stepped into the square, and the heat nearly felled him.

He had forgotten. He had forgotten, like a first-time traveller in the air-conditioned comfort of the train. Out of the shade sweat poured from him, blinding him in seconds. His hurt lungs ached with the heat of the air. It was seven o'clock and still high into the hundreds without any breeze at all.

He turned to the *fiacre*-driver at his side. The man was grinning at the folly of the foreigner. He did not look like an informer.

"The ferry," Chas said, hardly daring to move.

"Ferry closed."

I know that, Chas thought, unable to be angry, too hot for an argument. He didn't want the tourist ferries from in front of the Winter Palace and Savoy hotels. He knew they were closed by now. He tried to explain:

185

"The Egyptian ferry, people's ferry." In front of the temple of Luxor. By the Mina Palace. The one real people use.

"Monuments closed."

I know that, you fucking barbarian. I want to go to Qurna. The driver shrugged at the crazy man before him and held five fingers in the air. Chas held up one. He hardly had the energy to haggle. He did not have to. The businessman from the train came up beside him, surprisingly quietly for such a big man.

"You are going across the river?" he asked. Chas nodded. The Egyptian smiled. "I too. My wives' house is across the river, near El Gezira." It was the village directly across the river. "You like to come with me?"

Chas nodded gratefully. The businessman looked contemptuously at the *fiacre*-driver who still hovered before them, shifting his weight from foot to foot in incomprehension and hope. The businessman spat, once, a long green squirt into the sand, before saying, "Not licensed, no good." He clapped his hands, and a big black Nubian driver, waiting patiently at the head of the authorized rank, strode towards them, elbowing the illegal driver out of his way. The businessman turned to Chas as the Nubian shouldered the luggage, eyeing the parcel Chas refused to surrender.

"My name is Mohammed Kabir." He held out a big broad hand.

Chas took it, saying, "I'm Chris Harrison."

The merchant nodded. "Please, you must stay at my house. It would be welcome." Chas did not reply. As they climbed into the *fiacre* Mohammed barked out his instructions, and turned to Chas again. "Forgive, please. I must stop at the Post Office to check my post box."

"It's nothing," Chas answered, knowing the Post Office was on their way to the ferry.

They stood outside the Post Office for some minutes, before Mohammed emerged clutching a handful of envelopes already torn open. "Nothing of importance."

But can he be trusted? Chas asked himself. He could think of no reason why not. Theirs had after all been a chance meeting, and as he well knew the Egyptians were a legendarily friendly and hospitable people. It would be useful for him to have a base across the river, away from the authorities' eyes and the influence of the scoundrels he would have to deal with at Qurna. And it would be best to leave the Letter somewhere safe, somewhere where its value was not recognized or understood, before going up the mountain to Abdel Amr. But. But.

Suspicion, the gentle rocking and jangling of the *fiacre*, the steady clop of the horse's hooves on the beaten sand of the road, the slight breeze created by the movement, were all helping to restore him from the first shock of the heat. If there was some plot between Mohammed and the driver to turn him in to the police, he could not identify it. Nothing the driver did was at all out of the ordinary. The road passed round the Temple. Chas had no eyes for it. It was a small, low, ordinary town which only existed because of tourism and as a rail-head for the local farmers' produce. It was impossible to get lost in it or go astray. Chas relaxed. He knew they were going in the right direction.

"It is most kind of you, Mohammed," he told the merchant. "There are some matters I must deal with across the river, but I would like to meet your son, and to eat and stay with you, if I may?"

Mohammed smiled again, spreading his palms in agreement. "Is nothing. A guest is always welcome in my house and the house of my wives."

The People's Ferry was waiting when they arrived. It ran irregularly in the evenings, waiting for enough passengers. It was a paddle steamer with two decks, one stacked on the other, supported by fluted and leafy iron pillars, its sides open to the river air, built in England unimaginable years ago. Rickety, erratic, cheap and when it moved, alive with laughing Egyptians. The driver helped him from the *fiacre*. Mohammed paid him, one pound fifty, Chas noticed, the Egyptians' rate.

They stood on the upper deck, alone, most of the other passengers preferring the presumed safety of the lower deck. Nearer, indeed almost under, the waterline it would be easier to begin swimming from it if the ferry should begin to sink. But the old boat roared and belched acrid smoke, and shuddered and muddied the dark blue waters of the river, and began its steady trudge across to western Thebes.

187

Mohammed tapped Chas's parcel, and spoke in Arabic.

"You have business across the river?"

Chas nodded. He could understand the big man's curiosity.

"Buy or sell?"

"Bargain."

"Who do you want to bargain with?"

Chas considered for a moment. The less he told anyone the better. Already he had been lucky, luckier, perhaps, than he deserved. But everyone across the river knew of Abdel Amr and of Qurna's activities. They might keep themselves distant from it, but they knew what was going on, and a successful businessman was bound to have contacts with *le chef* which might make life easier. He had to play his luck, and it seemed worth the risk.

He might have felt differently if he had asked the big man what business he was in. The answer would have been cotton, with all that could mean in terms of business associates. He would certainly have felt differently if he had gone into the Post Office and seen Kabir hand over a fat bribe for an immediate telex to Cairo, to his colleague David Medina, telling him he believed he had Medina's man and would take him home. For Chas Winterton's luck was running out, and the convincing open envelopes Kabir had borne out with him were the usual debris of an Egyptian businessman's pockets. But Chas knew none of that, as he replied.

"I want to see Abdel Amr."

The Egyptian showed no surprise. Why should he? He had been brought up in these parts, and business was business. What else should an Englishman travelling without luggage want in Thebes?

He indicated Chas's parcel, still clutched achingly into his armpit. "Are you going to take it with you?"

Chas agonized for a moment. He knew how dangerous it would be to take so precious an object alone up into the caves. It was not that the villagers had any great record of violence in their criminal pursuits down all the millennia, except among themselves, but theft was their speciality, and they could easily remove it from him. On the other hand, it was all he had. It had been a kind of talisman for him since the Wadi. He shuddered at the thought. Could he really leave it behind, especially with someone he barely knew?

"I don't know," he answered at last.

Mohammed shrugged his shoulders.

They had arrived.

They spilled out with the crowd into the cluster of donkey-hire stands and the little market filled with fruits and shouting children. Mohammed hired a porter with three donkeys, one each for himself and his guest, one for his luggage. The donkeys began their stagger into El Gezira.

Mohammed turned to him, ignoring the slow strain of the small animal beneath him, "You know Abdel Amr?"

"I have met him once. I am a scholar."

Mohammed smiled to himself. He knew all about corrupt scholars. Everyone in these parts did. "Can be arranged," he said quietly. "Is best you go see him in the morning."

Chas could not agree. "No. I have to meet him sooner. Tonight."

Mohammed seemed to be thinking about it. "Is possible," he said finally, then, turning his attention to the donkey driver, gave his instructions. "Wait at the house," he said. "When my guest is ready, take him to Qurna. And tell El Amr that El Kabir wants him returned safely, to his house, tonight. Understood?"

The driver nodded. They were passing the central crossroads of the village. A single plane tree, an expensive import, stood at the village's heart. Mohammed turned to Chas again.

"He will bring you here," he informed the Englishman, "to wait for a car to Qurna."

"What car?" Chas asked innocently.

Mohammed smiled again. "Any car which passes." Chas should have known. Here, at least, locally, Abdel Amr was as great a power as Medina. They fell silent till they arrived at the house.

Unlike most of the houses in the village proper, it was still built in the ancient fashion, from sun-baked bricks faced with fine mud from the river and white lime paint ground from the rocks of the mountains. Like all houses here it had no exterior windows, and its roof was made of a cool lattice of reeds and layers of palm leaves. Mohammed went in first, alone. Chas

189

knew it would be unlikely for him to be introduced to the wives.

Mohammed returned some minutes later. He looked depressed. "My son has not arrived. But, please, come in."

Inside was the main courtyard. It occurred to Chas that it was still laid out like a local farmhouse because once, quite recently, that was what it must have been. Mohammed led him into the main room. A wife (or daughter?) fully robed and veiled was laying out watermelon, dates, sweetmeats and tea, but she hurried away as soon as she was done.

"*Sharabi?*" Mohammed asked, meaning alcohol. Chas accepted, and the Egyptian went to a locked cupboard to pour them each a glass of colourless fire-water. It tasted rather good. Dates, Chas guessed.

Mohammed spat out a long rattle of watermelon seeds into the plate at his elbow. "Would be best if we ate before you went up the mountain."

Chas had anticipated the suggestion. "I think, my friend, I should do my business with Abdel Amr first. Then I could best enjoy your kind hospitality."

"As you wish. Perhaps my son will be here when you return."

"I hope so, for his father's sake." Chas knew better than even to refer to the women of the household. This was clearly, at least in some ways, an orthodox family. Mohammed acquiesced, admitting that it would, in any case, soon be time for him to pray. One thing, however, Mohammed had not forgotten.

"And your parcel?" he asked.

Chas had had time to think it over. Outside the company of thieves it would be better to trust to the ancient, honest Egyptian traditions of hospitality. "Do you have a store-room where I might leave it?"

Mohammed nodded, and took him through to it, just beyond the main room. It was, as usual, as large again, and full of the valuable things in the house; sacks of grain and pulses, earthenware and brass pots, pottles of kerosene for cooking with. Chas set his parcel against the wall, removing the gun and tucking it into his waistband. Mohammed saw him do it

190

but merely shrugged. It was to be expected. The Egyptian steered him away from the other store-room door, into the kitchen where the women were cooking, back instead into the main room and the courtyard. Outside the donkey driver merely nodded and mounted a donkey, gesturing to the Englishman to do the same.

Mohammed took Chas's right hand between both his vast ones, saying, "Later, we eat, we talk, with my son."

"*Inshallah*," Chas replied: God willing, "I look forward to it." Then they set off.

They did not have to wait under the plane tree long. About ten minutes after they arrived a beaten-up Peugeot 404 came bouncing up through the village, clearly on its way to the ferry. The donkey man stuck out an arm. The car bounced to a halt. The driver (again a Nubian; this was the south) stuck his head out of the window, explaining angrily that he was going to Karnak, that he had no time to waste. The donkey man's answer was simple.

"Visitor for Abdel Amr."

The driver scowled. He had just come from the mountain. Still, defeated, he opened the back door. *That was power*, Chas thought as he got in. "Any car," Mohammed had said.

The donkey man leaned down to the Peugeot's driver. "Tell El Amr that El Kabir wants him returned, tonight."

The Nubian nodded, and gunned the engine.

Half an hour later, they were scaling the steep path up the cliff-face, Chas's damaged hands and muscles straining in the dying heat of the day. Occasionally he stopped, gasping. The Nubian merely stopped and watched him from the rocks above, neither complaining nor helping. Chas started forward again, trying not to think of heat or discomfort, keeping his eyes on the mountain top beyond, the mountain high above the Valley of the Kings whose peak was a natural pyramid cut out of the rock by wind and time. He tried to think of freedom and escape, but all he could think of was Medina, so he fuelled his footsteps with hate.

But as they came to the highest cliff-mouth, as they entered into the cool dark dryness of the cave, his worries fell away from him. He began to laugh. They had passed through the intricate wooden doors into an outer hall, with a Persian carpet on the floor and simple furniture. He was led down a corridor past rooms where the men of the cave were sleeping, eating, talking on rich divans in the comfort of the master-cave. Chas was still laughing, with relief and stupefaction as the Nubian brought him to a door inlaid with silver filigree grilles and ivory birds of paradise.

He was laughing because he thought he knew why there had been no search at Asyut, and why, with Abdel Amr's mercenary help, he would be safe. He had forgotten, it had occurred to him, about the monastery. He had forgotten it was an accident at the monastery which blew Deir el Baramus earlier than Medina had planned. He was laughing because he believed Medina would have assumed that he was already dead. That his corpse lay rotting with those of Yacoubu, Esa, Carfax.

He was laughing because he did not know the depth of David Medina's desires, nor how much, in the world as it is, good men like Mohammed Kabir are answerable to others like his enemy.

The Nubian opened the door and let him in, but did not follow after. As the door was locked behind him Chas turned to greet Abdel Amr. Federigo Paolozzi rose to meet him.

Qurna

"You won't need the gun in here, Doctor." The priest was smiling.

"I'm not so sure."

"Oh, really, Doctor, I know you very well. Much better than you imagine. I know how much you hate priests, and how much more you have to hate me for. I know that you would kill me if I tried to attack you, even though you must know that if you were to do so you would be dead yourself in seconds. I don't want to harm you. Not here, not yet. Please be seated."

Chas no longer knew what to do or think. He only knew he was afraid, and that he hated Paolozzi. He motioned the priest back to his divan, and sat in the far corner of the room from him.

"By the way," the priest added placidly, "if you were going to kill me, Doctor, you might have released the safety-catch."

Chas swore. He hated the priest even more. He hated being patronized. Paolozzi was looking at him with interest, his black eyes flaring yellow in the lamplight. The air was heavy with incense, and Chas was grateful for the occasional gusts of clean air let in by a duct cut into the rock.

"Where's Abdel Amr?"

"Busy. I thought it would be more convenient."

"How much did you pay him?"

The priest smiled again, patronizingly. "I didn't pay him anything. I gave him a present, but all that will be explained." The priest halted to examine his fingernails, unhappy with something which had occurred to him. "I almost hate to have to say it, Doctor," he explained, "but I feel I ought to. You're very good, Doctor. Much better than I had expected. On occasions you have almost been a nuisance."

It was the kind of compliment Chas could have done without. "What do you want, Paolozzi? Where's Medina?"

"All in good time, Dr Winterton, and please don't worry about Medina. If I may say so, that has been your mistake all along. It is true that you never stood a chance, but not because of him. Because of us. You ought to have known that, being a Catholic."

Chas's revulsion had cooled. His anger was steady again. "And you should know better than to think me a Catholic," he replied.

The priest was indulgent. "Really, Doctor, that won't do. We caught you much too young. You remember what the Jesuits say? Give us a child till he is seven and he will be ours for ever. We had you almost twice that long. You're a recognizable type. The tormented unbeliever. What else do you think made you turn your research into a Crusade, and forced you into the desert for a decade, like one of the Early Fathers?"

Chas's mind rejected the thought. "You've been reading too many psychology text-books, Paolozzi. It won't do at all. You should stick to the things you know."

Paolozzi's face showed no expression as he answered softly, "Which are murder, kidnap, torture." He closed his eyes. He looked as if he was praying. There was reverence in his voice as he continued: "Your mistake was in thinking Medina was your main problem, when all the while it was Rome. And they ask, 'How many battalions has the Pope?' "

Chas tried to dispel the Roman's odour of sanctity. "What has the Pope to do with this?" he asked sharply.

Paolozzi's eyes opened, shining yellow in his smiling face. "Why, nothing at all. He does not have to. Popes come and go. Rome endures. You do not think we would trust the Pole with anything so important, do you?" Paolozzi shook his head, like a teacher with a stupid pupil. Chas shuddered. He knew how Paolozzi treated his pupils. But the priest was in the mood for explanations, enjoying a sense of his own success, his own intelligence.

"There are five of us, Doctor, at any time. There always have been. We are not very good priests, as I think you may remember, but we are not selected for the priestly virtues. Hand-picked, hand-trained, reporting to the Secretary of State and attached to the Holy Office. Attached to the Inquisition. And none of us knows the others' names. It is the best-kept secret in the Vatican."

Chas was almost past caring. He could see no way out, not yet. He bought time by indulging the Roman. "Five of what?" he asked.

"Five Keepers of the Faith," Paolozzi replied, as though that should be enough, but went on to explain, smiling: "Sometimes called The Plumbers. . . . Faith is a strange thing, Doctor. It is never rational. And if it is shaken at all it is shaken by things which seem unimportant to a rational mind. That is why we have never permitted full tests on the Turin Shroud. It makes no difference if it is the Holy Shroud or not. You and I know that. There have always been false relics. But there are millions of simple people whose simple faith would be destroyed if it were proved to be something different. We cannot abide such revelations. We have always believed it is better to lie, or to hide the truth, than to shake the simple faith of simple souls. It is what we were trying to explain to Galileo when we showed him the instruments of torture."

Chas's stomach turned over. He had heard it before. Men from the Curia speaking as though they were as old as the Church itself and had been a witness to all its troubles. It offended him. It unnerved him. It showed immense contempt for literal truth and time.

"The Turin Shroud is only an example," Paolozzi continued. "But we knew, of course, we had always known, that there were two truths we could not tolerate, which had to be destroyed. It was your misfortune to discover one of them."

Chas simply waited, intrigued now, using silence to make Paolozzi continue. It did not take long.

"We had always known St Peter died in Alexandria, on his way to visit Paul in Rome. It was unfortunate. But it was brilliant of the Early Fathers to ignore the inconvenient fact. We always knew there was evidence against us. So for centuries we fought Alexandria and the Copts who were its inadequate heirs. We cheated, we lied, we destroyed. We destroyed the evidence. And we did our best to destroy the legend, the memory. We destroyed the library at Alexandria.

195

And we did our best by Inquisition to destroy the Western Jews who had spilled into Europe out of Alexandria, lest they carry the contaminated truth."

He seemed to have forgotten Chas altogether, who sat appalled at these mad ravings, not daring to believe they might be true.

"One piece of evidence always evaded us," Paolozzi went on. "The last Letter. We always hoped it had been sent to Jerusalem, and destroyed in the sack of the city by the Romans, but we never really believed it. In the fifth century the Copts of Alexandria made their last great stand against us, issuing copies of the letter. Since then we have always had to assume the original still existed and to prepare for its discovery. It was then that Keepers were first created. It took us time, but we destroyed the copies of the letter. The First Crusade was fought to cover the destruction of the last one, in a mosque library in Acre. Three copies we preserved. Three only. Against the finding of the original. One of those copies, four hundred years too recent to be original, is now in the hands of Abdel Amr. Whatever happens between the two of us, that letter will eventually be released on to the market. As a fake. An early, Coptic, fake. It should dispose of any rumours of your excellent work of the past ten years."

Chas could think of nothing to say. He understood at last why the priest had been so certain at Medina's party that the letter was a fake. He realized how carefully, and how long, Rome's plans were laid. He was astonished to see that Paolozzi looked unhappy, as though he had somehow failed.

The priest had more to tell him. "We would rather not have to release the copy, of course, but at least copies can be discredited. There are too many legends woven round the Church for another one to matter. But my commission as keeper is to secure the original, and that is now within my power."

Chas released the safety-catch with a click. Paolozzi put out an open hand to reassure him.

"Not now, I told you. Not here. Though I cannot help believing I killed the wrong child at that school so many years ago."

196

Chas willed himself to play along. Whatever else he needed, he needed information, and Paolozzi was being talkative.

"You tell me you were always my real enemy. You tell me you were always more important than Medina. How?"

Paolozzi clasped his broad killer's hands together. Somehow it made him look more like a priest. "The Church has no battalions," he explained, "except for influence, faith and intelligence. We would not have preserved our power so long, nor our authority, if we had not always attracted so many great intelligences. They have taught us to concentrate our endeavours always along the line of people's deepest desires and fears."

Chas could not tolerate Paolozzi's arrogance further. "What has that got to do with beating Martin Foster to death? What has it got to do with trussing Aaron Adams up like a turkey?" He was silenced by the contempt of Paolozzi's reply.

"That is a matter between myself and my confessor. Do not presume to judge me after what you did to Stanshall."

Chas felt suddenly humbled, suddenly aware Paolozzi was, after all, a priest. "I did what I did in self-defence," he murmured lamely.

"And I do what I do in defence of something far greater than myself." The priest had stood up. Chas fingered the gun. Paolozzi rolled up the sleeves of his cassock. His forearms were covered with a network of scars and scabs. They looked as though he had been wearing barbed wire. *Oh, shit*, Chas thought. He had been. Chas knew the kind of people who did that; they had come out of the woodwork since winning the approval of the Polish Pope; the members of Opus Dei, the storm-troops of conservative Catholicism. They had the men, they had the guns, they had the money too. How much of what Paolozzi was saying could be true?

The priest was glaring at him.

Chas turned on him. "Don't bare your scars on me, Paolozzi. I've heard it all before. I know your kind. The kind who look down on the rest of us because we won't make ourselves suffer the way you do for the things you believe in. You think a little masochism, a little pain, makes you better than we are, Paolozzi? That's crap, Paolozzi. That's horseshit.

All it means is that we're sane and you're crazy. You're wrong. You're quite wrong. I'm not like you at all. I'm not one of you. I'm not a weird psycho."

For an instant Chas thought the Roman was about to fell him. He raised the gun. Paolozzi only smiled. His teeth were ragged. He looked like a fox caught at the hen-coop. He straightened up, shrugged, sat down again, a picture of priestly self-control.

"Your trouble, Dr Winterton," he said, as though speaking of the common cold, "is that you still think too much like a Jesuit. Everything you've done since you found the Letter has been done on the assumption that people and their motives are tricky, complicated. They're not. People are simple. Only the world is complicated."

Chas wondered what all this had to do with Medina and a cave in Qurna high above the Nile. The priest answered him.

"You nearly out-thought them all, even Medina. I am impressed. Truly. Because you did it without once thinking to ask what it was each of your enemies wanted. It was the first thing I did."

The priest relaxed, pleased with himself and his little speech. Chas still had no idea why he was here, and why no attempt had been made to take the Letter from him. What plans did Paolozzi have for him? But the Roman was looking courteous again, with the look of a bishop in a Boston drawing-room asking for contributions to a hospital.

"You must forgive me, Dr Winterton. I am losing my manners in my excitement. Abdel Amr would not approve of my being such a bad host." He clapped his hands. The lock rattled and the door slid open. Chas reached for the gun. As the priest instructed the Nubian to bring them tea, Chas moved swiftly to the door, forcing the Nubian sprawling into the room. He picked up the keys. He backed out of the door. Then light-bulbs exploded in his head.

He came round a few minutes later, in the same room, in the same chair. Paolozzi was holding the gun, and smiling.

"That was stupid of you, Doctor. And, of course, expected. You should know by now there is no way out of these cave systems if the occupant wants to keep you here. And I haven't finished with you yet."

It was said in a tone free from malice, but the yellow eyes were gleaming in the lamp-light.

"What you forget, Doctor, is just how much we know. We have run a diplomatic service for nearly two thousand years. We inherited the administration of the Roman Empire. We may not have much military power, but we have information and influence. It is really all we need. When all is said and done, Medina wanted to preserve his power in the region, the Egyptian authorities wanted a chance to impose stability, and the Americans wanted the chance to show some muscle, to feel like men again after the incompetent years. I have been able to give them all precisely enough to satisfy them and no more. All I wanted in return was the destruction of the Letter."

He clapped his hands once more, and this time the Nubian, escorted by an armed guard, did serve them tea. The Roman was relaxing. Paolozzi rolled back his heavy sleeves as he drank his glass of tea. The scars again.

"We knew from our American Secretariat that the CIA were planning something big. We knew Medina would be involved. We applied some pressure on him."

Chas was surprised. "How do you lean on someone like Medina?"

The priest seemed surprised by the question. "He needs us. It's very simple. Who else can guarantee his labour relations in Latin America, his private network in Poland? Once I learned in Alexandria that you had turned to Medina, everything was very simple."

Paolozzi put down his glass, wiping his lips with a big linen handkerchief. He made the gesture seem strangely feminine. Perhaps it was the long skirt of his uniform that did it.

"I had to kill Foster to satisfy the Americans. They are such simple souls. They weren't convinced a priest was tough enough to be doing business with the CIA. They changed their minds after that. But it was stupid of them to leave Adams in place as head of the Alexandria Mission. They should have withdrawn or killed him first. Fortunately, in the end, everything he did played into our hands."

One more time, Chas wanted to kill him. They had killed

199

Aaron Adams as casually as stepping on an insect in the garden. He had been the only man of honour in the whole accursed business.

"The Americans' plot with Medina was ideal for my purpose. With only a little luck the monastery would be destroyed with you and the Letter inside it. I took the liberty of making some changes to the firing systems. But I could not allow the destruction of such a library as that of Al-Azhar. And one religious bomb would be enough for the government."

Chas was appalled. "You're mad. You say that about Al-Azhar, but you made sure Deir el Baramus was destroyed."

It was the priest's turn to be puzzled. "That is a strange remark for a scholar, Dr Winterton, and a stupid one for a Catholic. Al-Azhar's is a great collection, one of the world's greatest outside Rome. Baramus's was barely even good. And in any case, you know it has always been our policy to love our enemies but to burn our heretics."

The priest was fiddling with his rosary. He looked distressed by what he thought of as Chas's stupidity, like a teacher at the folly of a well-liked pupil.

"You should appreciate," he explained, "that warning the Egyptian authorities of the raid on Al-Azhar put them in my debt, as I had intended. I also helped them out by disposing of Gemayel, who had known too much too long. Besides, I thought it was time to introduce an element of confusion, a tiny measure of panic. I hope you enjoyed the ritual Islamic touches."

He's preening, Chas thought. *He's proud of himself. Why doesn't he get on with it? Why doesn't he ask where the Letter is?* But Paolozzi had not finished.

"It was the confusion caused by the deaths of Gemayel and Foster which persuaded Medina and the Americans to bring forward the date of the attacks. It was easy after that decision was taken to set up your accusation as Foster's murderer, and Carfax's little stratagem. To be honest, I thought that would finish you off, and the Letter with you. Your resilience surprised me. Once you finished off the American at Saqqara I had to take you more seriously. Which is why I am here now."

Chas could not help but ask him, "How did you know?"

The priest positively grinned. His mouth looked like an abattoir. "I knew you would run South. They always run South. They always have done, hoping to hide from the real world, with its heart in Rome, in the emptiness of Africa. We have pursued our enemies this way for millennia. The only decision I had to take was between Luxor and Aswan, and even if you had run straight to the border, I knew the ancient services of Luxor and Thebes and Qurna would be more use to me than the amateurs to the south. As you yourself decided, and discovered."

Chas wanted to know exactly what he was up against, and who. "How did you get down here?"

The priest did not even blink. "Army helicopter. I told you I had certain sources of secular power at my disposal."

Chas's blood ran cold. He knew what priests like Paolozzi meant when they spoke of secular powers. Their mouths were full of diplomacy, the modern world, the technocratic state, but their eyes and hearts were filled with Inquisition.

"Why isn't Medina here?" he asked at last.

The priest seemed to despair. "There is a matter only I could deal with. An area in which only I could be trusted. And you have never understood Medina. He is a great captain in the army of the damned. He is an utterly empty man. He is a vacuum. For him acquisition is a kind of rape. It isn't so much that he wants the Letter as he wants to have taken it."

The priest stood, thoughtfully, working through what he meant to say. "In normal circumstances," he continued at last, "that might have worked very much to our advantage. If it were any other object I would count on his corruption. I would tell him the price of our continued support in South America and Poland is possession of the Letter. Get us the Letter. Once you have taken it, once you have raped it, turn it over to us. There is nothing he has taken, he has ravished, I think, which Medina would not turn over, would not gamble, in return for the benefits of real power, or what he takes to be power. But this Letter is too important to us, and I think he knows that, so I have always had to be prepared to seize it. So, in the end I did not involve him. I have left him in Cairo, to dream his corrupt dreams of victory and seizure, while I conclude my business."

"What is your business?"

Paolozzi looked straight at him, out of the light, his eyes huge and black in the comfortable cave, before replying, "Two things, Winterton," he said at last. "The first, of course, is the Letter. You are going to tell me where it is and I am going to destroy it. The second thing, however, ought to concern you rather more. I do not know if I will have to kill you when all this is over. I rather suspect I will. But I have already, as you know, taken steps to destroy your academic reputation. If you do survive, no one will believe your bleating. But when all is said and done, you are still a Catholic. It is my duty to offer you confession. It is my duty to offer you the Mass."

Chas threw himself at the priest, overwhelmed by anger, outrage and the sick smell of defeat. But as he struggled for Paolozzi's throat the Roman pulled back and brought his hand down, hard with the gun-butt still in it. Chas slumped to his knees, the blood gushing from his nose and broken lips. The priest stepped away, then reached down and seized Chas's waist-band in his powerful hand and all but threw him on to his back on the desk behind him.

"Take your trousers off, Doctor."

Chas looked up at him, bewildered. Holding the gun to the Englishman's head, the priest used his left hand to start undoing Chas's trousers. "Do it, Doctor."

Chas, like a child, on the verge of tears, began mindlessly to obey, fumbling with the buttons.

The priest was leaning over him, suddenly pale, his breathing heavier, faster, now, saying, "You should be grateful, Doctor, very grateful, that you did not find the other thing, the other truth we could not endure, or the Keepers would have denied you even such small courtesies."

He tugged at Chas's trousers, pulling them down to the knees. Then he reached up and took Chas by the left forearm, tugging once with a twist, turning him face down on the desk, his hand tucked high and painful up between his shoulder-blades.

Paolozzi stretched out above, putting all his weight on him, holding the gun to his right temple, whispering in his left ear.

"I talked it over, you know, Doctor, with Miss Carfax. A

splendid woman. Most professional."

The priest jammed his fingers between Chas's wounded thighs. Chas screamed. Phlegm filled his throat.

"She agreed with me," Paolozzi continued, "that the old ways, the simple ways, are best."

Paolozzi pulled back, and spread Chas's legs, investigating the wounds with his broad fingernails. Chas reared up from the desk but Paolozzi struck him back down with a blow of the gun-butt across the back of his head.

"She did a good job," the priest said, reaching into his pocket. He put a small polythene bag on the desk by his victim's head. It was full of white crystals. "Do you know what this is, Doctor? This is salt. You have a phrase, I think, in English, about salt in wounds."

He tugged at the bag, opening it with one hand, spilling crystals as he did so. Some spilt on Chas's lips, and he felt his lips crack and the blood spurt. Paolozzi shook a handful into his palm.

"Where is the Letter, Doctor?"

Chas shook his head, trying to lift himself on to his elbows, sobbing. Paolozzi moved, striking, rubbing the salt into the wounds. Chas screamed, one high, castrated scream, as every nerve-end from his stomach to his knees hit his brain at once.

Paolozzi stood back, leaving Chas senseless with pain.

The priest looked happy, a fixed grin on his fox-face, but Chas did not see him. Nor did he see him tugging at the skirt of his vestment, or saying, "Whereas her colleague, Ismail, of course, believes in simpler, more personal methods, of physical humiliation."

Then Paolozzi was on him again, with all his weight, forcing Chas's legs apart and tearing at his own skirts, unconscious of all else, and taken unawares as Abdel Amr and the Nubian both broke into the room.

The Nubian sent the Roman flying as his master scooped up Chas, dragging him by the armpits to a chair.

Paolozzi was up again, in an instant, unsteady on his feet but aiming, till the Nubian with one quick blow struck the gun from his hand.

"He's mine," Paolozzi roared impotently. "You promised

203

him to me."

The Man of the Mountain looked at him with contempt. "I struck certain bargains," he admitted, "but if you wanted this you would have had to pay much more."

"I'll pay. . . ."

El Amr ignored him. "And now there are other considerations I must take into account. I will keep our bargain, but nothing more. If you want what this man had, then all you need to know is he came from the house of Mohammed el Kabir outside El Gezira. Now take the gun and go."

There was no arguing with him, big, barrel-chested, like all his predecessors a great survivor. Paolozzi glared at him with his yellow-black eyes, but surrendered. This was the Mountain, and this was its Man. He scooped up the gun, looked at it, thought about it, and decided against it. "Very well. I will go. But keep him alive. If what I want is not there, I will come back for him. It is our bargain."

The old man acknowledged it. "It is our bargain."

Paolozzi seemed almost petulant beside him. "I need a car."

Abdel Amr smiled, and stepped aside, pointing to the door, saying, "You have feet."

Qurna/Between the Valleys of the Kings and Queens

After they had bathed his wounds, and cleaned them, and painted them with iodine, and wrapped them in lint, Abdel Amr returned to him. The old man sighed, thinking to himself, before saying, "It is a bad business, English. It is a new wife you are keeping me from."

"I'm sorry," said Chas, sounding foolish even to himself.

Abdel Amr shrugged. "Women are nothing," he explained. "But it is a difficult position you put me in." He stared at Chas, as though expecting some kind of explanation, but none came, so he went on. "You have something the Nazareni wants very badly, something which is probably at the house of El Kabir, so in return for you and your information, if you come to me, he gives me something very valuable, almost priceless."

"It's a fake," Chas explained desperately.

The Man of the Mountain nodded. "Oh, I know that. The Nazareni was honest enough to tell me, though I knew already. I have a good eye."

Chas could believe it.

"But even so," Abdel Amr continued, "it is very old and, to certain people, valuable. A good bargain for me. Is the thing he wants at El Kabir's?"

Chas nodded. "You must send to warn him. The priest will kill him."

Abdel Amr looked up at the roof of the cave. It was black with centuries of tobacco smoke. "I have already done so," he explained, "that is what is so difficult. That it should be El Kabir. You do not need to worry about him too much. He is a difficult man to kill."

"I wouldn't have guessed it."

Abdel Amr looked at him, as though suddenly interested.

205

"No, you wouldn't," he said quickly. "You do not know him as well as I. We have been friends and partners many years."

Chas found that hard to believe. Mohammed had seemed, if nothing else, honest. Was he losing his touch, he wondered? Was he losing his ability to sum people up?

"Partner?" he asked weakly.

Abdel Amr almost laughed. "Oh, yes. Do you think any serious criminal can survive without the aid and support of honest businessmen? He has been my counsellor for many years. And can take care of himself, though I have sent him guards as well as warning. I wish I had known he was coming home. His son?"

Chas nodded. "He hadn't arrived when I left."

Abdel Amr scowled. "A bad business, armies. He should be working for his father."

The old man sat down and clapped his hands. Whisky was brought in to them. Good whisky. And a narguileh toked with hashish for the old man. "You are too weak for this, I think," he explained.

Chas agreed, and found it thoughtful.

After he had puffed some of the sweet smoke into its water bottle and inhaled the pure fumes the old man went on.

"You see my difficulty. I have a bargain, though the Nazareni tried to overreach it. Then I find it involves my old good friend who has sent you to me, doubtless with another bargain."

Chas risked it. "I have a bargain. Something more valuable than the Nazareni could ever dream of offering you. I have the original of the ancient copy which he gave you. I also have contacts in the places which could offer you most money, the big Western institutions. Museums, libraries, universities. And my price is only safe passage out of Egypt for myself and the object and ten per cent of any sale price."

Abdel Amr closed his eyes. Chas wanted to explode. Every minute Paolozzi was closer to the Letter, but he knew he was entirely in the old man's hands. And the old man gave away nothing. "Forget the percentage. We would keep the object and get you out of Egypt. As a gesture of goodwill, if you found a buyer within a month I would pay you perhaps ten thousand dollars. With something like this, we do not need your contacts. We have our own. If nothing else, Medina would be interested in something of this nature."

Chas could not keep the recognition, and alarm, from his face. This time Abdel Amr did laugh, though quietly. "I see you have had dealings with Medina. Most of us in this business have. El Kabir, in fact, introduced us."

Chas felt suddenly very cold, and realized how foolishly trusting he had been. Suddenly, he feared absolutely and completely for the safety of the Letter.

"I wonder," Abdel Amr asked, "how much Medina might be prepared to pay for you? But that is unethical. El Kabir is Medina's agent. It is a question he should ask."

The old man took another suck of hashish and closed his eyes again, momentarily lost in a world of infinite reflection. His skin looked very brown, very hard, in the half light, like the skin of a mummy, or the papyrus of the Letter. When Chas thought about what the foreigners had done, it seemed appropriate that these last considerations of the future of the Letter should fall to this representative of an older Egypt, before power-plays or morals. At last the old man decided.

"It would be wrong of me," he explained, "simply to ignore the Nazareni's agreement, but I would like what you have offered. Whether or not I get it is a matter I will leave to fate. You and the Nazareni must settle that for yourselves. It is a matter between you two. I will send you after him. If you survive, and save it, bring it to me. And do not tell El Kabir till it is done, or Medina will be down upon us. Can you walk?"

Chas didn't know. He stood up and tried. The answer was yes, if he forced himself. He would force himself. Abdel Amr led him to the cave mouth himself. Once there, he made Chas wait till a gun was brought to them. The old man handed it over saying, "He has one. It is best you have one too."

Chas thanked him and weighed it in his hand. The gun felt good. Abdel Amr had one thing more to say.

"All of you are mad, you foreigners, and I do not know what the hate between you and the Nazareni is, but you have borne great wounds bravely, and I want the Letter, so, let us hope not for the last time, I wish you well."

They shook hands, then Abdel Amr was gone, back into the cave, leaving Chas to the rock-paths glimmering whitely in the moonlight.

Night had fallen, the indigo Egyptian night. He tried to get his bearings by the pale silver moonlight. The caves of the village ran back into a spur of the mountain. To his right was the Valley of the Queens, which would lead him nowhere. To his left was the Valley of the great queen, where Hatshepsut's temple lay cradled in a natural rock amphitheatre. It looked like every child's tiered dream of an ancient Egyptian temple, for it was the one most drawings were based on. If he took the path round the amphitheatre it would bring him gently down on to the main road back to the river, but it was a longer way about. The longest way lay behind him, up the bluffs past where the natural pyramid peak of the cliff and valley system loomed, then down into the Valley of the Kings, and the long way round into the plain and El Gezira.

Chas realized with a start that he was avoiding the issue, for he knew what he must do, regardless of what Paolozzi might have done, whichever route he might have taken. He would have to take the quickest route, down the cliff face before him directly into the plain. It wasn't the safest way, but it was the fastest.

Even in the moonlight he could see the sudden change of colour before him. Around him everything shone white, white limestone cliff which in the daytime, when the temperatures climbed into the 130s Fahrenheit, became a vast oven where no one could survive without water. A full-grown man needed three litres a day just to replace lost fluids. Without it, he would fall into a stupor. Then he would die. So Chas gave thanks it was night, and almost cool.

Below him, the desert began, a drift of sand, but in time there came a single, almost straight, line. Beyond it, everything was black, and in the daytime brilliantly green, for the line marked the edge of the water table, the extremity of the river's reach, the dream and destiny of desert travellers. Out there were the last crops of summer, ripening date palms, wells. Out there was the kingdom of the river. And somewhere out there, down there, was Federigo Paolozzi.

208

He set off down the path, his footsteps alternating between the scrape of limestone and the slide of the sand the desert wind blew into pools in the hollows of the rock. All the time he listened, listened for the trace of the Roman. He left Qurna and the great tombs behind him, left behind the temple of Hatshepsut and, beside it, the smaller, yet more perfect temple of Mentuhotep, Winlock's great discovery.

I'll show Winlock, he thought irrationally. *I'll show all the Yankee bastards. Just wait till I reveal the Letter. Goodnight, Winlock. Goodnight, Cambridge.*

Even in the darkness, the thin light of the moon, he sensed shadows crossing him, and froze. The Roman? Behind him? No. No. It came as a relief. It was bats.

All his bones and muscles ached. They wanted him to stop. The raw skin where three fingernails had been was bloody and matted with dust. He was thick with limestone powder. Already. Scarcely half-way down the cliff-face. In his eyes, in his mouth, in his nose, in his hair. It stuffed his pores. It lay thick in every crease of his body, chafing the burns beneath his clothes. Whatever else he needed, he needed to get to decent drugs and good clean water. He had to stop himself breaking into "Ol' Man River". Was this delirium, he wondered? How infected were his wounds? How far was it, out to the village? Two miles? Maybe three? *How long, O Lord? How long?* He kept on sliding down the rock face, cutting out where possible the twisting of the path. How far ahead of him could Paolozzi be, not knowing the terrain as he knew it, not knowing the innermost heart of Egypt?

He spent too long thinking about it, instead of listening, instead of trying to quieten his passage. Paolozzi nearly killed him.

One clear shot, in the moonlight, was all the Roman got. It was nearly enough. Ringing out of the darkness from below the big bullet passed close enough to his shoulder to spin him round and send him falling, bouncing down the cliff-face as every inch of his body screamed its pain and derision.

He was almost senseless when he stopped falling.

The priest. Where was the priest? The beast. The beastly priest. Stop it. Delirium. Nice word, delirium. Yum, yum.

Illyrian delirium. Stop!

He shook himself to as, somewhere above him, Paolozzi switched on a flashlight. Chas must have fallen past him. He must have fallen clear. The flashlight was probing now, searching. Trust him to be prepared. The trace of the flashlight began reaching downwards, towards him. He had to get away. But how to avoid Paolozzi? If they met face to face everything became a question of luck, of timing, of reflexes. And he was sick, delirious.

Nor could he aim back up the beam of the flashlight. He could not see it. Paolozzi was concealed by the spur on which he stood. He had to find some way to hide so that the priest would be forced to come past him, never knowing where he lay in ambush. He had to get into a tomb.

It struck him suddenly. Of course. A tomb. The cliffs here were riddled with them. With caves into which the royal bodies had been transferred from the great tombs to save them from grave-robbers. Not far from here had been the Royal Cache itself. He had to find a cave and force Paolozzi to follow after. He had to choose one of the black holes in the white face of the cliff.

The flashlight beam was swinging nearer. Chas threw himself out into the air down the cliff face, catching with his heels, kicking scree behind him. Another shot rang out, wildly, and the lamplight flickered.

He came crashing to a halt with his legs twisted beneath him on an outcrop. His legs felt cramped and twisted into knots, but nothing was broken, nothing was not working. Behind him the thin slit of a cave mouth filled a white defile with darkness. It was enough. It would serve.

It was time to tell Paolozzi who he had been firing at, not some mere spy sent out by Abdel Amr.

"Nice try, Paolozzi," he called up into the darkness, "but you really must try harder."

The lamplight flickered again as Paolozzi tried to establish where the voice had come from. Then the Roman's voice oozed gently into the thick night air. "And you should have made confession, Doctor, because now I'm going to kill you." Then his footsteps scraped and scrambled on the limestone and the sand. Chas pulled himself inside the cave, making sure he left clear signs of his presence in the sand outside.

The dark came swiftly past the cave-mouth, extinguishing the moon and stars. Chas trailed his left hand against the cave wall, trying not to think of Saqqara. The cave curved round and opened out. He stood in absolute darkness, darkness deeper than any night.

There was a rank animal smell in the cave, of something old and warm and murderous. There was a strange sound in the air, almost not a sound at all, like the distant whisperings of millions of manic children, or the sound of old men's toothless mouthings magnified beyond the point of hearing. More a feeling than a sound. A feeling of the darkness of the cave, as strange as the spongy substance underfoot. Chas braced himself and waited.

It seemed an age before he heard what sounded like human breathing, almost comforting in the not-sound mumbling of the dark, the silencing sponge underfoot. He waited. He knew what people did in caves.

He was clever, Paolozzi. He knew the torch-beam made him a target, so he set it on the spongy ground and stretched away from it, barely in contact with it. He would wait for the gunfire and aim for it. He stretched out for the switch. The first time it failed him, a fade in the darkness. But the second time he succeeded, and switched it on.

The not-sound exploded beyond endurance as the bats rose in their panic, a whole column in its thousands, flying this way and that in an orgy of terror, careless of other dangers. Paolozzi screamed, louder and louder, caught in the ageless fear of the night. Chas fired.

It would not stop, the not-sound of the night. Chas closed his eyes, for despite their sonar, bats flew into him, or close. A whole flickering of wings about his body, a catching of their all-too-human thumbs, fluttering, flying. In his clothes, in his hair. It seemed to him that they were clawing, feeling, nuzzling, spitting. Bat spit all over him. And he almost broke and ran in terror. About one per cent of all bat-column members carry rabies.

Paolozzi was moaning, moaning as the blind bats took him

211

for a rock, a shelter, settled on him, dug in, still terrified by the blazing stab of light. The priest was lifting something, almost as though he were pleading. Chas aimed again, barely able to open his eyes. He fired, and the flashlight exploded and a wet thing spattered his legs. Then there was a roar as Paolozzi flung himself back out the way he had come.

Once more the sudden gunfire, the explosion of the lamp, drove the bats to frenzy, hurling them helpless in every direction. Then one of them was scraping at Chas's tight-closed eyes. He shouted, he shook it free, he ran, out of the ancient terror of the night into the present torment which awaited him beneath the the cold gaze of the moon.

Bats were tumbling out of the cave in their thousands to the shrill chittering of their not-sound, seeking refuge in the air, and it must have been the haze of them which filled the cave-mouth which saved him, for when Paolozzi fired he fired wildly, striking rock and bloody bat-flesh but sparing his adversary.

Chas fired without aiming as he dived to his right, down the cliff-face once more, rolling, banging, shaking, breaking. He knew enough by now to land on his feet, twist, turn, and drop and fire in one movement, up at the shadow looming over the spur against the moon, but he did not see what happened, for Paolozzi fired as well, and Chas felt his right arm jerk, as though somebody had seized him and was lifting him off his feet.

He heard a shout, as though from far away, but it sounded like him. Then he fell and rolled over, throwing up blood, phlegm and whisky.

Then there was nothing at all.

212

Luxor

Medina raced down the steps of his Lear Jet. His driver and his pilot, good men the both of them, had thrown away their rule books. It was a bare two hours since the telex had come from Kabir, and Cairo lay more than four hundred miles away. But it was also already night, and everything remained to play for.

Inspector Sennari was waiting for him on the apron with a car. They said he was a good man. Good man or not he certainly had his instructions. Ismail pulled the official driver from his seat, leaving the man to tumble to the ground, and took his place.

As they pulled away in a squeal of tyres, Medina leaned back in his seat and turned to the inspector.

"You know this is a private business." Sennari nodded, privately sickened. "Is there any news?"

Sennari pulled out a cigarette and offered one to Medina, who with a single movement turned it down and struck Sennari's from his lips. He had no time to waste.

"Is there any news?"

The inspector wanted to hit him, just once, but he had his instructions, and the Secretary was no more a man to cross than was Medina. "I'm just getting reports of shooting, from the mountain, on the cliffs below Qurna, but I have no confirmation."

"And El Gezira?"

"Peaceful. No trouble reported. Some men of Abdel Amr's, he is the headman of Qurna. . . ."

Medina interrupted him impatiently: "I know who Abdel Amr is."

Sennari continued regardless, "Some of Abdel Amr's men have called on Mohammed el Kabir." He paused, wondering if he should explain. Medina hurried him on.

213

"I know Mohammed too. There's nothing unusual in that. No disturbances, I take it?"

"None."

"And the priest? Any sign of the priest?"

Sennari wondered how much he should tell him. He wondered what the Secretary was playing at. The priest had arrived that morning in a military helicopter. Why were two men being helped, but each kept in ignorance of the help the other was receiving? It was no business of his. He had a wife and family to think of. He played it by his instructions.

"Not so far as I know."

"For your sake, Inspector, I hope you know every damn thing that you're supposed to." Then he stopped threatening, for he was thinking of detail. "You have transport across the river?" It was a pity western Thebes had no airstrip.

Sennari was ready for him. "We have a police launch. I assumed you would prefer not to wait for the people's ferry."

Medina looked at him long and quizzically. "You would be surprised, Inspector," he said, almost smiling, "at some of the transport I have had to use in a long and not uneventful life. But you are right. Because of all the things I have had to use, I would prefer the police launch. And on the other side?"

"Is an ordinary taxi." Sennari looked at the American, wondering if he would ask the intelligent question. He did.

"Police driver, I suppose?"

Sennari nodded. "With strict instructions not to intervene in any circumstances. The same instructions every policeman on that bank has tonight. All of them are members of my squad. I shall be going over with you. Just to make sure you have an open field. Tonight, from the river to the mountain is yours."

Medina patted him on the thigh. It made Sennari's skin crawl. "You're being too hard on yourself, Inspector, and your men. Your driver is perfectly entitled to intervene, only providing my life is at risk."

Sennari could not bring himself to smile.

They were approaching the river, its big black rolls of water coiling and sliding over each other like muscles. The police launch bobbed in the unnatural glare of the streetlights strung along the corniche. It all looked like a film-set, artificial. Something laid on for Medina, as almost all this was, except for those things laid on for the priest. Sennari would be glad when all of this was over, whatever all this was.

But Medina had no such cares as he climbed into the launch. He turned to the policeman who followed after. His teeth shone falsely in the light. Dentures, wondered Sennari, or merely capped? Capped, he decided, as the American asked him, "So the Englishman is still with El Kabir?"

It took the inspector aback. He had assumed Medina would know. "Oh, no," he explained, "he left for Qurna a good three hours ago."

Medina swore. Three hours? Three? It didn't make sense. He swore again. It was Egypt. How long had they taken, even with a bribe, to send the telex? How long had they taken to get it to him? One hour? Two?

Why hadn't they told him? He swore one last time as the launch pulled away. What was happening up there, in the cliffs below Qurna?

The Valley System/El Gezira

He lay gasping in a rock-pool of sand. It was all he knew. The not-sound had receded, leaving its twittering feeling etched deep into his joints and bones.

He tried to move his arm.

As the pain hit him, everything went slow, everything went silent, except for something whimpering near by. What was it that whimpered? *Whimpering impotent's limper whimper. . . . Stop.* He had to stop. Was this the thing itself, the ancient enemy, death? He tried to force himself to think. He had to think.

There was something wet and salty in his mouth. He had bitten his tongue as he forced himself to concentrate. He used his good arm to roll himself over onto his back, pain shouting at him all the while. Above him the moon still shone, but the shadow he had fired at was gone. He lay sobbing dry gouts of air. He tried to remember.

He remembered what had happened to his arm. Through the numbing effects of shock, he remembered the whiff of burning meat.

The priest had done it. It was the priest he had to kill.

Why? Why try? Why not fly? *Fly away, try away, fly, fly, fly. . . . Stop!* He lifted himself enough to run his good hand down his arm. All there. Nothing broken. Except for the tangle of blood and torn flesh at his biceps which made it impossible to use.

Nausea and pain both hit him again.

He was on his own. Abdel Amr had told him that much. So had Aaron Adams, a lifetime ago. And Paolozzi, if he lived, was his one great enemy. How long ago had that been? What kind of start did Paolozzi have?

He kicked out, using his legs to push him against the cliff-face, to force him into a sitting position, sliding his skinned back up against a rock. He looked at his arm again. *How the hell am I going to write with that?* he thought, then had to struggle to stop himself giggling. He had to guard against hysteria.

It occurred to him forcibly for the first time in his life that he was going to die. He understood it, and it held no fear, for he had no intention of dying where he lay.

Something, something out of his long years in the desert, out of his years of searching, something troubled by images of Carfax's face suddenly melting, of Adams revolving on his steel hawser in a tomb in Saqqara, and of a gentle man on a train out in the Western Desert bringing him help when all hope had been abandoned, refused to let him lie down, let him die here without fighting, without doing something to make them know it was Chas Winterton they had struggled in contention with. He would not die alone, if he had to die. If nothing else, he would leave the Roman's bones whitening before the sepulchres of kings.

Now he rested, as he tried to think. Even though it was night, the air about him was thick with flies, flies licking at the blood he had leaked into the sand. Where did they come from, he wondered? There were few flies in the desert, but whenever something died or rotted, suddenly they were there, in scores and hundreds. Somewhere he had read that the insects would outlast us, would survive the temporary humans, whatever wars and weapons we might turn to. He could believe the world would one day be a province of the Lord of Flies. It made him think of Paolozzi. He stood up. He had to move.

Movement nearly forced him to his knees again, but somehow he kept going, not knowing what reserves he called on. He knew that somewhere out there something feral, something bestial, which went by the name of Federigo Paolozzi, still eluded him. And he was unarmed. Once again he had to stifle giggles. He must have dropped the gun. He was badly wounded. He was in shock. And he could not know how much, or how little, damage he had inflicted on his adversary.

He began by checking the ledge before the cave, but wherever Paolozzi was, he was gone from there.

217

Afterwards, he would never be able to explain what kept him going, what drove him forward, down into the valley floor and on towards the village, but he remembered lapping water in irrigation canals and not tasting it at all. And he remembered thinking on his ghosts, on each of the additions he had made to the unquiet spirits who rose up out of Africa and swept down to the sea on the blue-gold green-gold waters of the Nile to find some rest in Alexandria. Carfax. Adams. Yacoubu. Gemayel. Esa.

Most of all Esa. Poor foolish grinning monk.

And he dreamed of murder.

And at El Gezira he found his dreams enacted.

Once he got down to the road he did not have to wait long for a lift into the village. Not that there was ever much traffic, but there are always farmers returning home late after a night's revels, and no Egyptian would have failed to stop for someone as damaged as Chas was by now.

He discouraged conversation and turned down all offers of a detour to a doctor. All he could think of was getting back to Mohammed's. He hoped against hope that Paolozzi would have to rely on his feet all the way back, but he could not believe it. So he urged his driver on in the hope that they might still pre-empt the priest. Deep down, he did not believe it, but nothing could have prepared him for the scene which awaited them on their arrival.

They crossed the El Fadliya Canal. Mohammed's house was just before the village, on the right. At the very least, Chas counted on the Roman being delayed by having to ask his way to the house.

What he had not expected, as they drew to a halt, was to see a car parked before the house, with its windscreen blown out and the three men in it sitting very dead, and Medina and Ismail before it carrying guns.

Everything which had been building up inside him snapped at once. He got out of the truck and ran, defenceless, at Medina, screaming obscenities.

As in slow motion, he saw Medina, bewildered, turn to Ismail and another man he had not noticed and could not identify to tell them to keep their weapons down. As he crashed towards Medina, the old man seized him with one big fist and lifted him from his feet, shaking him, shaking sense into him, trying to make him understand, and at last the words went in.

"No!" Medina was shouting. "No! Not me. The priest, damn you. The priest!"

And at last Chas understood. Paolozzi had come down from the mountain, murdering Abdel Amr's guards as casually as children. He was in the house now, with the one thing Chas and Medina most wanted.

They turned to the main door of the house together. Then the shooting began.

As they heard the first shots from within the house Medina turned to Ismail, snatched the long-barrelled .357 Magnum from his hands and shot the main doors clean away from their hinges. Then he swung up his left leg and kicked, almost gracefully. The doors fell in like playing cards. He did not even bother to look before running into the courtyard. Chas followed hard behind him.

There was another shot, and another, from the open door beyond into the main room of the house, sending Medina diving to the left and Chas to the right, almost blacking out again as he landed on his wounded arm.

There were women in the courtyard, sheltering behind the wall by the door into the main room. They were weeping, pointing helplessly to the door. Medina began squirming his way forward towards them, on his belly.

Christ! thought Chas. *He's using them as cover.* Possession now was everything. He had to get to the Letter. Unthinking, unarmed, he jacked himself on to his feet and kicked himself forward across the courtyard into the main room, diving to the left as he breached the door, thinking wildly, *Not my fucking arm this time!*

Two more shots rang out, ripping fistfuls of lath and plaster from the door-frame.

Medina was on his feet in an instant, heading for the door with a shout of "Cover me!" to his men beyond. He came through the door horizontally, barely a foot off the ground, heading for the inadequate cover of a hardwood and rattan couch as two more shots cut through the room at chest height. There was a shout, and something like a gargle, from the courtyard beyond as one of Medina's men went down with a hole smashed through his throat.

Chas saw Medina sizing up the room. *Where's the fucking priest?* he thought.

The answer came as something flew through the air from the door of the store-room beyond them, beyond the main room. It rattled across the floor, spinning like a top. It was a revolver, an empty revolver. Then Medina was up and taking aim, but the priest was ready for him, and the old man had to dive away as another shot rang out of the store-room, tearing the back off the couch behind which he sheltered in a puff of flying splinters and horsehair stuffing as his own shot smashed harmlessly into the thick old mud-brick wall.

What kind of armoury, Chas wondered, had Paolozzi taken from the three dead men in the car outside?

They knew where he was now, in the store-room, with a clear view into the main room and a partial one into the courtyard beyond. He was in there with the Letter. Chas looked around him, remembering suddenly, beginning to slide along the floor on his stomach, no longer thinking about the pain. If he could only get around the priest. If he could only get to the Letter.

Medina had seen it too, from his shelter in the far corner of the room, out of the immediate line of fire, the other door, into the kitchen, which ran beside both the main room and the store, which had another door into the store-room, where Paolozzi was, where the shooting came from, and now the smell of burning.

Burning. It struck them both at once. One of them had to get through into the kitchen and round the side of Paolozzi, because of the smell of the burning. Chas was nearer the door.

Medina shouted to his men once more, "Cover!" and bullets whined through the room, smacking shards out of the lime-stone floor of the best room, ricocheting wildly. But there was a noise from the store-room, a noise like a grunt or strangled

220

roar, of pain and of baffled rage.

Chas kicked himself up and ran, rolling through the door of the kitchen as Medina pulled away from the wall and loosed round after round at the store-room door to offer him cover. He crashed back to the wall to reload.

What Chas saw then made him hesitate for an instant.

The priest was standing in the store-room with the body of Mohammed stretched out before him. He stood at an angle, so he could cover, and was shielded from, the doors into the main room and the kitchen, while he did what he had come for, while he achieved the end of a lifetime's training and desire.

He had dragged one of the cooking rings and its kerosene bottle into the store-room from the kitchen. He was holding the cedar board face down into the flames, scorching the papyrus, burning the Letter away.

Paolozzi saw him, but did not stop what he was doing, what he was good at, burning. Flakes of papyrus and resin were coming away from the board now, and glowing into ash. His hand was burning too, but he ignored it. What he did do was raise the gun and aim it between Chas's eyes.

But before he could fire, he stumbled, for Mohammed was up, from the floor, his face almost white, his hands clawing at the priest's vestments, at his throat. Paolozzi shouted, defiant, and turned the gun, and squeezed the trigger. Blood, and something thicker, exploded out of Mohammed's back. The force of the shot lifted him from his feet. Then he crashed to the ground, on his knees, and his body slumped to the ground, twisting as it fell. Paolozzi turned his attention for an instant back to the papyrus and the flames.

It gave Chas and Medina the time they needed. It gave Chas time to know he needed a weapon.

The fire, Chas thought. *The kerosene bottles. You could break a man's head open with one of those.*

There were kerosene bottles piled in the kitchen, heavy and squat and lethal, if only he could get to them. He had to rely on Medina now.

The old man rolled across the main room, firing as he went. Paolozzi raised his gun and released three anwering rounds, his hand never wavering for an instant from the flames it was

221

feeding. Chas dived into the kitchen, flat and low across the floor, flying into the pile of heavy cast-iron kerosene containers. He grabbed one with his good arm, and turned as the priest turned towards him, cocking the gun one last time.

"Medina!" Chas yelled, and Paolozzi hesitated for an instant, not knowing who to fire on first, as Chas swung the bottle weakly, as best he could, into the air at the priest.

Instinctively, unthinkingly, the Roman fired, and the bottle punctured, spraying kerosene everywhere, dousing them both as it crashed ringing to the wall.

Medina had risen to shoot, but he did not need to.

The priest was no longer looking at them. His gun-hand lay limp at his side. He had returned his attention to the flames, as though there was something about them which puzzled him, which he did not understand.

They saw Paolozzi looking down at the Letter, held by a hand, on an arm, on a body, under vestments, all sprayed with kerosene from the bottle Chas had thrown at him. He was watching the fire licking round the edges of the Letter, licking up his hand and up his arm, catching on the kerosene on his skin, his clothes, his hair. They watched him watch himself catch fire.

Then Paolozzi bloomed with fire, from head to toe, a fireball, and turned, and they saw, in the midst of fire, his half face wrench into the semblance of a scream, but no sound came, a silence ringing through their minds, the emblem of some soundless, unclassifiable rage.

He filled with flame. Then everything exploded, in the heat, and the Roman's clothes crumpled, as though they were empty, and the other kerosene bottles, the tins of clarified butter, the cooking oil all exploded, one after the other, like diabolic fire-crackers, in a heat so intense that it drove Chas and Medina back, away from whatever might have been left of the Letter, as the bricks of the walls shattered and the roof died in a lick of flame.

So they dragged Mohammed out with them, consigning the Roman priest and the Egyptian Letter to an orange pyre so consuming in the still night air that afterwards all they would find was ash, more ash, and bones.

222

Cairo

He was better. If this was being better.

He had spent three weeks in hospital. They had set his broken bones, cleaned out his poisoned flesh, and stitched and taped his wounds. Now he was well enough to be allowed out on his own. He would discharge himself today.

Medina had paid the hospital bills. It always came back to Medina. Chas looked down at the crumpled sheet of expensive rag-paper in his hand, unfolding it, smoothing it, reading it once again.

You lost, it read, in Medina's scrupulous hand. He could not know how rare any specimen of the old man's writing was.

You may say that I lost too, it continued. *I do not have the Letter. But I have the copy, bought from Abdel Amr, and I accomplished everything else I set out to achieve.*

While you have lost the Letter, your reputation, and your livelihood.

But you are a resourceful and inventive man. You must know I could make use of you.

Do not dismiss the notion too easily, Doctor. . . .

Chas screwed the paper up again, into a ball, with his one good hand. "Christ," he said, to the brown waters of the Nile, to the flat white light of the afternoon, to the children playing on the decks of feluccas downstream from where he was standing.

He didn't have to read any more. He didn't want to read any more. He pulled his good arm back and tossed the paper out over the water, into the thickly moving air. The wind snatched it, and it was gone.

He knew what it had said. He remembered all too well. He

223

turned and stepped back into the city's dust and heat and haze, remembering the old man's final words:

    . . . *I am your last best hope.*

He scowled, and put it behind him.

He was running low on hope.